Praise for A W...

"Aside from good writing, ...
unusual aspect of falconry, it's nice to ...
along with a new PI who is not drowning in wise...
Andy Straka has managed to avoid the more obvious
clichés of the genre while continuing to pay homage to
the conventions of it. This is a goal that many of today's
PI writers have failed to achieve. Straka should be
proud."
—Robert J. Randisi, Founder,
The Private Eye Writers of America

"An exciting investigative tale [with] an entertaining
story line. . . . The plot never slows. . . . Frank [Pavlicek]
is a strong character. . . . Andy Straka has introduced a
winning new sleuth." —*Midwest Book Review*

"Straka writes a good novel. His writing style is clean,
at times lyrical." —*C-Ville Weekly*

"Straka paints a detailed picture of the modern South,
which has still not completely escaped its turbulent past.
The descriptions are apt, the dialogue is fast-paced, and
the plot will keep the reader guessing to the end."
—*I Love a Mystery*

"The writing is smart and interesting; the dialogue and
settings are good. . . . Comes [close] to capturing the
Robert Parker Spenser formula. The PI is a literary man
with a hands-off love interest and a semi-mysterious
sidekick." —*The Mystery Reader*

Praise for A Killing Sky

"Straka's storytelling is as sharp and strong as talons,
and once he's got you in his grip, he never lets go. *A
Killing Sky* is sure to confirm his status as one of the
rising stars of the mystery genre."
—Rick Riordan, author of *The Last King of Texas*

Also by Andy Straka

A Witness Above

A
Killing
Sky

A Frank Pavlicek Mystery

ANDY
STRAKA

A SIGNET BOOK

SIGNET
Published by New American Library, a division of
Penguin Putnam Inc., 375 Hudson Street,
New York, New York 10014, U.S.A.
Penguin Books Ltd, 80 Strand,
London WC2R 0RL, England
Penguin Books Australia Ltd, Ringwood,
Victoria, Australia
Penguin Books Canada Ltd, 10 Alcorn Avenue,
Toronto, Ontario, Canada M4V 3B2
Penguin Books (N.Z.) Ltd, 182–190 Wairau Road,
Auckland 10, New Zealand

Penguin Books Ltd, Registered Offices:
Harmondsworth, Middlesex, England

First published by Signet, an imprint of New American Library,
a division of Penguin Putnam Inc.

First Printing, April 2002
10 9 8 7 6 5 4 3 2 1

PUBLISHER'S NOTE
This is a work of fiction. Names, characters, places, and incidents either
are the product of the author's imagination or are used fictitiously,
and any resemblance to actual persons, living or dead, business
establishments, events, or locales is entirely coincidental.

For Kelci, whose faith is more precious than words.

ACKNOWLEDGMENTS

I owe a debt of gratitude to the following in the creation of this book: Jane Rafal, Sergeant Richard Hudson of the Charlottesville City Police, Deborah Prum, Michael Martin, Lucy Russell, Jennifer Elvgren, Kate Hamilton, Tom Nolan, Mara Rockliff, and Kathy Craig. I also greatly appreciate the help I received from falconers Mark and Lorrie Westman, Lee Chichester, Gavin Sutherland, Craig Nicol, Michael Garst, and Steve Jones and Laura Culley at *American Falconry* magazine—all of whom, in one way or another, took the time to contribute their expertise to my meager but growing store of knowledge.

Genny Ostertag, my editor at Signet, deserves a tremendous amount of credit for helping to shape and fine-tune the story. This book would not be what it is without her thorough, professional insight. Many thanks as well to my agent, Sheree Bykofsky, for her dedication and integrity handling the business side of things. Finally, I wouldn't be able to continue to write at all without the loving support of my wife, Bonnie, who is always my last and best editor.

1

Old age, they say, comes at a bad time.

It had certainly come at a bad time for George and Norma Paitley. A copy of an almost twenty-year-old *Washington Post* article, complete with photos of the elderly couple's Buick, pancaked almost beyond recognition, lay front and center on my desk. According to the story, an eyewitness to the aftermath of the early-morning accident on Connecticut Avenue had reported seeing what looked like a city garbage truck speeding away from the scene. A check of the city's fleet, however, revealed no damage to any of its vehicles. In fact, the day of the accident had been a federal holiday, and none of the official trucks were working. Another photocopy, this one of a follow-up piece several weeks later, indicated that the police still had no solid leads about the identity of the truck or its driver.

The plain manila envelope containing the two articles had arrived at my office in Charlottesville, Virginia, via courier. No note or explanation of any kind. No return address or information about who the sender might have been, either. I was trying to figure out if someone had mixed me up with someone else when the phone rang.

"Okay," I said a few seconds later, "so you say you're Cassidy Drummond."

"Not only say it, Mr. Pavlicek. I am."

The call was a prank, of course. Had to be.

The voice on the phone sounded confident, if a tad weary. During TV coverage of the sex scandal that had nearly ended her father's political career, the real Cassidy Drummond had sounded younger, more unsure of herself. I remembered juxtaposed images of her and her sister in matching school uniforms, some Richmond news producer's quixotic idea of evoking pathos. My Caller ID screen read NUMBER BLOCKED.

"Jake Toronto put you up to this?" This was just the kind of stunt my ex-homicide partner might dream up.

"Who?"

"Never mind."

"Did you get the articles I sent over?" she asked.

I looked down at the clippings. "Oh, they came from you, huh?"

And just when the reading was beginning to get interesting.

"Yes. Or I should say from my sister, Cartwright. I found them in her suitcase."

"I see. . . . Nice touch. You're not one of Nicky's friends, are you?" I said.

"Nicky?"

"My daughter. I thought you might be one of her friends."

"I'm sorry. I don't know her."

The radiator in the corner moaned. Its rust-speckled pipes might have served as savior to my dilapidated potted plants, Filbert and Flaubert, but the heat in the old renovated warehouse had been overperforming so regularly of late I was giving serious thought to the idea of adding orchids to my collection. With the office windows thrown wide open, the only evidence of the raw March morning outside came from the faint din of traffic on Water Street below.

"Didn't I see a blurb in the paper the other day that said the congressman's daughters were still overseas?"

"In Japan," she said. "Yes, we were there for a couple of months. A foreign study project in Kyoto. But we flew back into Dulles yesterday. We're both still enrolled at the university, and midterms are coming up. Be careful about the newspapers, Mr. Pavlicek. They're always late and often inaccurate."

"Maybe you should've thought of that before you sent me these articles."

She was silent for a moment. Then she said, "I wanted to give you someplace to start."

Start? At this point, as any private investigator worth his lack of fear or tarnish will tell you, I should have hung up the phone. The world is filled with enough real problems. Why waste an ear on tabloid-bred charlatans bent on some thrill? But the articles in front of me looked real enough. Being the curious and maybe sometimes slightly sadistic sort, I leaned back in my creaky swivel-tilter and decided to wait her out. The half-finished report on my computer screen for the attorney who needed a witness to bolster his client's claim for negligence against a half-blind librarian who had U-turned her minivan through the client's storefront window had long since ceased to stir my imagination anyway. Plus, how often do you get to speak intimately with celebrity, even the counterfeit brand?

"You still there?" my faux-famous caller asked.

"Yup."

"You sound as if you still don't believe I am who I say I am."

"I don't. You and your sister really as identical as you look on TV?"

"Pretty much." Annoyance in her voice.

"Where are you two planning to live now that you're back in C-ville?"

"Can we get back to why I sent you the articles?"

"Just trying to establish the extent of your credibility."

"*My* credibility? What about *your* credibility?"

"You called *me*, remember?"

"I was given your name by Marcia D'Angelo."

"Marcia?" A referral from my girlfriend was not one to be taken lightly.

"She's an old friend of my family. She said you know her."

"I know her, all right." I'd even harbored thoughts, for going on two years now, of knowing her in the biblical sense. Marcia was a woman with strong beliefs, however, and I respected that. We weren't exactly talking marriage, although popping the question had been crossing my mind of late. Funny, though— she'd never mentioned any friendship with the Drummonds. Then again, we didn't talk much about politics. It was not always an area of agreement between us.

"She was a volunteer for one of my father's campaigns a long time ago, you know."

"Wonderful."

She went on. "Wright and I are supposed to be moving into an apartment on Gordon Avenue after the first of the month. Right now we're staying at the house our father rents out in Ivy. He's just about to leave on a trade mission to Greece."

I didn't know about Greece, but she had the local spot right. Congressman Drummond had recently made the move to Albemarle County, following his divorce from the twins' mother. The man had been acquitted of sexual harassment, though he'd admitted a long-standing affair with a staff member. Now he and his family were "healed," as Tor Drummond put it, at least enough for him to be running for reelection.

Most often, celebrities move quietly to the Charlottesville area, hoping to gain a modicum of anonymity among the horse-dotted hills. They drive their clay-splattered SUVs or pickups between town and their farms like any other rural Virginian. But Tor Drummond, from a line of patriarchs who had made their fortunes processing tobacco, was an exception. He drove a banana-yellow Hummer, wore a ten-gallon Stetson, and despite the furor over his latest extramarital exploits, seemed to have little interest in voluntary obscurity.

"I would've thought you'd want to avoid your father's place," I said, finally reaching for the recorder on my desk and a new cassette. "You mind if I record the rest of our little chat?"

"No," she said.

According to law in the enlightened Commonwealth of Virginia I wasn't required to ask her the question, but since we were talking celebrity and politics here . . . well, I'll say no more.

"And as far as my avoiding the house," she said, "my sister and I are students here and I don't see why I should."

"Not taking sides between Mom and Dad?"

"Of course not. We've all agreed to put what's happened behind us. Besides, Mom's been really busy lately."

"Uh-huh."

If I remembered right, the twin's mother, Karen, was a respected and—if you believed the papers—

blameless pediatrician from Richmond. Doctor and Congressman Drummond had married when both were medical residents. Our intrepid congressional representative was a physician too, at least by title, although he hadn't actually practiced medicine for years.

"So will you help me?"

I still had little idea what she was talking about, but something in her tone suddenly told me she was legit. Why was I not surprised? Why did it feel like this call was going to lead to something much bigger than a couple of old newspaper articles about an unsolved hit-and-run? Something about Marcia?

I stared at Fauntleroy, the eagle owl that presided in taxidermic splendor over the corner of my office opposite the plants, a gift from an old man who saw into the soul of birds. The owl stared back.

"All right, Miss Drummond. I'll bite—you say you found these newspaper clippings in your sister's suitcase?"

"Yes."

"Why were you going through her bags?"

"Well"—she hesitated—"that's where it begins to get complicated."

"Complicated."

"Yes."

"You and your sister are close?"

"Of course."

"She in some kind of trouble?"

"Yes. I mean, she might be."

"Have you asked her why she was carrying these articles around?"

"No—I can't."

I picked up a stray marble that had been rolling around among the papers on my desk and turned it over in my hand while I waited for her explanation. It was blue, with swirls of white and gray that made it resemble the planet Neptune.

"My sister has disappeared," she finally said.

"Your sister's missing?"

"Yes."

"Well, I'm sorry Marcia gave you my name, then. If what you say is true, you and your parents need to be talking to the police, not to me."

"But this just happened. My parents don't know anything about it."

"I see. And you don't want them to."

"No. Not yet, at least."

I thought about all that. "How long has your sister been missing?"

"Since late last night. Mom and Dad were both there to meet us at the airport, and we all went out to dinner after. Then Wright and I drove back down here to Charlottesville with my dad. Mom went home to Richmond."

How new millennium—divorced parents both there to meet the kids. I wondered if Drummond's campaign manager had brought along a photographer to document how healed they all were.

"Okay. Then what?"

"The flight was like, fourteen hours or something. I was exhausted. Wright was tired too, but she said she was going to drive into town to meet her boyfriend."

"What time was this?"

"Almost midnight."

What we do for love.

"Your sister must really be into this guy. How come he wasn't at the airport too?"

"It's not like that, Mr. Pavlicek. I mean, it was . . . but she was planning to break up with him."

"Is that why she went to meet him?"

"Yes, that's what she said. I think she just wanted to get it over with."

"Did your father know she was going out?"

"No. She made me promise not to tell him."

"Okay. Then what?"

"Then nothing. She never came back. She's not in her room this morning, and the rental car we were using is missing. I've tried calling her cell phone and everything."

"Maybe she and the boyfriend made up," I suggested.

"No. Wright would've called me."

"Isn't your father curious about your sister being gone?"

"I told him she's with Jed—that's her boyfriend. Anyway, Dad's pretty preoccupied right now with his trip and all. Besides, he and Cartwright haven't exactly been getting along lately."

This smacked of trouble. Being the father of a teen myself, I heard alarm bells sounding.

"Let me level with you," I said. "There could be any number of innocent explanations for your sister's behavior. The police won't even become involved until after twenty-four hours have gone by. I sympathize, but I'm sorry. I don't really see how I can help at this point. If your sister hasn't shown up by midnight, you need the police. And if I were you, I'd be sharing what you've just told me with your mom and dad."

"Please, Mr. Pavlicek. I can't wait until midnight. I just know something's happened. Jed's capable of almost anything."

"The boyfriend? What do you mean?"

"He's gotten real possessive. When we were in

Kyoto he would send her these crazy E-mails. Sometimes three or four a day."

I glanced again at the picture of the crushed automobile. "He the one who sent your sister these articles?"

"Maybe—I don't know."

"Have you tried reaching *him* this morning?"

"Yes. He was just headed to class, then swim practice. He's on the team, you know. He said he had no idea what I was talking about. Said he didn't even know Wright was back. He thinks I'm making up a story so she doesn't have to see him.

"I just want to make sure my sister's okay, Mr. Pavlicek, and I don't want my parents or the police or anybody else—especially Jed—to find out about this."

Confidentiality, under the right circumstances, was something I could handle, but were these the right circumstances?

"How come all the secrecy when it comes to your parents?" I asked.

"I'm sorry. I'd rather not discuss any more of this over the phone. Is there someplace we could meet?"

I picked up a number two pencil and started drumming it on the copies of the articles on my desk. Maybe I'd had crazier calls. I just couldn't remember one. Most likely Cartwright Drummond had gotten cold feet about the boyfriend. Maybe she'd been too embarrassed to admit this to her sister and gone to spend the night somewhere else. Then again, why would she be carrying around these old newspaper clippings? One of the high-tech spy catalogs I get sells a little device you can hook to your phone and, its makers claim, use to determine whether or not the party on the other end is telling the truth. Not for the first time I wished I'd had such a gizmo. Trouble was, like everybody else, I feared being replaced by a machine.

A road grader, or something that sounded very much like it, roared by outside. I haphazardly flipped through my appointment book. Wouldn't you know? No pressing crimes, no other damsels in emergent distress. Nothing but an arrangement to spend an hour or two hunting that afternoon with my daughter, Nicole—we'd be flying Armistead, my red-tailed hawk. We were nearing the end of the season, the wind was down today, and I didn't want to miss the chance.

"I could meet you at a restaurant down here on the mall," I said. "The Nook? Say in about an hour?"

"Okay. I'll be there. But—"

"But what?"

"You haven't mentioned anything about money."

"Is it a problem?"

"I can offer you five thousand dollars."

"Whoa. Hold on now. I charge seventy-five bucks an hour, plus expenses."

"All right."

Fauntleroy was still staring, but Filbert and Flaubert seemed to have perked up a bit at the mention of money.

"If this is a hoax, tell Toronto, or whoever put you up to it, that I said you are very good."

"I promise, Mr. Pavlicek," she said. "No hoax."

2

"She's for real," Marcia D'Angelo said. Her soft Southern drawl oozed conspiracy. "She called here a couple of hours ago."

Thw-aack. A Granny Smith apple, the target of her knife, split in two. She stood in bare feet at the butcher-block table in her kitchen, dressed in a flannel shirt over cutoffs that nicely displayed her shapely legs. The heat was turned up high. The public schools might have been out on spring break, but my girlfriend's idea of fun—while a number of her students and fellow teachers were reclining down in Tropicanaville—was to stay home and clean out all her closets and drawers. To think, if only I could have talked her into joining the crowd in Florida, instead of chasing down lost celebrity children, I could have been snuggling right there beside her, rum swizzle in hand, warm sand between our toes.

"I was afraid that's what you'd say," I said. "What did she tell you?"

"She said she was worried about the way her sister has been acting lately and that she'd found an item she wanted someone to check into, an old newspaper article or something. Didn't want me to tell her mother and especially not her father. So I thought about it and sent her to you."

Not exactly the spin I'd been given, but I let it pass. "Why me?"

"She wanted someone she could trust. And it's the kind of thing you do for a living, isn't it? She made it sound like she and Cartwright were having a disagreement. Seemed like she was just after information."

"That's all she told you?"

"That's all. Why? Is there something more?"

I avoided her gaze. "You know this family well, then?"

"Of course. I've known them for years. Karen and I met at the office when I worked on Drummond's first campaign. We really clicked and have kept in touch ever since. She and the girls are good people."

"Tor Drummond parades around like he's the next Bill Clinton. How come you never mentioned them before?"

She shrugged. "I guess I just didn't think you'd be interested."

"You worked for Drummond's campaign?" She snickered, tossing her hair. She was wearing it in a semishag cut, a look I favored. "Were you on staff?"

"That was a long time ago. And I was a volunteer. There's a difference. Believe me."

She finished cutting the apple into wedges and sat down next to me with the lithe, subtle movements of a dancer. I suppose she *was* a dancer of a sort—she had talked me into the ballroom and swing classes offered at one of the county middle school gyms. Marcia, hardly trying, moved better than anyone else in the room.

"So what's up with Cassidy and Cartwright?" she

said. "You still haven't answered my question." She stared at me across the table.

I was on thin ice here. I swallowed my bite of apple. "It could be nothing," I said, "but I don't think so." A phone call to the D.C. police had already confirmed that the hit-and-run described in the article was still an open case—not that anyone was paying much attention to it after all this time.

"Oh?"

Somewhere I was supposed to find a balance between professional and personal obligation. "It might be serious," I said.

She put down the bite she had been about to put in her mouth. "You're not kidding, are you?"

I shook my head.

She started to push her chair away from the table to stand up. "I need to call Karen," she said.

I put out my hand to stop her. "Don't," I said.

Her eyes turned smaller. I'd seen the look before, thankfully not too often. Reluctantly, she sat back down.

"I'm meeting Cassidy in half an hour down at the Nook," I said. The Nook was a small family restaurant on the downtown mall. "I'll find out the details and determine just how serious we're talking about."

"But this is my friend, Frank. These are her daughters."

"And they're also adults, if I'm not mistaken. Cassidy Drummond may be about to become my client, and she's asked me not to reveal what she's told me to anyone else."

Now I had her curious as well as angry.

"What did she tell you?"

"You know I can't do that, Marcia. Not when the client asks for confidentiality."

"But I'm the one who sent her to you."

I said nothing.

She glared at me. "Don't do this, Frank. Turn it over to someone else, some other private investigator."

I was stunned. "Why?"

"You don't want to have anything to do with Tor Drummond."

"Why not?" She was probably right, but now she had *me* curious.

"You—you didn't grow up around here like I did. You don't understand."

"I didn't move into town yesterday, you know. What don't I understand?"

"The Drummond name goes back generations. Tor Drummond, despite his many obvious failings, still has a lot of old friends."

"So? Just because I'm an old Yankee doesn't mean I can't figure out Tor Drummond. Besides, it's his daughter I'm dealing with."

"What about the police?" she asked. "If it might be serious, shouldn't you be talking with them?"

"If it gets to that point."

She said nothing. All at once her eyes began to tear up.

"What's wrong?" I reached across the table and grasped her hand.

She shook her head and pulled her fingers away. It's something Marcia and I seem to share a knack for. Tiptoe up to the past—then turn away. My own history is discomforting enough without trying to exorcise all her demons. But right then and there I felt like I needed to. We'd been over marriage notes, compared divorces, our experiences raising kids—talking about all of that had never been easy. Here came a new and heretofore unknown chapter. I wasn't about to drop it.

"It might help if you could tell me more about your experience with Tor Drummond," I said.

"Who cares about Tor? He made his bed a long time ago and he has to lie in it. Haven't Karen and her daughters been through enough?"

Those alarm bells were sounding again.

"You've obviously known them for a long time."

"Huh." She tossed her head again.

"I've read what the newspapers have to say about the congressman. The way things are going he might even manage to get himself reelected."

"Good for him. For all the good it did his wife and children." She dabbed at a corner of her lips with a paper napkin and threw it down on the table.

"What's the congressman like in person?"

She shook her head some more and rolled her eyes. "You really want to know?"

"Yeah, I do. If it helps me figure out what's going on with his daughters."

"I think Torrin Drummond is the most tortured individual I have ever known."

"Tortured?"

"Yes."

"What makes you say that?"

"On the surface he's brilliant. Caring demeanor. Incredible gift for putting his thoughts into words—"

"And underneath?"

"Underneath?" She seemed to be summoning up memories she would just as soon have left buried. "Underneath he's nothing but a selfish little boy."

"That doesn't make him much different from most of the rest of us selfish little boys."

She fixed a listless stare on a point on the wall behind me. This was not the Marcia I knew and loved.

"Except that most boys grow up eventually and learn how to control their impulses," she said. "I'm not sure this boy ever has."

3

Cassidy Drummond entered the restaurant like a slumming princess and looked around tentatively. I recognized her from the last time I'd seen her photo in the paper. Almost innocent green eyes, hair more strawberry than blond, little or no makeup. At the moment, she seemed to be doing her best to look like any other student. She wore blue jeans and some kind of heavy sweater under a well-worn L. L. Bean shell. On her feet were Tevas and wool socks. Something about her reminded me of my daughter, Nicole, who was a student at the university herself.

I was seated in a back corner booth, decked out in my usual cold-weather hunting attire: lined combat fatigues and a shabby but functional Boston Celtics sweatshirt under a khaki traveler's vest. I smiled when she looked at me and stood up. She made a beeline in my direction, extending her hand.

"You must be Mr. Pavlicek."

"You weren't a hoax." I took her slender hand in my own and we shook. Her skin was cold.

"I told you," she said. She unzipped her jacket and took it off as we slid into the booth opposite one another. The waitress came over to refresh my coffee and poured a cup for Cassidy as well before buzzing on to another table. "You're taller than I expected. You look like you're dressed for camping."

I shrugged. "My daughter and I may try to get a little hunting in later on."

She nodded. If it bothered her or if she were curious about it, she didn't let on. She took a test sip of the steaming coffee. "I just got off the cell with Marcia. She said you dropped by to see her."

"Had to check you out," I said.

"I guess I must've passed the test."

"I wouldn't be here otherwise."

"Marcia doesn't seem too happy with you." She had that right.

"For every wound there is a healing," I said.

"Somebody famous say that?"

"Not that I'm aware of."

"Anyway, thanks for not giving me away."

"Doing my job."

"Marcia also told me you were a really good detective."

"*Investigator* is the proper word. Officially, the only detectives in Virginia are those still on the force."

"Investigator, then. Whatever." She seemed to have a barely contained nervous energy about her as she dumped sugar and cream into her coffee.

"Still no word from your sister?"

She shook her head.

"Okay. Let's start where we left off. If you really think your sister is missing, why all the secrecy?"

She crossed her legs. Her foot began tapping reflexively on the floor. She kept her eyes on me, but she said nothing.

"If I'm going to work for you, Miss Drummond, rule number one is you need to be honest with me." I waited.

Finally she said, "I told you about her boyfriend."

"Right. She went to dump him. I should be able to check that out easily enough."

Her voice dropped to a more intimate tone. "What if . . . what if I told you I suspect my father might have something to do with Wright being gone too?"

Instinctively, I glanced around the restaurant. Not too busy this time of day. None of the few other patrons appeared to be paying us any attention. "I'm listening."

"Well . . . it's not like I have any evidence or anything—"

"What do you have, then?"

"Wright has been acting a little strange lately."

"Oh?"

"It's just that she and I have always been so close, you know? She's always been my best friend. But lately—lately it seems like there's been this distance between us. I mean, when we were in Kyoto, we weren't staying with the same family or anything, but we would meet together every day.

"Then, about a week ago, she started making excuses, saying she was too busy. She missed three days in a row. Yesterday on the plane, when I tried to talk to her about it she just got mad at me, told me I should mind my own business. I thought it might be about Jed, her boyfriend. I told you, I think he's crazy. He might do anything. But now I'm not so sure."

"Why is that?"

She looked around the room herself for a moment and lowered her voice even more. "Last night after I went to bed I couldn't sleep, even though I was really tired—it must be the change in time zones. Anyway, I came down to the kitchen about one o'clock to get something to eat. I had to pass by our father's office—

it's a separate room built off the landing between the first and second floors. His light was on, and he was on the phone with someone. I don't think he knew I was there. That was when I heard him say something that made me wonder."

"What did he say?"

"He said Cartwright might have to go away for a while."

"Anything else?"

"No. I was afraid he might hear me on the landing, so I just went on down the stairs. When I went back up to my room later, the light was off and he'd gone to bed."

"It might've been just a passing remark," I said. "Without knowing the context, I have to say he could've been talking about anything. Who knows? Maybe an internship or something."

"But who would he be talking to at one o'clock in the morning?" she said. "And why hasn't Cartwright come back? Or at least called me?"

"You said your father's getting ready to leave for a trip, right?"

"Yes."

"Won't he become suspicious if Cartwright isn't around to see him off?"

"No, she told him she had some stuff do this afternoon over at the university. And it's like I said earlier on the phone. Dad and Wright haven't gotten along lately. Even being away on our trip didn't help. They had an argument last night over dinner."

"About what?"

The waitress swung back by and asked if we wanted more coffee. We both took refills and waited until she left.

Cassidy's voice was just above a whisper. "Wright wants Dad to drop out of politics. Says it's the whole reason our family's not together anymore."

"What does your mother have to say about that?"

"She stays out of the argument. I don't think she cares anymore."

"How about you?"

"I pretty much agree with Wright, but I don't think it'll do much good. Dad's always been more married to his work than he ever was to Mom."

"You've been through a scandal and a divorce," I said. "Why would Wright care now whether or not your father tries to stay in politics?"

"I don't know. I just think it's weird."

I thought it over. "It seems more likely, from what you've told me, that your sister's boyfriend may be involved. If—and it's still a big if—it turns out she's really missing, that is—"

"She's gone, I'm telling you. She would've called me."

"Tell me more about this boyfriend. What's his full name?"

"Jed Haynes."

I took out my notepad and wrote it down. "You said he's a swimmer on the university team. What year?"

"He's a third-year, and he's very good at swimming, like nationally ranked or something."

"How long have he and your sister been dating?"

"About six months. Since we all came back to school in September. She met him at a party. They saw a lot of each other until we left for Japan in January."

"They been sleeping together?"

The question seemed to catch her off guard. Her eyes cut away from me again, and her hand came up to scratch at her ear. "Some," she said. "I guess."

"Jed belong to a fraternity?"

"No. I don't think so."

"Where does he live?"

"He shares a house with a bunch of other guys. I can give you the address."

"Okay. You said you talked with him earlier and he thought you were making up an excuse for Cartwright. Did he seem agitated?"

"Jed's always agitated."

"Sounds like a potential world leader. Do you have any idea where he might be in the next couple of hours?"

She shrugged. "Class, maybe? No—wait. I know he has swim practice around four. I remember Wright telling me, because she said if she couldn't catch up with him last night, she'd have to try to go see him then."

"All right. I'll go pay a visit to Mr. Haynes. Odds are, I'll find he's just playing coy with you for some reason. Probably secretly shacking up with your sister."

"Cartwright wouldn't do that, Mr. Pavlicek. Not without calling. I'm telling you."

Maybe it was true. The twins could've possessed a bond, the extent of which only they could understand. What must it be like to know another so intimately, to be linked, in some ethereal way, from as far back as the womb? I thought of Nicole again and wondered what it would have been like if she had had a sister.

Cassidy must have caught something in my eyes because she said, "Is something wrong?"

"No," I said. "I was just thinking how you remind me of my daughter."

"Oh. You mentioned her earlier. Does she live with you? Marcia said you were divorced."

"Nicky's mother had some problems, so Nicky lived with me while she finished high school. She's at the university too, now, a first-year, so I guess you and she have something in common."

"That's great. She know what she wants to study?"

"Not yet—not exactly."

Nicole had been making a lot of noise lately about joining me in my PI business. I had better things in mind for her, however. No way was I going to let her end up chasing down reluctant witnesses over insurance claims like her old man. I was trying to nudge her toward English or history, maybe even something practical like computer science. Private investigation was an occupation I supposed few university students aspired to, so I let it drop.

"What if Jed Haynes tries to tell you the same story he told me? What if you can't find out anything?"

"Well," I said, "there's always these." I'd brought the copies of the articles she had sent me. I pulled them out of my pocket, unfolded them, and laid them on the table.

"Do you think they have something to do with Wright disappearing?"

"You tell *me*. Ever hear of these people before?" I skimmed through the article again. "George and Norma Paitley?"

She shook her head.

"I already made one call. This case was never solved. I can check into it further, but that'll take time. By then, if you still haven't heard from your sister, you'll need to go to the police."

"But what about Dad?"

"Look, you're hiring me to try to find your sister.

This is the way we need to do it. One step at a time. We'll worry about your father, if we even need to, when the time comes."

"My father is a very influential man, Mr. Pavlicek."

"That's okay. I've dealt with a few. What other information can you give me? Didn't you say your sister was driving a rental car?"

"Yes. We picked one up at the airport to use for a couple of weeks. Mom and Dad are going to buy us both new ones for our birthday later this month."

"Happy birthday," I said. "I need to know the make and license of the car, if you have that information, or at least the name of the rental company and the approximate time you picked up the vehicle."

She pulled out a piece of paper. "I thought you might want that. The paperwork's with the car. But here's the name of the company. We picked it up at Dulles."

"Good." Her handwriting was flowery and elliptical. "You also said you've tried calling your sister's cell phone number several times?"

"Yes."

"She always have that phone with her?"

"Yes. We both have them."

"Do you know if Cartwright has her charger with her?"

"No. The charge usually lasts a couple of days."

"Does she have an adapter for the car?"

"I don't know. I can check her bags again."

"Okay. I'll need that phone number."

"All right. How do I pay you?"

"A five-hundred-dollar retainer to start. I'll either bill you for any additional charges or refund the difference."

She pulled a small camel-colored purse from her

jacket pocket. She took out a checkbook and an expensive-looking pen and wrote out a check, then tore it off and handed it to me.

"Anything else you can tell me?" I folded the check into my pocket without looking at it. "If this thing ends up going to the police, you and your family will have to answer a lot of questions. You might as well try to think of everything you can right now."

She pressed her lips together for a few moments. "I suppose there might be something."

I waited.

"You remember I told you about my sister's boyfriend Jed sending her some crazy E-mails while we were in Japan?"

"Uh-huh."

"He signed most of them. You could tell they came from his college mail address. But some of them were signed differently, poems and stuff, and they came from a different address. They were just so crazy. Wright didn't even tell me about them until recently. I guess she assumed they were from Jed. She said she'd been getting a few of them off and on since the school year started."

"Which is about when she started dating Jed."

"Right."

"You said Jed's agitated and possessive. Why would your sister want to go out with someone like that?"

"He might become famous, for one thing," she said.

Like we need more of that, I thought, but said nothing.

"Plus he looks like Brad Pitt with a body like Patrick Swayze. I think Wright thought she could tame him. Turns out he's just a jerk."

"Did you and your sister communicate a lot via E-mail when you were overseas?"

"Sure. We both have laptops. It was just like being at home. We'd E-mail each other sometimes three or four times a day."

"Did Cartwright take her laptop with her last night?"

"No. She left it. I saw it when I went through her bag."

"All right. We may need to check on that later. What time did you say your father was leaving?"

"In a couple of hours."

I took one of my business cards out of my wallet and gave it to her.

"Anything else you can think of right now?"

"No, I don't think so."

"If something else occurs to you, or if you hear from your sister, my cell number's on the card."

"Okay."

"Either way, I'll call you on your cell phone after I talk with the boyfriend. Okay?"

"Okay."

She gave me the number, along with her sister's cell phone number and Jed Haynes's number and home address. When we finished, I paid the bill and walked her out of the restaurant.

The spring sun was still a no-show. A gunmetal-gray sky arched over the downtown mall. The chill hit us and we both zipped up.

"Thank you," she said, standing on the bricked-in pedestrian Main Street, steam rolling from her pretty mouth. She stuck out her hand and I took it again. The fingers were still cold.

"Don't thank me yet."

I had a troublesome inkling neither one of us would be so grateful when we found out what was happening with her look-alike sister and Mr. Jed Haynes.

4

The cold washed over me like a purifying balm as I tried to shake the feeling, trudging back down the mall toward my office. I picked up the turnip when I made the turn down Second toward Water Street. It was all the guy could do, I noticed, to keep from breaking into a run. Not much experience, apparently, running a tail.

He had been standing at the kiosk at the far end of the mall as we left the restaurant, pretending to talk on the phone. A pudgy little man in a long black raincoat. He kept shifting his gaze our way as Cassidy Drummond and I parted company, and for a few moments afterward he seemed uncertain about which one of us to try to follow, but then he took off after me. I'm sure he wouldn't have found my nickname for him flattering, but that was my first impression. Purplish skin with a bushy mustache and bulging eyes—a ripe, overgrown turnip packed into clothes.

After rounding the corner out of his line of vision, I stopped, folded my arms, and leaned against a lamp-post. It took only a few seconds for him to come panting around the corner in pursuit. At the sight of me waiting, he pulled up short.

"We need to talk," I said.

We exchanged hard looks. His mustache twitched. He knew he was made. He shook his head and put his index finger to his lips as if to shush me, but what he was doing with his other hand interested me more. He moved it deftly beneath his long coat and came partway out with the barrel of a very large handgun, loosely pointing it in my direction.

Not so obvious to anyone behind him or walking past, but he made sure it was plenty obvious to me. Since I'd left my .357 hanging in its shoulder holster over the hat rack in my office, I was in no position to play Wyatt Earp. Even if I had wanted to, the barrel of his gun looked about the size of your average red-wood, so I would have been decidedly outgunned. Oh, well, you know what they say—the bigger the gun, the smaller the . . . ah, brain.

"Here? In broad daylight?" I said. "There must be twenty witnesses within earshot who could ID you before you'd make it out of sight."

Something in his eyes told me such a problem was not a big concern for him. *My* identifying him, on the other hand, might be. He seemed to reflect on the possibilities for a moment. Then he put his finger to his lips again, turned, and disappeared back around the corner.

When I got around to breathing, I decided—discretion in this instance being the better part of valor—not to follow. He'd made his choice when he came after me, so he had little if any chance of picking up Cassidy Drummond again. It was cold consolation as I made my way back to the co-op.

"Sounds wild, my man." Jake Toronto lifted his mustang boots onto the edge of my desk, put his hands behind his head, and leaned back in his chair. "Even if I wanted to pull a hoax, not sure I could come up with something that good."

Toronto is my ex-homicide partner from New York. He is also my falconry sponsor and best friend. Now and then we even manage to still do a little work together. He lives like a monk in the mountains, flying his goshawk and surviving mostly off his investments, but he's also been known to perform "certain security functions," as he puts it, for a select clientele, not all of whom I would want to meet in broad daylight.

Today, however, I felt like I was grubbing next to him. He was decked out in a dark Jos. A. Bank suit, indigo shirt, rep tie. Said he'd come over to Charlottesville to take care of "some legal work and some banking." All legal, he assured me. His slicked-back hair made him look like a compact version of Steven Seagal.

"I just heard one of Drummond's ads on the radio coming over here," he said. "Guy's starting early. The election's not for seven months."

"Guess he figures he's vulnerable. Wants to make sure he keeps the party's nomination."

He shrugged. "Politics," he said.

"I'm pretty sure the other twin's just shacked up with this swimmer. Maybe something she doesn't want her sister to know about. On the other hand, I'm not too keen on strangers sticking howitzers in my face."

"Don't recognize the guy you described. You said he seemed pretty familiar with the piece?"

"With the gun, yes. Didn't seem to really know much about tailing somebody."

"Unless he wanted you to pick him up. Maybe send you a message."

I nodded. The thought had occurred to me as well.

"We'll see . . . You bring Jersey with you?" Jersey was Toronto's falconry bird, a woodland accipiter a little like Toronto himself, a street fighter with near-

mythic killing prowess. Bird or mammal mattered not
to the northern goshawk. The element of surprise was
one of its biggest weapons.

"Nah. We hunted this morning. How's that pretty
redtail of yours?"

"Better than ever. Almost makes me think twice
about letting her go."

"Your call. When it's time, you'll know." He stared
out the open window, then up at Fauntleroy.

"Nicole and I are taking her out crow-hawking in
an hour or so."

"Ambitious."

"Care to join us?"

"No, thanks. Got appointments." For Toronto to
turn down a chance at hunting must have meant something important.

"All right," I said.

"Hey, you say Marsh used to be a volunteer for the
congressman?"

"Yup. Seems pretty emotional about it, too."

"Think he hit on her?"

"She wouldn't say so, but that would be his M.O."

"Kind of makes things a bit personal, don't it?"

"Doing my best to reserve judgment."

"Folks start waving iron in the air, gets your
attention."

"That it does."

"You gonna need some help on this Drummond
thing?" he asked.

"Thought you'd never ask. Can you check out a cell
phone number for me, find out any numbers that
may've been called since midnight last night?"

"Not that easily. Who's the carrier?"

I gave him the name of the company and Cartwright
Drummond's cell phone number.

"It may take a while, but I think I can come up with what you want. You wanna know how much her last bill was too?"

I smiled. "Just the calls. Depending on what I hear from the swimmer, the way this thing's headed, I may have need of some of your other . . . uh, talents as well. I'll let you know."

"I got the time. I got the talent," he said. "I'll be around."

After he left, I made a few more calls up to D.C. about the newspaper articles Cassidy Drummond had given me. Left a couple of messages. Talked to a couple of clerks and basically came up empty.

Old news is hard to find.

5

Not many people put a lot of stock in this anymore, but falcons used to be considered arbiters from God. When I say falcons, I mean hawks and eagles too, all species of birds of prey. Longwings, such as the peregrine or the prized gyrfalcon, often drop in a stoop from a thousand feet or more like a bolt commissioned by a sudden killing sky to choose among their slower-flying quarry. From antiquity birds of prey have been revered, even worshiped. To this day eagles are considered sacred by many Native Americans, and in many parts of the world falcons retain a mystique often associated with royalty.

Here in old Virginny, however, I wasn't feeling particularly royal at the moment.

Nicole drove the bouncing pickup down the farm road while I worked at holding Armistead low enough on my fist to keep her from seeing over the dash. Smoky clouds hung like a solid ceiling overhead. The temperature hovered in the forties. We hadn't spotted any crows yet, but that didn't mean they weren't somewhere about. Armistead was impatient, footing my glove.

"Pretty bird. Sit still now." Nicole tried to soothe the redtail with her voice.

We were closing in on the end of Armistead's last season with us, and I wasn't sure who would miss the hawk more, my daughter or me. My apprentice bird was now a mature adult, a skilled hunter, ready to be released back to the wild to find a mate.

She would probably never find it necessary to try to take crows for food when on her own. They would be impossible game for your average redtail, and easier fare was almost always plentiful. But introducing her to new game at this point, I figured, would at least broaden her experience. Besides, I thought she just might be up to the challenge. The vineyard owner had approached me about ridding his acreage of the blackguards. Whether we caught anything or not, the very presence of such a raptor in the area would help keep the crows at bay.

"Hey." Nicole held tight to the wheel as the truck bounced over another rut in the road. "You know, Congressman Drummond's house is just a mile or so over those hills." She was looking at the highest point in the vineyard, a pair of swells covered, like the rest of the landscape surrounding us, with rows of arbors.

"Is that a fact?"

I had made the mistake of mentioning my new client to her before leaving the house with Armistead. Technically, Nicole was on my payroll, since she did some part-time work, mostly computer-related, and she was always interested in my cases. Nearing the end of her first year at the university, she was also talking about the possibility of moving to a house with a couple of male classmates to save money in the fall. I liked the saving money part. Not so sure I was wild about her sharing quarters with the male classmates.

La Casa del Pavlicek had seen some upheaval when my daughter had arrived on the scene a couple of years before. My on-the-job crash course in young-adult parenting had involved everything from late-night curfews to learning what a Def Leppard was, and though I wasn't exactly up for a remedial effort, since she was so determined to save money, I'd offered her the option of moving back in with me for a while. After all, I hadn't had to scrape the remains of lavender shaving cream off my shower wall in months. And my elderly landlords were getting bored by all the peace and quiet after a year of wall-shaking stereo.

One thing was certain. Nicole Mae Pavlicek, a.k.a. Nicky, a.k.a. my wanna-be partner in Eagle Eye Investigations, had a mind so quick it was all I could do to keep up with her at times.

"Aren't you curious about what your newest client might be up to?"

"You've got it wrong, Nicky. Normally, we spy *for* the client, not *on* the client."

"I've never met them, but I've heard Cassidy and her sister are nice, not stuck up or anything." She had already offered to cross-reference a bunch of search engines on the Web and print out a file of background material on Congressman Drummond and the twins, including photos. "You know this case could make you famous," she said.

"Or infamous." I was beginning to regret even mentioning Cassidy Drummond to her in the first place.

"You're always so negative, Dad."

"Not negative. We're talking public figures here. No telling all that's going on. It's best you stay as far away as possible. You're still a student. You've got other priorities. Trust me, I'm being realistic." At least I'd stopped short of giving her any details, especially about my encounter with the turnip and his oversized gun.

The truck jolted through a bigger-than-usual washout. We had been climbing gradually, and now I noticed we were approaching the top of one of the hills. Nicole must have sensed this a long time before I did, which explained the grin that had been plastered on her pretty face.

Still no crows. Maybe they had heard we were coming and convened a powwow someplace to plan their escape. If we did manage to scare any up, our own plan called for lifting Armistead into the sight position and launching her out the window to start a tail chase. It wasn't all that elegant. But it was the tactic best suited to our habitat and our bird. Even Toronto, who had taught me most of what I knew about hawking, had adapted his falconry to suit the piedmont terrain.

Nicole was sitting higher in her seat, peering over the break of the hill. "I'm stopping here," she said.

"Why? You see a crow?"

"No, but I'm pretty sure I can see the Drummond place down there in the valley." She set the parking brake, jumped out, and began pulling her heavy jacket and a pair of binoculars out of her backpack.

"Nicky! We're supposed to be hunting here, not playing games."

But my words fell on deaf ears. She was already several yards from the truck, bounding over the rocky terrain to a better vantage point. I could either sit there with a couple of pounds of anxious redtail tethered to my wrist or follow my daughter.

I jumped out with Armistead and opened one end of her giant hood, which was secured to the bed of the pickup. The hawk stepped inside onto her perch, and I latched the door.

"It's okay, girl. We won't be long." At least I hoped we wouldn't.

By now Nicole had moved farther down the ridge to a break in the arbors. From up here you could see across open fields to another hillside and beyond to the Blue Ridge. She had the field glasses trained on something. As I came up beside her, I followed her line of sight to a cluster of buildings hugging the opposite hill in a grove of bare walnut trees maybe half a mile distant.

"That's gotta be it. We're closer than I thought. Look at the size of that limousine."

She handed me the binoculars, I'm sure expecting me to raise them right away and look, but I stared wordlessly at her.

"C'mon, Dad. Don't you want to see what the Drummonds are up to?"

I would like to think it was only business on my part in agreeing to look for Cartwright Drummond, but to tell the truth, I bore a bit of the same sleazy curiosity as your average *National Enquirer* connoisseur. Why the rich and powerful incite such morbid nosiness is anybody's guess. Maybe we need to show they aren't really any better than the rest of us. Nevertheless, the feeling didn't sit well with me. Titillation coiled like a menacing viper in the pit of my stomach.

I shook my head and raised the glasses to my eyes.

The main house came into focus first: a contemporary design of glass and stone. There was a large terrace to one side that opened to a courtyard of sorts. Behind this stood two or three outbuildings, around which several vehicles were parked, including Tor Drummond's trademark Hummer and the black stretch limo to which Nicole had referred.

"It looks like Drummond's place."

"Are they leaving for a trip or something?"

I focused more closely on the limo. I could see a garment bag and a roll-on suitcase propped against a retaining wall to one side, partially obscured by the rear fender. I wasn't sure, but I also thought I saw wisps of exhaust coming from the back of the vehicle and the silhouette of a driver behind the darkened glass.

"Something like that," I said, lowering the binoculars.

"See anything to help you?"

"Not really."

"What about the guy standing by the corner of the house?"

I'd missed that. I raised the glasses and scanned the house again. "There's nobody there."

"He was just there a minute ago."

"Wait a minute." My stomach did a little rumba. Two men came around the corner of the house. One was clearly Tor Drummond. He hadn't donned either his Stetson or his trademark boots today, but he was easy enough to spot: a tall, angular man with a jutting jaw, dressed semicasually for travel. That famous jaw seemed to be working overtime at the moment. Next to him, listening intently, stood the same turnip in the trench coat I'd met a little while ago on the street.

"Something wrong?"

I let the eyepiece drop from my face. "No. It's nothing," I said.

"For a father who makes his living exposing liars, you aren't a very good one yourself."

I smiled, said nothing.

"Why won't you let me help you more with your business? I'm not a child, you know."

"No, but you're my daughter. You can do better than mucking around with the likes of some of the folks I have to deal with."

"You could at least give me a chance."

I looked at her. Her hair blew about in the cold

wind, but she didn't seem to mind it a bit. "What are you trying to prove, honey?"

"Nothing." She glared at me.

I waited.

Gradually, her gaze softened. "You remember when you found out what really happened with Mom and Uncle Cat?"

"You cried."

"Yup. And I told myself that was never going to happen to me again. In order to protect me, you kept going until you found out the truth. That's the kind of thing I want to do."

I stared at the ground. She'd just ennobled what for me had became a very ignoble profession. "All right," I said. "How about that computer search you offered to do? You can start with that. Should save me some time."

She brightened considerably. "Now you're talking."

"But classes and studying come first. Right now your most important job is to get your degree."

"I'm getting all A's."

"Good. Let's keep it that way. And remember, anything I ask you to do is confidential. You should be able to find plenty on Tor Drummond, but I'm especially interested in his family."

"Sure thing. I think I remember reading something about the daughters in *C-ville Weekly* last year. It was right about the time the scandal over Drummond's affair broke."

"Okay. Check it out."

We walked in silence back to the truck. We took Armistead from her box and released her to hunt from a soar above us while we drove back down between the rows of arbors, hoping to scare up some game. I scanned the surrounding arbors and hedgerows with the binoculars. The crows, if there were any, had vanished into deep cover.

Nicole spun the wheel deftly to avoid a washout. "You know I would've voted for him last time if I'd been old enough."

"Who, Drummond?"

She nodded.

"Still feel like voting for him?"

"Well, let's see. Mr. Congress-boy intimidates his secretary into bed with him, cops a plea, dumps his wife—I don't think so."

"Awfully hard on the guy, aren't you? Remember, we need to maintain some professional distance."

She rolled her eyes and shook her head. "The guy's a first-class sleaze, Dad."

So much for professional distance.

6

The university's new aquatic and fitness center is an impressive glass-and-brick affair on Alderman Road next to the even more impressive football stadium. (I wonder if Thomas Jefferson would've liked football.) Parking outside the building in one of the few spots open to visitors is a virtual impossibility, although that never stops a determined few from hovering like vultures in hopes of grabbing any opening. If a riot of undetermined location ever breaks out on the university's grounds, this would be one of the first places I'd tell them to look.

I settled for a spot on a shady side street a few blocks down Alderman and walked to the swim center from there. I'd almost called Cassidy Drummond after taking Armistead back to her mews and feeding her and dropping Nicole back at her dorm, but I decided to wait until I'd talked with Jed Haynes. Whatever Congressman Drummond was up to with the turnip, I needed to talk to the swimmer first.

Groups of students, individuals, and pairs moved around this area, some as joggers or cyclists, all keeping a wary eye on the sporadic stream of traffic. I entered the lobby behind a long-legged young woman wearing tights and a sweatshirt, carrying a backpack.

"Excuse me," I said. "Do you happen to know if the swim team is practicing here right now?"

She paused and gave me the once-over. I was still wearing my hunting garb. She must have decided I was okay, though, because she said, "I think so, unless their practice is already over."

"Thanks," I said.

She turned and disappeared quickly into the depths of the building.

I pulled out my wallet and rifled through a stack of laminated cards. Since Marcia's father was affiliated with the university, she had managed to finagle a card that allowed me to use the athletic facilities. I had been down here a few times before to work out on the vast complex of fitness and weight machines that overlooked the pool, although all things being equal, I still preferred my free weights at home. The student checking IDs at the entrance off the main lobby waved me through the turnstile without so much as a second glance. Lucky for me, camouflage had never stopped being a fashion statement.

The entrance to the pool deck was on the lower level, between the men's and women's locker rooms. Two male swimmers came through the doors, laughing about something.

"Excuse me, fellas. I'm looking for a member of the swim team—Jed Haynes?"

"Jed?" one of them answered. He looked me over. "He just finished practice. He's probably in the locker room. Locker number's thirty-seven, I think."

"Thanks."

"Hey, you a reporter?" the other swimmer asked. "I hear Jedi's up for all-American."

"Jedi?"

"Yeah. That's what all you guys call him, isn't it? The Jedi knight. Dude's more like Darth Vader." They both laughed again.

"What's his event?"

"Freestyle."

I pulled a pen and piece of paper from one of my pockets and made a show of writing it down. "Thanks," I said.

"Hey, you sure you're a reporter?"

I smiled and pushed through the door into the locker room.

It was a big place with several rows of metal lockers. A wall of warmth washed over me, saturated with dampness and chlorine. I followed the numbers around to find a lanky young man pulling jeans on next to locker thirty-seven.

"Jed Haynes?"

"Yeah?" He slipped a T-shirt and sweater over his head. There was an overly self-assured air about the voice. His eyes blazed into mine, intense. I saw what Cassidy Drummond had been talking about. He seemed to sense right away I was no reporter. I didn't think he looked like Brad Pitt. More like a leering version of Tom Cruise.

"You have a minute to talk?"

"What about?"

"Like to ask you a few questions about Cartwright Drummond," I said, offering him one of my cards.

He took it and stared at the information. Then he turned it over to examine the back as if the card wasn't real.

"Christ—I don't believe this." He shook his head and rolled his eyes.

I said nothing.

"Not here," he said. "C'mon."

He extracted a small duffel bag from the locker, closed and locked the door, then slung the bag over his shoulder. I followed him out of the locker room, back up the stairs, and out past the turnstile to the main lobby. There was a snack bar off the lobby with vending machines, a few tables and chairs and such. No one else seemed to be using it at the moment, so we went in and sat down.

The soon-to-be all-American slumped in his chair and glared. "What's the bitch been saying about me now?"

"That remains to be seen."

"What's that supposed to mean?"

"You and Cartwright have been dating, haven't you?"

"Yeah—we're supposed to be, anyway."

"Were you with her last night?"

"No, man. I've been trying to get her to call me all day. She's supposed to be back from Japan, but the little cunt all of a sudden acts like she's too good for me or something."

Someone needed a lesson in manners.

"That's probably true," I said, standing up to lean against the table. "But let's put it aside for the moment. Did you know she left the Drummond house late last night on her way to see you?"

"She what?" It took a moment for him to realize he'd been insulted. "Listen, asshole, I don't know what you think you're—"

He didn't quite get to finish his sentence. Instead, he grimaced in pain. It might have had something to do with the fact that the heel of my left hiking boot was pressing firmly down on the toe of one of his soft sneakers. He tried to push it off, but couldn't. He looked around for help, but it was obvious he didn't want to make a scene, especially in his current position.

"I'll sue you, you ba—"

"Ah-ah." I held up my hand and he got the message. "I'm not from the police, Jed, so I don't have to be nice. I'm usually a lot more easygoing than this. But I need information, and you need to tone down the language a bit. You understand?"

He scowled but nodded.

I took my boot away, sat back down, and watched him rub his sneaker. "Don't worry. It'll just be a bruise. I didn't even give you full pressure."

He seemed to be working very hard to stifle an impulse to speak.

"As I was saying—Cartwright Drummond left her house last night on her way to see you. Did she arrive at your place?"

He shook his head.

"You're *sure* about that?"

"Yes," he said through gritted teeth. "I told her sister that."

"Where were you last night after midnight?"

"I was at the house. Myself and a couple of the guys were playing foosball, then we watched Letterman. Then I went to bed."

"Your roommates can confirm this?"

"Sure—ask 'em. Ask anybody you like."

He was thinking through his situation. Maybe thinking about throwing me a punch. Maybe even thinking—really thinking—for the first time about Cartwright Drummond.

"Where is she?" he asked.

"Cartwright?"

"Yes."

"That seems to be our problem."

We both ruminated about this for a few moments. His countenance darkened. "If anything's happened to her, I'll kill whoever did it," he said. Passive-aggressive on steroids, perhaps.

"You're leaping to an awfully big conclusion, aren't you?"

He grunted and glared. "I mean it," he said.

I could have told him then that the object of his obsession had been about to abandon him and that he was going to have to learn to accept that, but I didn't. "Well, that's just wonderful, Jed. But remember, those who try to kill often end up getting killed themselves."

He didn't care. He was maybe twenty, twenty-one. He was bulletproof—except, at the moment, when it came to his toe.

"What happens now?" he wanted to know.

"Now I keep looking."

"You calling in the cops?"

"Potentially. I'm still hoping she'll turn up. You know anyplace else she might go? Other friends, maybe?"

He shook his head.

"Really get to know a girl when you date her, huh, Jed?"

"Well, what do you expect? Cartwright's usually hanging with her sister, if anybody. And they've both been out of the country."

"Where are you headed right now?"

"Me? Probably pick up some dinner at the Tree House and head over to Alderman to work for a couple of hours." The Tree House was a snack bar, and Alderman was the main university library.

"What's your major?"

"Biology."

"Premed?"

"Nah. My uncle's a surgeon and he tells me, the way health care's going, to forget it."

"What will you do when you graduate?"

"Maybe research. Maybe something else. I don't know. I wanna keep swimming as long as I can."

"Olympics?"

"Maybe. Coach says I got a shot."

"Know anything about history?"

"History? Not much, why?"

"Ever hear of some folks named George and Norma Paitley? They were an elderly couple, died together almost twenty years ago. Car accident up in D.C."

His face showed not the slightest sign of recognition. "No. I never heard of them. What do they have to do with Wright?"

"That's what I aim to find out." He still held my card in his hand. I reached over and tapped it. "You think of anything else, you give me a call right away. You understand?"

He crossed his legs, looked at his toe as if it were no longer a part of his body, and began rubbing it again. He nodded.

"Oh, and let's just keep this conversation confidential. Be easier for me to try to find her that way."

"All right. But you find her, you tell her I want to talk with her."

"I'll do that," I said.

He was still rubbing his toe when I left.

7

I whistled between my teeth. Up close, Tor Drummond's rented mini-estate looked solid enough to withstand an earthquake, maybe even an atomic blast. Someone had also spent a fortune on landscape architecture and planting beds. I wheeled my truck in through the open gate. Crushed brownstone snap-crackle-popped beneath my tires. The limo was no longer in sight, of course. The place looked deserted.

I was about halfway up the driveway when a dark blue Chevy Suburban shot over the rise beside the house and approached me in a hurry from the opposite direction. The drive was steep and it had the uphill advantage. The vehicle pulled to a stop, blocking my way, and two suits got out, the first a muscular type who could have been a robotic clone of Al Gore and the second none other than my friend Mr. Turnip, who hopped out from behind the wheel. Unlike our earlier encounter, however, neither the turnip nor his partner appeared to be armed.

Since I had the gun this time, I decided I could afford to turn on the charm. I rolled my window down and spoke to the other driver. "Fancy running into you again."

"I'm sorry, sir. You're on private property. You'll have to turn around." Turnip's voice—he obviously now had one—boomed as if he were wearing a built-in megaphone. He gave no acknowledgment or indication of our earlier meeting.

"I'm here to see Miss Drummond," I said.

"Which Miss Drummond would that be?" He knew darn well which Miss Drummond.

"Cassidy Drummond." I opened my door and stepped out of the truck, handing him my card. "She'll be expecting me."

He looked at it, as if he needed to, and grunted. Then he spun around without a word, walked back and climbed into the Suburban to talk on a cell phone, leaving the robot and me to stare at one another.

I zipped up my Virginia Cavaliers parka. "A little chilly today," I said.

The robot said nothing. I wondered if he were programmed to talk.

After a minute the turnip got out of their vehicle and came back to where we stood. "Got any ID?"

I gave him a smirk. Some game we were playing here. I produced my license from my wallet.

"He's carrying," the robot said. Atlas speaks.

The turnip searched my eyes for a moment. "Mind leaving your piece with us?" Suddenly the professional. Polite.

I shrugged, unzipped my parka, and handed him my .357, figuring if they'd been going to have some sniper shoot me down, there on the driveway, they would have done it already.

"We'll back up and turn around. You can follow us up to the house."

We climbed back into our respective rigs. They executed a fast three-point turn—not an easy feat with that much truck—and I followed them. We passed under the limbs of one of the walnut trees, just beginning to bud. Rows of blooming daffodils and crocuses ringing a stone foundation came into view. Then the back of the house, every bit as impressive as the front. On the patio, standing with her arms crossed, was Cassidy Drummond. She looked none too pleased.

The security types motioned me into a spot along the driveway before disappearing in their Suburban around a corner of what looked like the main barn. I pulled into the space and let the truck idle for a few moments before shifting into park, watching Cassidy in the side mirror.

"Nice welcoming committee," I said as I climbed out. I nodded in the direction of the goons.

"What are you doing here? I thought we agreed our arrangement would be confidential. You said you would call."

I signaled for her to lead me inside. No telling if the lion and the tin man were still within earshot.

She ushered me inside onto the richly tiled floor of an enormous kitchen. Sub-Zero refrigerator/freezer built into the wall. Top-of-the-line appliances, made for entertaining a small army. A huge rack of gleaming pots and pans hung overhead. Everything about the room was big, from the center island, complete with integrated entertainment center, to the massive Shaker table in its own eat-in alcove.

She closed the double patio door and turned to me with her arms crossed again. "Well?" she said.

"No one else is in the house right now?"

"No. My father left for the airport a while ago. His staff either went back to Washington or headed for his campaign office in Richmond. The only problem is, by showing up here like this, you've just alerted my father to the fact that you're working for me."

"I've got news for you, Ms. Drummond. He already knows."

"What?"

I explained to her about my encounter with the turnip, leaving out my little nickname for the man. Her eyes grew wide.

"Oh, my gosh," she said. "Oh, my gosh."

She sat down at the big table and motioned to me to sit across from her. The last time I'd seen a kitchen chair so large was in a giant's castle at an amusement park.

"I told you," she said. "Dad might be involved."

"Let's not go jumping to any conclusions just yet."

"Would you like some coffee?"

"If it's decaf," I said. "Already had my stimulant for the day."

She got up and went over to a gleaming metal urn, poured two mugs, came back, and set one in front of me.

"How long have Ike and Spike out there been working for your father?"

"I don't know, a couple of years maybe."

"He always have this much security around?"

"Ever since the Diane Lemminger scandal." Lemminger was the staffer with whom Drummond had been carrying on an affair. "I thought it was mostly just to keep the media away."

"How come they didn't go with him to the airport or accompany him on his trip?"

"Oh, he has Mel for that."

"Mel?"

"Mel Dworkin. He's been Dad's chief aide for years. Helps run his campaigns. He's also a bodyguard. Knows martial arts. I think he sometimes even carries a gun."

"Sounds like a handy guy to have around."

"Cartwright hates him. She calls him 'Blow-Dry' 'cause his hair always looks so perfect."

"Still haven't heard from your sister?"

"No." She began chewing on one of her nails.

"I had a chat with Jed Haynes."

"You did?" Her eyes grew wide again, as if she were surprised I'd actually done what she'd hired me to do. "What'd he say?"

"Claims he hasn't heard a word from your sister. I'm going to check out his place and talk to his roommates to be sure, but it seems like he's telling the truth."

"Oh, my gosh," she said again. "You think something else happened to her? She was taken by some weirdo or something?"

"It's a possibility. It's also possible she decided, for some reason, to disappear on her own."

"Why?"

"I was hoping you might be able to help answer that."

"Did Jed know anything about those articles I found in her bags?"

"I don't think so."

"Have you been able to find out anything more?"

"Not yet. Like I told you, that's going to take some time."

We sat in silence for a moment. I looked at my watch. It was almost six o'clock. In six hours Cartwright Drummond could be officially listed as missing.

"I have to tell you, Ms. Drummond, I really had expected to find your sister with Jed Haynes. I'm not sure what's going on with your father and these goons outside, though I plan to find out. As far as the articles you found in your sister's suitcase, they might be related. Then again, they might not. The way this thing

is headed, I'm afraid you're going to end up needing
to deal with your parents and the police."

She shook her head. She stopped biting her nail and
bit her lip instead. "Keep looking," she said.

"You sure?"

"Yes. I want you to keep looking, no matter what
else happens."

"What about going to your mother?" Marcia's
anger percolated in the back of my mind.

"Not yet—maybe later."

I tried to search her face for some hidden meaning,
but there was none. "All right. I can go talk to the
roommates, see if they back up Jed's story. Then I can
start making sweeps of the area, looking for the rental
car. I've also got somebody doing some background
work on your sister's phone and those articles."

"I've found something else I want to show you,"
she said.

We stood and I followed her from the kitchen into
a mudroom and storage area. There were two large
closets filled with coats and shelves brimming with
outdoor gear and various paraphernalia. Right in the
middle were a pair of colorful, oversized duffel bags
and some smaller satchels. A long bench stood against
the opposite wall.

"I've been so worried about Wright that I haven't
even finished my own unpacking today." She bent
over one of the smaller bags. "Remember I told you
about those E-mails? Here it is. She carried it on the
airplane." She lifted out a dark gray laptop.

"Are there some on here?"

"Yes. At least I think so. We both use AOL. She
always saves important ones as files."

"You want to try to read them now?"

"I already did. That's what's so weird."

"What?"

"There are files listed in her box, but they won't open. And she must've changed her password. I can't get into her E-mail."

"You two know each other's passwords?"

"Yes. We've never kept secrets from each other."

"Until now."

She nodded. "Do you think you could—I don't know—break into it somehow?"

Sounded like something right up Toronto's alley. If it wouldn't be corrupting her too much, maybe I could get Nicole to help too. "I think I might be able to manage something."

I took the machine and the power cord from her.

"Please call me if you find something," she said.

"Roger that. But you'd better start thinking about what you're going to tell your mother."

"Okay."

She walked me back through the kitchen. I took one last look around. Never knew when or under what circumstances I might have to come back.

Outside, the daylight was beginning to fade into the clouded combination of pastels that precede a gray dusk. For a brief moment, the dying sun cast a crimson glow on the hillside and the patio behind the house. No sign of the security men.

"What about your safety and these supposed security types?" I asked.

"You think I should leave, find someplace else to stay?"

"Your father's not here anymore. I think that would be wise."

"Where should I go? Our new apartment's not ready yet."

"I've got an idea," I said.

8

"This is crazy, Frank." Marcia paced back and forth in her living room. "Just what, exactly, did you hope to accomplish by bringing her here?"

Cassidy was taking a shower upstairs. It had been easy enough to gather up some of her and Cartwright's things, mostly still in their suitcases, toss them into the back of the pickup, and drive her into town. I pulled over twice and checked my rearview mirror the whole way to make sure the turnip and the robot hadn't tried to follow us.

"She just needs a safe place to stay for tonight, maybe longer."

"A safe place to stay? What in the world is going on? First, she calls to tell me she needs to find someone to help her find out some information regarding her sister. You show up and tell me it's something serious, but you won't tell me what it is. You don't even want me calling her mother, who's my friend. The next thing I know, you're rushing her in here like she's some sort of fugitive or something."

"Wright's missing." Cassidy's voice came from the top of the stairs. Apparently the water from the shower hadn't been loud enough. Still dressed, she came partway down the steps.

"She's what? Are you sure?" Marcia asked.

"No one's seen her since midnight last night," I said.

"I was just coming back down to get my shampoo," Cassidy said.

Marcia looked horrified. "But there's been nothing on the news. And the police—"

"It hasn't hit the news," I said. "And the cops don't know yet either. We're trying to keep it quiet, until we figure this thing out."

Marcia gave me the same kind of worried look she might have given had it been her own child. "Do you think she's been kidnapped? Is she in some kind of danger?"

"Too early to tell."

"I told him not to let anybody know, Marcia. Not even you," Cassidy said.

"Why not?" she asked. "What about your mother?"

Cassidy looked at me.

"It gets complicated," I said. "Why don't I leave Cassidy to fill you in on whatever she wants to tell you? Every minute I sit here talking is another minute the trail grows cold."

Marcia looked back and forth between the two of us, settling her gaze on Cassidy. "Go ahead, then." She dismissed me with a wave of her hand.

I took it as a sign that meant I was to remove my Cro-Magnon brain from the premises, so I did.

My cell phone rang as I was backing out of the driveway. I fished it out of my pocket and answered.

"Well?"

It was Nicole. Psychic.

"Well, what?"

"Any more developments on the big case? I came

over here to your place and let myself in to use the computer. Didn't want to use one at the university. I've got that folder ready for you."

"Thank you very much. I've got something else for you."

"You do?'

"Has Jake called, by any chance?"

"No. Why?"

"He's getting some information for me."

"What else do you have for me?"

"A laptop computer. Got some files on it we can't seem to open. Also need to find a password to get into somebody's E-mail."

"Cool."

"I thought Jake might be able to help you."

"Where are you? What's going on?"

"Can't get into that right now, sweetheart."

"C'mon, Dad. Don't hold out on me. I'm the one who gave you some great advance surveillance of the Drummond place." Technically, she was correct.

"I love you, Nicky. And because I love you, I'm not going to get into any more of this right now."

"But—"

"No buts."

She let out an audible sigh.

"How was your late class this afternoon?" I asked.

"It was the most boring class I've ever been to. Charlemagne."

"Charlemagne was actually quite a fascinating fellow."

"Yeah? Well, maybe you can come take my class next time."

That'd be the day. I'd last about fifteen minutes with one of those profs.

"Dad?" she said.

"Yeah?"

"When are you going to bring me the laptop?"

"Later."

"All right. I'm meeting Jerry at seven-thirty to play racquetball."

"Jerry?"

"Just a friend, Daddy."

"Uh-huh. Shouldn't you be studying about Charlemagne?"

"It's just a history class. I wouldn't even be taking the stupid course if it wasn't a requirement."

" 'Don't know much about his-to-ry. Don't know much bi-ol-o-gy . . .' "

"I hate it when you sing the oldies," she said.

9

Potential Olympian Jed Haynes, it appeared, preferred the Spartan lifestyle. His house was a sixties-style ranch wedged between apartment buildings off Fourteenth Street. Brown paint peeling over the doorway, broken shutters askew at the front window, a trio of empty Coors Light cans decorating the muddy microchip of a front lawn. There were a couple of cars in the driveway and the lights were all on inside, so I parked along the curb, went up to the door, and knocked.

A girl with long blond hair answered.

"Yes?" She wore bell-bottom jeans with bright panels sewn into the legs, the kind a lot of us used to wear years ago. A blue nose ring pierced one of her nostrils. Her halter top left her midriff bare.

"This where Jed Haynes lives?" I asked.

"Yeah, but he's not here."

"Oh, no." A mocking voice came from inside. "It's another autograph hound trying to track down Jedi the Great."

Over her shoulder I could see two males gripping handles, switching from offense to defense on either side of a foosball table. *Crack*. The ball slammed into one of the goals.

"Yea-a-ah!" The winner performed a touchdown-celebration kind of dance.

"That sucks!" his opponent exclaimed. "I was distracted. Two out of three."

I showed my card to the girl. "I'd like to ask you folks some questions, if you can spare a minute or two."

"Hey, guys," she called over her shoulder. "This man's not after an autograph. He's a private investigator."

That got the foosballers' attention. They left their handles behind and came to back up the girl at the door. The taller one, a square-jawed kid with curly hair, spoke first.

"What's up, man?"

"Like to ask you all a few questions about Jed."

"No shit? What'd he do now, run into some little old lady's car?"

"Not quite."

"Let the man in, let the man in," the shorter of the two said. "Let's get some real dirt on Jed." He had dimpled cheeks and hair that was slick with some type of gel.

His buddy snickered. "All right, Mr. Investigator. C'mon in."

The girl opened the door to let me pass. I entered a living room trashed with fast-food wrappers and old pizza boxes. The main furnishings were a lumpy couch and a recliner not unlike my own throne at home, except that this one had several rips and tears in the upholstery.

"You want to sit down?" the girl asked.

"That's okay. This won't take long."

They all sat down. The girl and the kid with the gel in his hair took the couch while their friend slumped into a torn beanbag chair from which little balls of foam sprinkled onto the carpet.

"Who are you working for?" the guy on the couch wanted to know. He slipped his arm around the girl. They were obviously a couple.

"That's why my card says 'private.' Sorry."

He didn't look happy.

"What's his name again, Kayla?"

"Pavlicek," the girl said. "That's what it said on his card."

"Maybe I can start by getting all your names," I said.

"You still haven't told us what this is all about." Gel-head puffed himself up from the couch a little, trying to play the alpha male thing with me. I wondered if he and Haynes took lessons from the same instructor.

"Yeah, man." Square-jaw was backing him.

I saw no reason to embarrass either one of them when all I was after was information. "Pretty routine, really. I'm just trying to establish Jed Haynes's whereabouts last night."

"What for?"

"Look, folks, I'm not here to cause you trouble, if it's not warranted. I'm just trying to keep a private problem from going to the police. You can either give me what I'm looking for, or I'll find out the information some other way. Jed says he was here with you guys last night. He telling the truth?"

Gel looked at the others and shrugged. " 'Course he was here, man. All night. We hung out, played some foos, watched TV."

"What time did you all go to bed?"

"I don't know, man. Maybe one o'clock. It was after Letterman. You remember, hon?"

She giggled. "It was real late."

"Yeah," he said. "Jed was definitely here. All night."

"He couldn't have sneaked out after the rest of you went to bed?"

"No way, man. I'm a light sleeper."

"Uh-huh. You guys been roommates long?"

"Since the beginning of the year."

"You guys know Cartwright Drummond?"

"Wright?" Square-jaw smiled. "You mean Jed's obsession."

His roommate punched him in the arm. "Jed's not obsessed with her, man."

"Yes, he is."

"No, he's not. Besides, she's still overseas, isn't she? Japan or someplace." Gel-head looked at me.

I shrugged. "Guess you'll have to ask Jed," I said.

"What do you want to know about her for?"

"No particular reason."

The four of us stared at one another for a second or two.

"That's all I needed to know for now," I said. "Thank you very much."

I turned to go, and they all got to their feet.

I paused on my way to the door. "I would like each of your names, though. In case I need to talk to any of you again."

"I'll bet old Jedi stole a couple cases of beer from that restaurant down on the corner again," Square-jaw said.

"Yeah, right," the girl said.

"Your names?" I repeated.

They both looked at Gel-head. He shrugged. "Why not? Hersch," he said. "My name's Penn Hersch."

The girlfriend said her name was Kayla Vestervelt and the other roommate's name was Chad Lippman.

"Hey, Pavlicek," Hersch said. "We gotta tell Jed you were here, you know."

"Fine with me," I said. "Thanks for your time."

My cell phone rang again.

"O-ooo . . . a busy man."

I pushed the button and answered.

"Frank, it's Jake."

"I was wondering what became of you."

"Information takes time, my man."

"I'm just finishing up with some people. Let me get out to my truck."

The foosballers were both thinking it was some kind of big joke now, laughing and poking at each other as the girl went to the door and opened it. Chuckling herself, she avoided my gaze as I passed her on the way out.

I waited until she closed the door, then walked back down the sidewalk and climbed into the privacy of my cab. "Still there?"

"Just painting my nails. How'd you make out with the crows today?"

"Nothing."

"Figures. It's hard enough scaring up a tail chase in wide-open country. Your vineyard owner might be better off trying to lure a wild resident redtail into setting up shop around his spread." I could hear his yellow Lab, Hercules, whimpering about something in the background.

"You've got the dog with you?"

"Thought I'd bring him along for the trip."

"You're still in town, then?"

"In the Jeep down across from your office. Sipping latte from some joint called the Mudhouse. Funky place."

"What'd you find out for me?"

"You're not going to like it. I checked on that number you asked me about," he said.

"Right. Were there any calls?"

"Something going on with these girls and their father, Frank?"

"Quite possibly."

"After you told me about the turnip-face pulling his cannon on you, I figured you'd want to know about this right away."

"Know what?"

"This is the missing daughter's phone, right?"

"Right."

"She or someone else made only one call after the time you gave me. It was to a Charlottesville listing," he said.

"What number?"

"Her father's unlisted cell phone."

"Wonderful."

"Not only that. She got a call back from him ten minutes later."

"How do you know that?"

"Don't ask."

"Interesting." I explained to him about my spying the turnip while Nicole and I were hunting and my encounter with him out at the Drummond estate.

"Sounds like you've got a gnarly one on your hands."

"Can you do me another favor?"

"What's that?"

"You have somebody at home who could watch the birds and the ranch for tonight?"

"I'd have to make a call, but yeah, sure."

"I've got Cassidy Drummond stashed at Marcia's house. I'm pretty sure no one knows she's there. Would you mind heading over there, keeping an eye on things? You could crash on the couch or something."

"No problem."

"Just tell Marcia I sent you for extra insurance and not to worry."

"You don't think she's gonna worry when she sees me show up?"

"Can't be helped, I guess."

"That all?"

"If you can hang around tomorrow, maybe you could find out a little more about those old newspaper articles I was telling you about. I'm stalled a bit on that. And if you don't mind swinging by my apartment on the way over to Marcia's, Nicky's got a whole file of background information on the Drummonds. Plus, I've got Cartwright Drummond's laptop. Maybe you could help Nicky decipher some files for me."

"What're you gonna be doing?" he asked.

I thought about that. "You ever see those kids' books where you have to try to find the goofy-looking little guy somewhere in the background surrounded by a whole bunch of complicated and colorful scenes?"

"Yeah, I think so."

"I'll be looking for Waldo," I said.

10

Waldo, however, must have moved his act to a different town. The rental car description Cassidy Drummond had provided—midnight-blue Nissan Maxima with D.C. plates—and the tag number I'd gotten from the company might as well have been phantoms, for all the good they were doing me. I had traced circles over an ever-expanding search pattern in the neighborhoods around Haynes's place on Fourteenth Street, sweeping out as far as Rugby Avenue. Nothing.

Moving on to the university lots, I cruised the areas around Alderman again, and up to University Hall. Then I switched tactics and headed across town on Barracks and Preston, perusing most of the streets near my office and those surrounding the downtown mall. I made fast runs through Belmont, around the Prospect Hill area, and Cherry Avenue. Not a sign.

I had yet to check out the Pantops area, and Park Street and Rio Road, not to mention the Georgetown Road area and the entire 29 North corridor. It was a long night, and shaping up to get a lot longer.

A half hour later I found myself parked along the curb on High Street, dialing Marcia's number on the cell.

"Jake just arrived," she said when she answered.

"Good."

"He told me you said not to worry."

"That's right."

"Making any progress?"

"Nada."

"Cassidy's told me everything."

"Okay."

"I'm sorry for being so short with you earlier."

"Forget it." I was watching the streetlights burn with life, watching the houses along the street burn with life too, lights ablaze, televisions and computer screens all aglow.

"What do you do now? Will you go to the police?"

"Most likely."

"I really am sorry, Frank. Now that I know—"

"I'm going to want you to tell me all that went on between you and Tor Drummond," I said.

There was a pause. "All right," she said softly.

"Can you put Cassidy on now?"

"Yes. Be careful, Frank."

"Always."

Another pause. "I—I don't want anything to happen to you."

"Me either."

Cassidy came on the line. "You haven't found anything?"

"Nothing," I said. "I'm sorry."

"I keep trying Wright's cell phone."

"I know." I'd tried it again too. Cartwright Drummond's cell phone number now answered with an ominous recording—"The subscriber you have dialed is unavailable or has traveled beyond the coverage area"—which meant either the phone had been turned off or the battery had died.

"Isn't there something else you can do?" Her voice sounded shaky.

"Keep looking."

"Okay."

"But I have to be honest. I'm not optimistic at this point. You're probably not going to be able to keep a lid on this thing."

There was silence. Then after several seconds: "I know, I know—" She began to cry softly.

I let her cry for a little bit. "I'm very sorry," I said finally. Seemed like I was getting good at saying that. "Listen. Time's getting critical. There are a couple of cops I know I can trust."

"No, please. Not yet. Please just keep looking."

I thought it over. "I'll keep looking," I said, "but don't get your hopes up."

"I'm afraid," she said. "You think . . . do you think Wright's been?" She couldn't form the words.

"We shouldn't go jumping to conclusions just yet."

"I've had this awful feeling ever since we talked earlier. I even had to go into the bathroom a little while ago to throw up. If Cartwright doesn't . . . we promised each other we'd always be there . . ."

I said nothing. Being a private investigator may sound glamorous to some. The truth is, a lot of the time it seems only incrementally different from picking up trash for a living. Right now the garbage detail looked pretty good.

"You believe in prayer, Mr. Pavlicek?"

"Sure," I said.

"I'm praying that God won't take Cartwright from me."

A cold wind swirled the trees along the street. A hunter's moon became visible for a brief moment through a break in the clouds.

"Me too," I said.

We hung up and I went on with my vigil.

C'mon, Frank. Charlottesville is not New York or

L.A.—not even Atlanta or Washington, D.C.
Shouldn't be that hard to find a missing auto. If it's
still in town, that is.

I checked out the areas around Park Street and Lo-
cust Avenue, then shot down the 250 Bypass to River
Road. It was well after ten by now. Traffic was light.
I looped back up on High Street to Martha Jefferson
Hospital, cruising through the surrounding streets and
lots. I was finishing up a check of the hospital's parking garage when it occurred to me I'd forgotten the
two parking garages at the larger university medical
center across town. I drove back down High Street to
Preston, cut across to West Main, and began trolling
in the direction of University Corner.

This was a transitional part of town, one that city
planners envisioned would one day serve as an attractive bridge between the college and downtown. The
vision had been at least partially realized. Between
the shells of older structures and vacant lots with their
sparkles of broken glass, there were a couple of new
hotels and a thriving, if eclectic, strip of eateries. The
city had recently upgraded the bridge that crossed the
railroad with attractive lighting, and the railroad station itself had undergone a major renovation—one of
the buildings now housed a trendy restaurant.

A minute or so later the medical center popped into
view on my left. I entered the first garage and started
my search.

Ten minutes later, still nothing. Five levels of vehicles, one older Maxima, but nothing remotely resem-
bling the Drummonds' rental car. Maybe Cartwright
Drummond had left the state. Maybe her father was
having her followed, like her sister, and for some
reason she'd decided to go underground in a Third

World country. I moved on to the primary-care-center garage.

I was cruising along the second level, momentarily distracted by a minivan backing out of a space, when a flash of dark blue up ahead on the left caught my attention. Another Maxima. In the amber light it gleamed almost black. I took in a deep breath as I came abreast of the vehicle. D.C. plates.

Checked the tag number. Bingo.

I sat there letting the truck idle for a moment, hardly believing my luck. Maybe there was a simple explanation to this whole affair after all. The vehicle appeared to be clean and unoccupied, just the way Cassidy and Cartwright had probably rented it. I scanned up and down the row of cars. Nothing unusual. Except for the van, the garage was quiet at this time of night—hospital visiting hours were over. Many of the spaces now sat empty. I reached across and grabbed my four-cell and, just in case, my .357 out of the glove box. Strapped on the weapon and stepped from the truck.

Nothing but the sound of my own engine, the cold and the sweet smell of my own exhaust, and the haze of steam blowing from some kind of vents on the roof of the hospital across the street. I slipped on a pair of leather gloves and carefully approached the rental car. In no way did it seem out of order—the inside was empty and the doors were all locked. I considered trying to break in, took a look around, and decided I better not. My flashlight beam swept across the seats, over the steering wheel and the dash down to the floor.

There. Something reflected the light a little, dark and wet on the carpet. It took a moment for my mind to register what my eyes had seen, and in that second I inadvertently angled the beam up toward the rearview mirror and an even more unmistakable image.

I'm a man rarely given to profanity.

"Sweet Jesus," I whispered.

Bloody fingerprints.

11

"You're in deep doo-dah, all right, Frank."

Carol Upwood twirled a strand of blond hair between her fingers as she leaned back against the wall of the elevator, used by detectives and brass only, that led from the garage to the third floor of the city hall, where the investigators from the Charlottesville Police Department worked. She was a five-foot-two spark plug of makeup, fingernails, and bluster. The only thing harder on a testosterone-laden ego than a brilliant woman is a brilliant woman cop, and Carol was most definitely that.

I stretched. It was late, almost midnight.

"Geez, Frank. You know, maybe you're gonna want to write a book about all this. . . . You oughta be takin' notes," Bill Ferrier said. A former Virginia State Police violent crimes investigator, Ferrier had been lured out of early retirement to work as a detective for the city in what was called the Crimes Against People Unit, which handled missing persons, not to mention homicides. Upwood was sort of his understudy.

When the doors opened I followed them down a short hall into the "big room," where the detectives all worked, their desks clustered together, backed by cork bulletin boards. The floor was a speckled gray terrazzo, the walls painted cinder block. There was a

drop ceiling with fluorescent lighting but no windows
to let in the outside view, not that there was much of
one anyway from city hall, tucked, as it was, in the
shadow of one of the city's downtown parking garages.
A Formica counter filled with files and other materials
ran the length of the wall around the room.

Ferrier sat in his chair, while Upwood propped herself on the side of his desk and crossed her legs. Since
it was after hours, she was wearing blue jeans and a
police department sweatshirt. Most of the detectives
worked irregular hours anyway, sometimes pulling
twenty-four hours at a stretch. The sweatshirt partially
obscured the Beretta she had strapped to her waist.

"Abercrombie's pretty hot about a PI sitting on a
crime scene," she said. Willard Abercrombie was the
chief of the Charlottesville City Police. My relationship with him went back a few years. My kinship with
the chief had been severely strained ever since the
time he had charged a local Baptist minister with sod-
omy: a crime that the man—imperfect as he was—had
not committed. I had stepped in to pull the preacher
off the hook.

"I wasn't sitting on the scene, Carol. I called you
guys as soon as I found the vehicle." I didn't tell them
I'd called and spoken to Marcia and Cassidy and Toronto first—a technicality. Marcia was going to call
Dr. Karen Drummond, bring her up to speed, and
arrange for her to meet with Cassidy.

After I called 911, the university police showed up
in less than three minutes, followed quickly thereafter
by the city people.

"Either way, some defense lawyer's eventually
going to play hell with it. Not to mention the media."

I shrugged and put my hands in the air. My best
"not guilty."

"How'd you know about the missing twin?" Ferrier said.

Bill is a good cop. Whatever happens, I know I can trust his word. When you're talking jail time or staring down the black barrel of some lunatic's personal protection device, that counts for something. When you're talking bureaucrats and power jockeys, it tends to take a backseat.

"I told you. I was hired by her sister."

"Uh-huh. And where is she, again?"

"Like I said before, my client doesn't wish to have her whereabouts divulged at this time."

He frowned, let out a long, exaggerated sigh. "That's just wonderful, Frank. We've got a U.S. congressman's daughter bugged out on us and you're playing a shell game with our major witness."

"Not my call."

"No?" He knew better than to try to shake me down. But he seemed disappointed. "This is the kind of shit that wrecks people's careers."

I was about to say something like I ought to know, but I figured it wouldn't earn me any merit badges at the moment.

He looked across at his understudy. She shook her head, but he spoke anyway. "Carol," he said, "maybe you oughta let me take the heat that might come down over this."

"Are you kidding?" she said. "I'd rather go back to working security at the university."

That Carol. Feeble little woman.

His eyes bored back into me. "What else do you know about this"—he looked down at his notes—"Cartwright Drummond?" Ferrier obviously didn't follow the news much.

"What do you mean?"

"She ever done this kind of thing before? Ever been in trouble? Maybe drugs or alcohol is involved. . . . And this swimmer you talked to, the boyfriend? We want to talk to him yesterday. I assume you know where to find him."

"Delighted to be of assistance." I smiled, but not too big.

"What about the names of the other friends you said you got?"

"Nothing remarkable, as far as I can tell, but I'm happy to share."

"And the parents? What about them?"

"I know as much as everybody else, I guess. What I read in the papers."

Politically incorrect Carol grunted. "Drummond's your basic scumbag. Trying to get reelected after the kind of crap he pulled . . ."

Ferrier looked to be thinking the situation over. I had come to him partly because of who he was, but also because in his current position he was a lot less likely to allow his chain to be jerked, if it came to that, by some higher-up.

"Lot of possibilities here, Frank, in what you're not telling us. Might just have to hold you as a material witness," he said. "You know, let you think about this whole situation with the other twin and everything."

"Aw, c'mon, Bill. Which of my lawyers do you want me to call first?"

I had employed several over the years, actually. Specialists. Some were even my own clients. In Charlottesville you can hardly walk across the street without tripping over an attorney. I don't always get the personal loyalty or attention of having only one, but then again, I prefer being on the side with the expertise.

Ferrier was twisting his lips, apparently formulating a not too kind retort to my bringing lawyers into the equation, when there was a little disturbance on the far side of the room.

"Where is he? I want to talk to him right now."

Chief of Police Willard Abercrombie waddled into the room like a walrus on quaaludes. He was better than two hundred and fifty pounds of impeccable grooming, a few inches taller than Ferrier, decked out in white shirt and tie, khakis, soft shoes, and navy jacket, his small blue-green eyes framed by tortoise-shell glasses.

"Well, well, well," he said. "If it isn't our guest of honor."

"Like I was saying about the lawyer—" I said to Ferrier and Upwood, ignoring the chief.

Abercrombie wasn't used to being ignored. He huffed and he puffed and he looked about ready to blow a circuit, but Ferrier cut in on him.

"We've explained to the chief your involvement in all this, Frank. I'm sure you'd agree that things have . . . uh . . . escalated a little beyond the scope of private investigation."

I said nothing. But my estimate of Bill Ferrier shot up even more. He'd helped bail me out of a jam once before. Maybe he would come through again.

"When'd you get such a high-profile client list, Pavlicek?" Abercrombie asked. "I thought you specialized in chasing husbands out of whores' beds."

Some people are made vindictive by circumstances. Some may have just been born that way.

I stayed focused on the detectives. "You may have a point there, Bill—about the escalation, I mean."

Abercrombie's eyes did a napalm. "Listen up, Pavlicek!" He moved right in front of me and shook his finger in my face. "I've got the governor demanding answers, the papers and TV stations beginning to call."

"Then I guess you called the congressman and the young woman's mom," I said.

"Of course I did. Left a message for the girl's mother. And I spoke with one of Congressman Drummond's people in Richmond. Fortunately, his flight was still over the Atlantic. The air force is diverting their plane to Iceland so Drummond can catch a different flight back to Dulles. Stopped a whole goddamn trade mission."

"Proud of you." I began to shake my head. Ferrier and Upwood stood like statues.

"You have a problem with that, my friend?" Abercrombie calling me "friend" was like Custer mailing a Christmas card to Sitting Bull.

"What, you mean besides the fact you may have just compromised the entire investigation?" I said.

"Frank . . ." Ferrier was saying.

Abercrombie turned to his detectives. "I want this idiot taken into custody. Arrest him, charge him—I don't care what you do, but I want him held."

"But, Chief," Ferrier said.

"Thanks . . . *friend*," I said.

The chief and I had never actually come to blows, but we came close now. He balled his fists, turned to glare at me, and his whole face contracted like a prune. He must have thought better of charging me, though. Either that or he thought it might not look dignified for the chief of police to be brawling in the middle of his own headquarters, especially with his white shirt and khakis on. Breathing heavily, he turned to Ferrier.

"I don't have time for this douche bag, Bill. I want

him out of our hair and away from this investigation."
He spun around and stormed out of the room.

Ferrier was right behind him. "Hold on a second,
Chief."

They walked down the corridor together, out of earshot. Ferrier seemed to be patiently explaining something while Abercrombie's voice kept blowing. I
picked out a couple of impressive-sounding phrases
like "obstruction of justice" and "probable cause."

Meanwhile, I was an instant pariah in the big room.
The two or three other detectives who'd been on the
phone or doing paperwork across the way, having bent
an ear toward the entire exchange, now went back to
their tasks as if I'd become the invisible man. Even
Carol turned to straighten some papers on her desk and
began writing something down on a yellow legal pad.

Ferrier returned and without saying a word grabbed
me by the arm and quickly walked me back to the
elevator. Surprised, Carol seemed to be undecided
what to do for a moment, but then made the choice
to tag along with us.

"Man's an emotion suppressor. Guys like that can
be dangerous," I said.

"Yeah?" Ferrier said. "Well, you better start doing
a little suppression yourself—of the tongue kind."

"I never saw anyone stand up to Abercrombie like
that before," Carol said under her breath.

"Don't encourage him." Ferrier finally let go of my
arm when we were in the elevator. "Listen, Frank.
I'm not going to BS you. You know as well as I do
that this thing's about to snowball. I'm not asking you
to tell us everything you know, but I am asking you
to think about what you're getting into."

"Sam Spade's dead, Spencer's fiction, and the rest
of us are just flesh and blood," I said.

"Something like that. You better watch yourself."

We all watched the elevator lights blink the changing floors.

"I used to hate this job, especially when there was no body," I said.

They said nothing. The elevator doors slid open in the parking garage.

"Am I free to go now?"

Ferrier gestured with an open hand, as if that should be obvious.

For a moment, I thought about telling them about the old *Post* articles concerning the hit-and-run, but decided I'd better hold off until I knew more. "Tell me one thing. You think Cartwright Drummond's been greased?"

"Don't push it, Frank." He craned his head out the door and took a long look down the garage to make sure no one else was within earshot.

"Pretty please?"

He coughed. "Wouldn't that have been your supposition?"

I nodded.

"Like you said, no body, though," Carol interjected. "For now, it's officially still just an abduction."

"I'm impressed," I said.

Ferrier cocked his head at me in a curious manner.

" 'Supposition.' You know, most people would've just used the word 'thinking' or 'guess.' "

"Get the hell out of here. And no leaving the state. You so much as breathe the wrong way and you'll be doing your peeing in a steel toilet where privacy ain't been heard from in years," he said as the elevator doors closed in front of them.

Ouch.

12

Marcia sat across from me in the Ford. We were headed west on I-64 toward Afton Mountain, sipping coffee from Styrofoam cups, Armistead tucked in her hawk box in the back of the truck. Marcia had only been hunting with me a couple of times, but she'd volunteered to come along and play bush beater this morning. The sun had just winked over the horizon behind us, spreading its flaxen light over the hills, the cold gray of the day before a distant memory.

"It always looks so beautiful," she said as we topped a rise in the highway and the Blue Ridge suddenly popped into view.

"Yup." I yawned and flexed my shoulders, just beginning to feel the effects of the coffee.

Needless to say, it'd been a night of little sleep for both of us. Dr. Karen Drummond had arrived from Richmond and turned out to be, for once, almost exactly the type of person the media had portrayed: an intelligent, compassionate, no-nonsense kind of individual. I could see why Marcia and she were friends.

Still in shock, Dr. Drummond was furious and maybe even a little frightened about the possibility of her husband's involvement in her daughter's disappearance. She agreed with the approach of keeping Cassidy's whereabouts a secret, although she was a little reluctant, at first, to keep that information from the police. By the time she left to go talk with them, however, Marcia had convinced her that Toronto and I could be trusted and that Cassidy would be safer where she was.

"Have you heard from Jason?" I asked.

Jason is Marcia's son. Has lived with her since her marriage ended years ago. A little younger than Nicole, in his senior year at Charlottesville High School.

"Oh." She swatted comically at the air. "He called last night from Nags Head. He said they're having a great time, even though it's still cold down there too. He caught a bluefish off the pier."

"Don't mind him spending time with his dad and stepmom?"

"Not really. In a way, I'm glad he can experience a husband and wife functioning at least seminormally. Lord knows, his father and I hardly ever did."

A mile or two down the road we approached the exit that would take us into the stretch of piedmont fields and woods where I had permission to hunt.

"You ready to talk more about Tor Drummond?" I asked.

She shifted in her seat a little. Nodded.

"Talk to me."

"What do you want to know?"

"He's got this goon tailing his daughter. The other twin's disappeared, and he's having late-night phone conversations with her. Then we find her bloody car. He capable of murder?"

She didn't answer at first. "I don't know," she said finally. "Maybe."

"What went on between you two?"

"Who says something went on?"

I checked the impulse to say something.

Her lip quivered a little; her eyes darted away from

me. She seemed to be marshaling her thoughts, perhaps arranging memories in a way that would make sense to someone else.

"I told you I was a volunteer," she said.

"Right. When exactly was that?"

"More than fifteen years ago—seventeen, maybe. Cassidy and Cartwright weren't even in kindergarten yet."

"That's when you all became friends."

"Yes."

"What kind of work did you do?"

"I worked on his first campaign. Phone calls, stuffing envelopes, that sort of thing. Art and I had only been married a few years, and Jason was still little too, of course. Karen had just finished her residency in pediatrics. She was working part-time for a practice here in Charlottesville, and she used to bring the girls and they would sit and play with Jason."

"Was Drummond still practicing at that time?"

"No. He never finished his residency. Said he'd decided he enjoyed politics too much."

"Quite a switch."

"I suppose."

"I take it money's never been much of an issue for the Drummonds."

"No, it hasn't. Tor's always had more money than was probably good for him."

"So you all became pals. Drummond's up for reelection every couple of years. You work on more than one of his campaigns?"

"No," she said. "I quit after the first one."

"How come?"

She hesitated. "I don't know. I got too busy, I guess. Karen and I have stayed friends, though."

She could tell I wasn't buying it. I took the Crozet

exit and turned right on U.S. 250. "Why'd you stop working on the campaigns, Marsh?"

Tears appeared in her eyes again. She sniffled.

I waited.

"Tor Drummond tried to rape me," she said.

I took my foot off the gas and looked at her. Her eyes were puffy, and her voice seemed to come from some far-off wilderness of grief and despair. I pulled the truck over to the shoulder, found a tissue for her in the glove box, and gave her a few moments.

"Witnesses?" I said.

She shook her head. "Of course not." She lifted her shoulders in a sob and leaned her head against the passenger door's window. She dabbed at her cheeks with the tissue and gently blew her nose.

I gave her a few more moments. This was no time to rush. "You want to tell me how it happened?"

She turned her head and looked out the window. Fog was lifting over the field beside the road. Testifying to a true Virginia spring, a few trees here had actually begun to sprout their leaves already, despite the recent cold. Some cars swooshed by, then a John Deere tractor followed by a line of frustrated motorists.

When she spoke, her mouth moved, but the rest of her seemed locked in some frozen section of her memory. "It was a couple of days after the election. At the time the district was mainly centered in Richmond, and Drummond had his headquarters there. Tor won by only a few hundred votes. When the official results were finally announced, he and Karen threw a victory party for the staff and volunteers. The hotel ballroom had been booked for the night of the election, so they held the party at someone's house in Richmond. A big house. Belonged to some big contributors. I don't remember the name."

She took a deep breath.

"Art stayed home with the children in Charlottesville, so I drove down with another volunteer. It was getting late. They were playing Rolling Stones music on the stereo, and there was dancing and a lot of champagne. Karen finally left to go home with the two girls, but Tor, the owners of the house, and a few of the staff and volunteers, including my ride home, wanted to keep celebrating.

"I went upstairs to use the bathroom. It was the kind between bedrooms—you know, with two doors. I thought everyone else was still downstairs. I'd had a little to drink, but I wasn't drunk. Tor must have followed me or something because I was just turning to lock the second door when he elbowed his way in." She shook her head in disgust.

"What did you do?"

"I was too shocked to react at first," she said. "I asked him to leave, but before I knew what was happening he had his arms around me, pulling my head back by my hair and kissing me hard. I wanted to scream, but I just couldn't. It almost didn't seem real. He started grabbing at my dress and was trying to undo his belt when, thank God, someone knocked on the other door."

"What happened then?"

"He broke away and slipped out the door he'd come through. I was so shaken up, I pretended I was ill. The girl who'd driven me down from Charlottesville came upstairs. They got me out to the car and she took me home."

"That's it?"

She nodded.

"You ever tell anyone about this?"

"No. Not for a long time, that is. The only other

person who knows about it is Karen Drummond. I told her after she decided she wanted a divorce from Tor."

"How about your ex-husband? Why didn't you tell him?"

"Are you kidding? Art would've tried to kill Tor."

"The thought's just been crossing my own mind," I said.

"Besides, what good would it have done? At first, I just kept telling myself Tor had been drunk, he didn't know what he was doing. Then I started wondering about myself. Had I done something to encourage him? Later I decided I hadn't, but I doubted anyone else would ever believe me."

I nodded. When I was a rookie cop in New York, I'd interviewed a rape victim, a young woman who worked on Wall Street, well educated, emotionally stable. But she'd decided in the end not even to press charges. She'd met the schmuck in a bar, gotten a little tipsy, and finding they both shared a passion for art, let him talk her into dropping by her place so he could see her small collection of paintings.

"Now you know why I never volunteered for another campaign," Marcia said.

"But you stayed friends with Karen and the girls."

"Yes. But to this day, I've always done my best to avoid Tor."

"How about him? He never approached you, never tried to get you alone to go for the grab-and-pull act again?"

"No."

Sophisticated sexual predators will sometimes move on once the thrill of the hunt is gone. "You ever try talking to him about it?"

"Once. It was a few months later, when Art and I

were beginning to have our troubles. He called the house looking for Karen and the kids—they'd been by to visit earlier in the day. Tor asked me how I was doing. I don't remember exactly what I said, something about Art and his drinking. Then I told him point-blank: 'You men need to take more responsibility for your actions with alcohol.' "

"What did he say?"

"He said I needed to be more careful how I presented myself around all-American studs like him and Art. I knew then and there I'd never be able to accuse him of anything and make it stick."

"You know if Drummond's ever done this to anybody else?"

She shook her head. "Like I said, I try to have as little to do with him as possible."

I put my arm out and gently pulled her to me across the seat. She leaned on my shoulder, and I kissed the top of her head and held her close. The curtain of fog continued to rise from the fields while we watched. Here it would be a while before the sun was able to burn through the haze.

13

Congressman Torrin Drummond looked haggard, most likely from lack of sleep. I caught glimpses of him on the phone as a secretary and an aide intermittently buzzed in and out of his office, triaging what appeared to be a blizzard of messages and calls.

I waited just outside the door in a conference room of his campaign headquarters. The building was an old double storefront in the Belmont section of town, just the kind of area where Drummond needed to drive home his slogan of "standing for the working people." The walls were festooned with REELECT DRUMMOND! posters. His chief aide, Mel Dworkin, the chunky man with bulbous lips and blow-dried hair that Cassidy had described, sat across the table from me.

"Wow," I said, "I hope it's not always this frantic."

Dworkin was stone-faced. "Man's lost his daughter. Wouldn't *you* be frantic?"

I had to admit he had me there.

"So the congressman must be pretty close to his daughters, huh?"

He shot me a look like he was swatting away a pesky mosquito. "Why don't I let Representative Drummond talk to you about that?"

Our conversation so far had been less than productive. Since he worked for the congressman, I thought he might know something about the security detail out at the house. He claimed he didn't. Since he'd been with Drummond for a long time, I thought he might be able to give me some hints about his boss's extra-curricular romantic activities. My subtle attempts at raising the subject had been received like flatulence at a press conference.

Dworkin allowed himself a small yawn. I noticed he was missing the top half of one finger on his right hand.

"Cartwright's disappearance is tragic," he finally said, as if reading from a script. "It's something you can't plan for. We're still hoping for the best. Politics sort of takes a backseat."

But even as he mouthed the words I could sense him calculating the prospects. The slightest trace of a smile crossed his mouth, disappearing almost as soon as it had materialized. He knew if they played their cards right with this thing, the sympathy vote would be huge.

A soft thud came from the direction of Drummond's office. The door swung open again, and this time the congressman himself stepped out. He was an imposing presence up close: about six-three with sharp-cut features, short black hair combed precisely across his forehead, white shirt and tie with the sleeves rolled up, and dark eyes well practiced in expressing empathy. I could see the Stetson hanging on a peg in his office. He closed the door behind him and made a beeline toward me, his hand extended. His leather boots creaked as he walked.

"Mr. Pavlicek?"

"That's right." I stood to meet his handshake and noticed Dworkin stood too, as if instant virtue had somehow been thrust upon us. The aide moved to close the door to the reception area as well.

Drummond's grip was firm but not too firm, and he held it a moment longer than was needed. "I want to thank you for your involvement in this situation . . . for helping Cassidy," he said.

"I'm not sure there's too much to be thankful for yet," I said, reminding myself I was talking to a potential rapist.

"Yes, but from what my ex-wife tells me, you've performed a valuable service, and I won't forget that."

I wondered how many times he'd uttered that line. He sat down in a chair next to his aide's seat and motioned for us to follow suit.

"Please," he said. "Sit down."

Dworkin and I resumed our seats.

"The police come up with any more leads?" I asked.

"No, I'm afraid not."

"We've asked that the congressman be immediately informed of any developments," Dworkin intoned, a little louder than the situation warranted.

Drummond shook his head. He placed his hands on the table and stared at them for a moment. He seemed to be looking inside himself at something he could barely stand to see. There were no tears in his eyes. Only uncertainty. Feigned or real, it was impossible to tell. "Now what's this I hear about my other daughter hiring you and you not being willing to tell anyone where she is?"

The two men stared at me the way they might examine an ugly insect.

"I'm afraid you've been misinformed."

"Oh? I was told that—"

"It's Cassidy who doesn't want anyone to know where she is. She's my client. I'm doing as she has asked."

"I see." The congressman digested this information for a few moments.

"Didn't your ex-wife tell you that?"

He shook his head. "Karen and I have generally limited communication these days."

"The cops ain't too happy with you, Pavlicek," Dworkin said. "You'd better watch where you step."

"Yes," Drummond said. "Wouldn't Cassidy be able to help with the investigation?"

"The investigation is ongoing," I said.

"What's that supposed to mean?" Dworkin's brow furrowed, and his syrupy voice suddenly switched to a snarl.

"It means I have some more questions for you, gentlemen. Starting with why the congressman has been having his daughters followed." The use of the plural, to include Cartwright, was a guess, but I figured it was a safe bet. Drummond, however, showed little reaction to the question.

"Look, Pavlicek," his chief of staff said, "I've hired guys like you before. This is serious business. Why don't you just bow out and let the police do their job?"

Drummond held up a hand to quiet him. "That's all right, Mel. I'm sure we all have the same thing in mind here: finding out what's happened to Cartwright." He focused his laserlike vision on me. There was an almost eerie serenity about his manner, which I didn't understand. "I believe you used to be a detective up in New York, Mr. Pavlicek—isn't that right?"

Here we go, I thought. This guy doesn't miss a trick. Probably has more than one ace tucked away in his underwear.

"That's right," I said.

"Didn't you get into some difficulty—a shooting or something, wasn't it?"

"That was resolved long ago, Congressman."

"The Department of Criminal Justice must know about that, then, don't they?" He was referring to the Virginia department responsible for regulating all private investigators and private security compliance agents in the commonwealth. If he thought he could somehow intimidate me, he was mistaken, but I sensed he might be up to something more.

"Absolutely," I said.

He pressed his lips together. "Mmmm," he said.

"Besides"—I thought I might as well play tit for tat—"don't we all have things we might have done in our past, things we might regret?"

"Hmmm." Louder this time. He smiled. "Could you excuse us for a few minutes, Mel?" he said without turning toward his chief. "I'd like to talk to Mr. Pavlicek alone."

Dworkin hesitated. He glared at me for a moment. Then he pushed away from the table, stood up without saying another word, and left the room.

"I know what you're thinking," Drummond said after he'd gone. "But people like Mel can be very useful. . . . He's very loyal and honest to a tee. Anyone offered you anything to drink, by the way? Soda, coffee?"

"I'm fine."

"All right. Now . . . to answer your earlier question. It was a question, wasn't it? Not an accusation."

"I have no basis to make any accusations at the moment. Only questions."

"Of course. I like you, Pavlicek. You see through things and get right to the point. That's a valuable trait."

"So is not giving a damn."

He smiled. "Everyone gives a damn about something, don't they?"

I said nothing.

"But back to your question. I assume you're referring to the unfortunate encounter you had with my employee on the downtown mall."

"That's correct."

"The explanation's quite simple. I've been worried about my daughters for some time, especially Cartwright. I'm in the midst of an important campaign, as you know. I decided, once they returned to Virginia from overseas, to have some of my people discreetly keep an eye on them for their own protection."

"Sounds more like spying to me. Why not just assign them each a bodyguard?"

He chuckled. "You don't know my girls, Mr. Pavlicek. They've both got minds of their own."

He was right. I didn't really know them, especially the missing twin. "Was Cartwright being followed the other night when she disappeared?" I asked.

"No, unfortunately. We didn't realize she was leaving the house." If it were a lie, he told it with such apparent conviction that the line between fiction and reality became blurred.

"Too bad. I suppose we wouldn't be here if you had."

He nodded. "The police seem to be suspicious of this swimmer from the university."

"That's where she told her sister she was going."

He ran his fingers through his hair and sighed. "I never was in favor of Cartwright dating that young man. He comes from California—did you know that? A fish out of water, if you ask me. You talked to him, didn't you, Pavlicek?"

"Uh-huh."

"What did you think?"

"I think the kid may just be telling the truth," I said.

Drummond flattened his hands against one another and bounced his fingers off his chin. "Which leaves us with practically nothing."

"What about the bloody fingerprints? Have they confirmed that they're Cartwright's?" Maybe I could pry some information out of him.

He visibly cringed. "Yes. I believe they have. They're also running DNA tests with samples from her sister and hair from one of her brushes."

"To see if someone else's blood might be in the mix as well."

"I suppose," he said.

"Have the police questioned anyone else?" I asked.

"They told me they're talking to anyone who may have seen anything unusual around that parking garage the night before last. Some other students, too. Friends of Cartwright's and this Haynes." His tone made the swimmer sound like a disease. "And Karen and I spent almost an hour and a half answering questions for them up there this morning. Of course, Cassidy was the last one to see her . . ." He dropped his hands and shook his head as if to clear it. "I'm sorry. I'm afraid I'm only running on caffeine and nerves here."

If it were an act, it was one of the best I'd ever seen. I let him go on.

"I've made some mistakes in my time, Pavlicek. Bad ones that everybody knows about. They destroyed my family and came close to destroying my career. But I don't know why my daughter would disappear like this . . . or what's happened to her. I just pray to God that she's okay."

"Cassidy says you and Cartwright had an argument the night she disappeared."

He blew out a sigh. "We did. Look, I know I may've done serious damage to my daughters—psychologically, I mean—with some of my actions. Not to mention Karen. It's something I'm going to have to live with for the rest of my life." He crossed his arms and stared blankly at the wall. At least he didn't bite his lip. If he had, I might've stood up and hit him in the face.

"Are you saying your daughter is in need of counseling?" I said.

"Oh, she's had counseling. She and Cassidy have always had nothing but the best. In fact, we've all had counseling, for all the good it did. And it doesn't really surprise me that Cassidy hired you. She doesn't trust me."

"Seems to me you haven't given her much reason to."

He looked at me in silence. Through the conference room door came the sound of a phone ringing. Someone picked it up. Drummond abruptly stood and went to the door and opened it. He leaned through, speaking to someone on the other side. Then he turned back to me.

"Why don't you come into my office, Mr. Pavlicek, where we can speak more privately?"

I nodded. I rose from my chair and followed him into his inner sanctum. A secretary was just exiting through another door, closing it behind her, as we entered.

Even in this temporary campaign setting, Drummond's office was appointed with an oversized cherry desk, a high-backed leather chair in matching burgundy, photographs of the famous and powerful. Not exactly working class in here. A testament, I guess, to what old money can buy. Drummond was a senior member of the House of Representatives. I wondered what his office up in Washington was like.

The congressman sat down behind the desk and bade me sit in one of the armchairs opposite. A power move designed to compensate for whatever he was about to tell me, I assumed. He leaned back in his chair for a few seconds, folding his hands across his lap, turning slightly to survey one of the pictures across the room before pulling his chair up and leaning forward to place his elbows on the desk.

"Suppose," he began. "Suppose I told you a family secret."

"I suppose I'd listen."

"You'd keep it private?"

"Unless it involved a crime."

"Fair enough." He smoothed the hair on the back of his head. "As you may know, the twins' mother and I were medical residents at the same time, here in Richmond."

"Right."

"I met Karen at a party with a bunch of other surgical interns. Those were wild times. The twins were, uh, to say the least . . . something of a surprise."

"I follow."

"We decided to go ahead and get married as soon as we found out. Karen's mom, who was living at the time, offered to help out with the children."

"Okay. But what does any of this have to do with Cartwright's disappearance?" I still used the milder term instead of "abduction" or "murder," which I was afraid might send the man over the edge.

Drummond sighed and crossed his arms, sitting back again.

"Nothing, I hope," he said. "It's just that Cartwright has recently developed what I'm afraid is this unhealthy obsession with the past. And, um . . . especially since the events of the last couple of years—"

One thing I knew about Drummond. It wasn't like him to stumble over words.

"You mean since the scandal and the divorce."

"Yes. Since the divorce, and especially while she was away in Japan—she seems to have decided she needed to put everything about me under the microscope."

"Maybe she's trying to figure out what would make you betray her mother," I said.

He grunted in disgust and shook his head. "I suppose . . . I suppose you may be right."

"What about Cassidy?"

"What about her?"

"Does she display this 'unhealthy obsession,' as you call it, too?"

"Not to the same degree," he said.

"But enough for her to want to hire her own private investigator."

"Touché."

I said nothing.

"Listen, all I'm trying to tell you is that Cartwright has always been the dominant twin, the one to question everything, the one to take the chances."

Chances. Could she have been taking some kind of risk the other night?

"What kinds of chances has your daughter been taking lately?"

"For one thing, she's been talking to Diane Lemminger."

My mind flashed through snippets of TV reports and newspaper columns. "Wasn't she the staffer with whom you . . . ?"

He leaned back a little more in his chair and nodded.

The scandal broke when Lemminger and Drummond had been photographed together in a restaurant, then later entering a hotel. Twenty years the congressman's junior, Lemminger looked like someone's dream of a Hollywood screen test. A true believer in the cause. She had lasted through three or four election cycles, until it became obvious that her relationship with her boss was more than just work-related. Later, there were even rumors of a pregnancy. Some had suspected Drummond of pressuring her into a quiet abortion, although none of his political enemies had ever come up with any proof.

"How does Cartwright know Diane Lemminger?" I asked.

Drummond shrugged. "Everyone around here knew Diane. The kids knew her. Even Karen knew her. Diane is, uh . . . quite something, to say the least."

"I'll bet. What would make your daughter go talk with her, the woman who broke up your family?"

"I'm not sure, exactly."

"What really happened between you and Lemminger?"

"Diane was never pregnant . . . not by me, at least, if that's what you're suggesting. A lot of lies have been spread around."

"But you had sex with her."

"Well . . . we were together."

"Which means you had sex with her."

"We were together. What more do you want me to say?"

Look away from the TelePrompTer? Read my lips? "And this went on for quite some time," I said.

"A period of time, yes . . . but Diane and I tried to keep things discreet. I'm not proud of this, Pavlicek. I lost Karen over it, the kids. I lost—" He seemed unable to formulate the words.

"When was the last time you saw Diane Lemminger?"

"It's been a couple of years now at least."

"How can I reach her?"

"I think she lives in Virginia Beach."

"How do you know Cartwright has been talking to her?"

"Cartwright told me in an E-mail."

"Odd that she would tell you if she really suspected you of withholding information from her."

He shook his head and shrugged.

"Suppose someone, a stranger maybe, were feeding Cartwright certain information. Information she thought was leading her to discovering something about your past. Accurate or not, would that've been a strong enough motive for her to take a chance on meeting this stranger?"

The congressman didn't answer. He turned his chair toward the window and looked outside. Sunlight struck the back of his head at an odd angle, the effect of which was to make his dark hair appear brown. When he finally spoke, his voice dropped considerably.

"I don't know," he said. "How can I know? Her sister told me she was going to meet with this swimmer Haynes, and now you and the police tell me the kid says he never saw her and you think he's telling the truth."

I decided to switch gears. "Who are you sleeping with these days, Congressman?"

He waved the question away. "Look, my friend, this is too much. This is my personal life. Even a politician is entitled to some privacy."

"Your daughters may not think so."

"I know that, goddamn it. That's why I'm . . . that's why I'm . . ."

"What?"

"That's why I'm telling you all this now. Just like you, I want to know if Cartwright mistrusted me enough to put herself in danger."

"Danger from what, Congressman? From whom?"

"I told you . . . I don't know," he said.

"There's something you're not telling me."

His face grew strangely passive. "I've been more than honest with you, Pavlicek. I'm giving you the truth."

"Okay. Then you won't mind answering some more questions. Ever heard of a couple named George and Norma Paitley?"

He glanced out the window for an instant. "Paitley? No, I don't think so. Why?"

"Their names have come up in the course of my investigation. You sure?"

He looked me square in the eye. "I'm sure," he said.

"Where were all your staff night before last when your daughter disappeared?"

"You'll have to ask them."

"You were on the phone with someone that night. About one in the morning. The call originated from

Cartwright's cell phone. Then you called the same number back."

"How do you know that?"

"Who were you talking to?"

"You've got no right to spy on me like this."

"No more right than you have to spy on your daughters."

We stared at one another. His smile was long gone. "I'll go to the right people with this, Pavlicek. I'll get an injunction if I have to."

I shrugged.

"You want more?" His eyes grew cold, indifferent. "I can see to it you won't even be able to get a job as a crossing guard in this state."

I stood up to leave. "It's been interesting," I said. "Thank you for your time."

"Now wait just one minute. I've told you some private things here."

"And they'll stay private, until I get together the evidence I need to nail you and whoever else is involved in your daughter's disappearance." I started to leave.

His chief of staff, Dworkin, suddenly appeared at the door. Maybe he'd been secretly summoned by his boss or maybe he'd been listening the whole time. "Problem, sir?" He stood blocking the doorway.

I looked back at Drummond, whose face had transformed. Now it appeared small and fearful and full of rage. His chief of staff wasn't all that big, but he looked plenty strong. Dworkin set his feet as I approached him and tried to push me back into the room. I took his momentum and grabbed him by his wrist, pulling him to the side and backhanding him across the mouth.

He fell backward. "Christ!" He took out a handkerchief and spit out some blood. "Here, asshole, take this." He pulled a blank sheet of paper from a stack on a table next to him and held it out to me.

I jerked it from his hand. "What's this?"

"It's all that's going to be left of your life when I get through with you."

I crumpled the paper in a ball and threw it back at him.

"You walk out that door now, Pavlicek, I'm not sure you know what you may be setting yourself up for," Drummond hissed.

"That's just it, Congressman," I said. "I'm not sure any of us ever do."

14

That afternoon I drove up to Washington, D.C. It's a pretty drive from Charlottesville, if you don't mind leaving the Blue Ridge behind and getting sucked up into the southernmost tentacles of suburbia that run practically all the way from northern Virginia to Maine. I spent all my years on the force living and working smack-dab in the New York middle of that great swath of civilization, so the short trip north to D.C. always makes me a little nostalgic.

Toronto had come up with a hot lead for me on the old *Post* articles. Neither the newspaper nor the police were all that helpful—no one much wanted to be bothered with a two-decades-old dead case file. But a check of the tax records revealed that George and Norma Paitley had lived in McLean, on the westernmost side of the I-495 Beltway, and that they had a son, still living in their old house, in fact. I'd sent him an E-mail the night before, claiming to represent a foreign bank. I wrote that I wanted to speak with him about some old offshore assets, possibly the property of his long-deceased parents. Perhaps with visions of the Caymans in his head, he'd responded that morning and agreed to meet me at the house after he got home from work.

South of Warrenton, development really starts to pick up. Traffic does too, as U.S. 29 merges into I-66 at Gainesville. From there, the last twenty-five miles into the nation's capital can take you two to three hours during the morning rush hour. But the opposite occurs, of course, in the afternoon, and as I drove along the interstate I was pitying the thousands of poor souls lined up in four lanes of bumper-to-bumper misery just across the median. The backup stretched all the way from Manassas to Vienna.

Half an hour later, I found the brown stucco Mediterranean with excessive plant growth climbing its walls, once the property of George and Norma Paitley, tucked on a side street in McLean. An old BMW was parked in the driveway. In front of it sat a brand-spanking-new Volkswagen Beetle.

I parked the truck behind the cars and went and rang the bell. The son didn't come to the door right away. Probably didn't want to seem too eager to collect on some more of Mommy and Daddy's old booty. I had to ring again.

When he finally did answer the bell, he turned out to be a tall, gangly man about my own age, with a full black beard and a head that was almost completely bald.

"Mr. Pavlicek?" he said.

"I am. Thanks for agreeing to meet with me on such short notice."

"No problem. C'mon in." He held the large oak door open for me.

I passed into an ornate front hall, outfitted with expensive old tapestry and Chinese jade. There was a coatrack off to the side and two pairs of men's hiking boots beside it, one appearing to be at least three sizes larger than the other.

"Can I get you something to drink? Iced tea? Saratoga water?"

"I'll take the Saratoga, thank you," I said.

He disappeared into a little alcove and popped back out a few seconds later with the familiar blue bottle and a tumbler full of ice cubes. I took the glass and poured my water. He led me through a door, and we settled on overstuffed chairs in what looked like the library.

"Before we begin," I said, "I should tell you I lied to you in the E-mail."

He had been straightening a pillow at his back when he looked up at me with alarm. "You what?"

"I lied to you about the bank. I'm sorry, but I needed information in a hurry, and it seemed like the best way to get you to meet with me."

He rubbed his beard, perhaps regretting he'd offered me the Saratoga. For the first time he seemed to take note of my size and the bulge created by the .357 in the shoulder holster beneath my jacket. "You're not planning to—"

"No, no. Not to worry. Just after information."

"Huh. I suppose I should've known better than to get my hopes up. You know how much it costs us to heat this place?"

"What kind of work do you do, Mr. Paitley?"

"I'm a lobbyist for a human rights group here in Washington."

"Bill, you okay down there?" Another man's voice carried down the hall from the upstairs.

"Fine. Everything's fine," Bill hollered back.

That explained the two cars in the driveway and the second set of men's boots.

"Just what kind of information are you after, Mr. Pavlicek?"

I set the blue bottle down on a coffee table coaster in front of me. "Are you familiar with Torrin Drummond?"

"The congressman? Why, yes, of course. I heard something on the news about him this morning, in fact. Isn't one of his daughters missing or something?"

"That's right."

"Are you working for the congressman? You could've just told me that in your E-mail."

"No. Let's just say I represent other members of the family."

He raised an eyebrow, then gave a shrug. "What is it you want from me?"

"Cartwright Drummond is the daughter who is missing. These were found in her suitcase when she got back from Japan." I reached inside my jacket pocket, pulled out copies of the two old newspaper articles, and handed them across to him.

He scanned both of them quickly. "These are from the *Post*. About my parents' accident."

I nodded. "Doesn't sound much like an accident to me."

He sighed. "I know. That's what the Metro police thought at first too, but after several months of investigation they concluded that the garbage truck must have been some wildcatter from out of town. Probably alcohol-related. Hit-and-run."

"Even if that's true, it's still manslaughter. Wouldn't you like to find out who's responsible for your parents' deaths?"

"Of course I would."

"Why would Cartwright Drummond be carrying these articles around in her suitcase?"

"I have no idea." He scratched his beard again. "Wait a minute—I just thought of something. Hang on a sec."

He disappeared around a corner, and I heard him

climbing the stairs to the second floor. I took another sip of my water.

A couple of minutes later he was back, carrying an old photo album. "I was right," he said. "I thought I remembered seeing this a long time ago."

He held the album open for me to look for myself. There on one of the pages was a color photo of an elderly couple standing arm in arm with a smiling, much younger Tor Drummond. They were under a large outdoor tent, obviously at some sort of event. Paitley took the album back and pulled the photo out of its sleeve.

"You know when that photo was taken?"

"There's a date on one of the other pictures on the same page, maybe from the same roll. It says August 1982," he said.

"1982. The same year your parents died."

He nodded.

"It was also the year of Drummond's first congressional campaign."

"If you say so."

"What did your parents have to do with Tor Drummond?"

"I don't know. Maybe they contributed money or something?"

"Can I keep the photo?"

He thought about it. "I'll tell you what. I've got a scanner on the computer in the kitchen. I'll just print you out a copy."

"Okay."

He disappeared again. On one of the bookshelves I noticed a small picture of him with his parents. This room, the entire house, had an old feeling about it, as if they were caught in some sort of time warp.

"Here you go." He came back into the room carrying the copy, a laser-printed facsimile almost as good as the original.

"Thank you very much," I said.

"Do you think my parents' association with Drummond might've had something to do with their accident?"

"I don't know," I said. "Maybe it did. Either way, it certainly looks like someone may have wanted Cartwright Drummond to think so."

"The news said the police suspect foul play in the girl's disappearance."

I nodded.

"If that's true, perhaps we'd all better be careful about this."

"I think that would be very wise," I said. "You know I've also got to ask you another question."

"Okay."

"About insurance."

He chuckled. "Life insurance, right? Like I might've had mommy and daddy bumped off to collect a big payout? Of course, the police at the time wanted to know all about that too. Only one problem: my parents had no life insurance at the time of their deaths. They were both in their seventies. When they died, I was left with the house and, after expenses, a very modest estate, most of which has now dwindled away just trying to keep this place up."

"So how could they have afforded to sink money into Drummond's campaign?"

"My parents were very kind, very generous people, Mr. Pavlicek. Besides the house and what they needed to live on, whatever money came their way, especially in their later years, was spread around to all sorts of charities and causes. I'm still on some of the mailing lists. Mom and Dad were even known to take in people who were in need."

"You must've been proud of them."

"Oh I was, but if you want to know the truth, before they died, I was beginning to think they were becoming suckers for every noble-sounding cause that came down the pike."

"How about the car? The insurance company must've paid off on the loss."

"Yes. The estate was paid a check for book value on their car."

"Did the company do an investigation?"

"Right. If you can call it that. They sent a fat young man around with a clipboard one afternoon. He asked me a bunch of questions about my parents' driving habits, then had me sign a form. That was about it."

"You mentioned your parents taking people in. Were any living with them at the time of their disappearance?"

"No. The last was a young woman from South America or something."

"I assume the police checked out all these people for any connection to your parents' deaths."

"Yes. They said they did."

"You remember any of the names?"

He thought for a moment. "I'm sorry. It's been a long time," he said. "Wait. Now that you mention it, I did have something odd happen regarding one of those people."

"What was that?"

"It was about six months ago. A young man called here and said he was doing some background work regarding a missing relative. I thought he was an attorney or something, although he sounded very young."

"What did he want?"

"He asked me about that woman, the one from South America I was just telling you about."

"Did the caller give you his name?"

"I'm sure he did, but I don't remember it."

"You remember anything else he might've said?"

"I'm sorry, I don't. I remember I was in the middle of working on a presentation when he called."

He showed me back to the front door.

I handed him my card. "You think of that caller's name or anything else, Mr. Paitley, please get in touch with me right away, will you?"

"Sure thing."

"Thank you for your time."

"Of course." He shook my hand. "I only wish what you said in your E-mail had been the truth."

15

It was a game of lies, wasn't it? Little lies we spun to others, maybe bigger ones to ourselves. Were Tor Drummond's lies what had taken him down a gray road that seemed to be growing ever darker?

"Let's see if there's any juice left in the battery," Nicole said.

She set the computer on the counter in Marcia's kitchen, opened the lid, and booted it up. Toronto and I stood next to her. The screen flickered to life, and within seconds we were staring into Cartwright Drummond's software.

It was after ten o'clock. Cassidy Drummond was already asleep upstairs. The stress of her long trip home, coupled with her sister's disappearance and the discovery of the bloody car, seemed to have taken their toll. She had been feeling ill all day, Marcia had said.

Toronto went to work. "Okay, Nicky, here's the way we do it." He slipped a floppy disk into the drive, tapped a few strokes on the keyboard. A series of letters and numbers appeared on the screen. This was no commercial software. This was some hacker's homegrown burglar tool kit. Toronto began entering code, walking Nicky through each step of what he was doing. I was lost after the second sentence, so I drifted out to the sunporch where Marcia and Karen Drummond were talking. Karen had decided to come stay with Marcia as well. I had picked her up with her suitcase from down at the Omni, where she'd stayed the night before.

"You two ladies mind some company?"

Marcia looked up and smiled. She was seated on a couch next to the doctor, who occupied a rocking chair. Both women held half-full glasses of white wine.

Karen Drummond's curly black hair swept in a half-moon across her forehead. She was normally a strikingly attractive woman, but now she seemed undone by fear and worry. Her lipstick had faded. Some of her mascara had run onto her cheek. She wore a black pantsuit with a white collared blouse underneath. The porch smelled of her perfume.

"Find anything on the computer?" Marcia asked.

"Not yet."

"I was just telling Karen about the conversation you and I had earlier today," she said.

I nodded.

"Do you think Tor could be behind Cartwright's disappearance?" Dr. Drummond asked. Her voice was lighter than Marcia's, soft and measured.

"Either that," I said, "or someone sure wants us to think he is."

She shook her head slowly.

"He seemed very concerned, when I talked to him in his office this morning, about Cartwright's 'obsession with the past,' as he put it. He mentioned he thought she'd been talking with Diane Lemminger," I said.

Dr. Drummond looked surprised. "This is the first I've heard of that," she said. "Why would Cartwright be talking to her?"

"I don't know, but I plan to find out. Lemminger's a reporter now, isn't she?"

"More like an on-air gossip columnist, if you ask me. Another one of my ex-husband's trophies gone sour." She took a sip of her wine.

I wasn't sure where she wanted to go with that, so I kept quiet.

"Your daughter was very kind to Cassidy earlier, Mr. Pavlicek."

Marcia had told me the two girls hit it off, but under the circumstances, of course, their budding friendship was a little muted.

"She's a good kid."

"More than a kid, I'd say," Marcia corrected me. A small bone of contention between us. She was always telling me I still treated Nicole like a child. That's what you get, I guess, from a divorced, overly protective father suddenly forced to take up residence with his teenager, as I had been with Nicole.

Dr. Drummond went on. "Marcia's told me Nicole's seen her own type of family trauma."

"Yes, she has," I said. Nicole's mother, Camille, lay paralyzed in an extended-care facility near Roanoke, the fallout from a nearly fatal overdose. Camille had money, so the cost was not an issue, but visits were hard. A feeding tube tends to stifle conversation.

"Karen said you showed her a picture earlier," Marcia said. "One you got from the gentleman you went to see in northern Virginia." I had shown Dr. Drummond the copy of the picture the Paitleys' son had given me. She hadn't recognized the elderly couple standing with her ex-husband. "May I see it?"

I unfolded the paper from my pocket and handed it to Marcia.

"That's George and Norma Paitley, all right."

"You remember them?"

"Vaguely. I think they showed up at a couple of early fund-raisers here in Charlottesville. Their son was in graduate school at the university or something. Aren't these the people who had the accident described in the newspaper articles Cassidy found in her sister's suitcase?"

"Uh-huh."

She nodded.

"Shouldn't we be going to the police with this information?" Dr. Drummond asked.

"On the way to your hotel to pick you up earlier, I stopped by my office and made another copy of both the articles and this photo. I put them in an envelope and dropped them by police headquarters for Bill Ferrier."

"But you'll keep investigating, won't you?"

"Yes."

"Good. The man in the other room with your daughter—Mr. Toronto?—you said he used to be a detective too?"

"Yes. A very good one. I may need his help on some things, but if he has to leave, we'll make sure someone is here with you."

"We should continue to stay here, then?"

"As long as no one knows you're here, I think that would be best."

"Is that all right with you, Marcia?" Dr. Drummond looked at her friend. "We seem to have invaded your home."

"Of course it is. You and the girls are welcome here anytime, no matter what the circumstances."

"Thank you. I don't know what we'd do up here

otherwise. I don't know how to thank you either, Mr. Pavlicek. My daughter says she's paying you."

"All taken care of in that department."

"What about the police?"

"It's your call, ma'am."

"Please, just call me Karen."

"Okay. It's your call, Karen. If you take your daughter and go to the police you might be better off. Then again, your husband will definitely know where you and Cassidy are."

"You really think Cassidy and I might be in some danger too?"

"Well, we've got a missing daughter whose car was found with blood all over it. We've got your husband talking to that same daughter late the night she disappeared and having both girls followed. And we've got a decades-old unsolved hit-and-run murder that your daughter had some interest in, also with links to your husband."

"Marcia said she told you earlier today about the incident that happened between her and Tor all those years ago."

"Yes."

"I'm glad she waited until after the divorce to tell me. I'm not sure I would've believed her before then."

"I'm sorry to have to ask you this, but do you think your husband has made unwanted sexual advances to other women? I mean, besides Marcia."

"I honestly don't know. I suppose anything's possible."

"Maybe something happened and Cartwright found out about it."

"But why?" The resolve that Karen Drummond had obviously called up in order to keep going began to waver. Her lips trembled. One hand pushed her hair back from her forehead. "Why would Tor want to harm one of his own daughters?"

"That's what I can't quite figure."

Marcia looked up from our conversation. I followed her gaze to see Cassidy, in one of Marcia's old bathrobes, entering the porch.

"Honey, you should be in bed," her mom scolded, but she stood up and hugged her. She and Marcia switched places, and mother and daughter sat on the couch.

"Can I get you something to eat?" Marcia asked.

Cassidy shook her head. She leaned forward with her hands cupped around most of her face and rubbed her eyes. I could see her cheeks were streaked with tears.

"You all right?" I asked.

"I just can't believe it, you know?"

I nodded.

"Do you think Wright's dead?" Her lip trembled as her eyes locked on mine.

"We don't know that, not for sure."

"But you think she might be."

"It looks—it looks like a possibility." I didn't know what else to say.

"But she might not be, either. She might just be . . . she might just . . ." Her eyes brimmed over with tears, and she covered her face again.

Her mother patted her hair and gently rubbed her back.

Then Cassidy said, "I still want you to find out for sure about Jed, and most of all I want you to find out if this has anything at all to do with my father."

I nodded. "There is the possibility that your sister might've been the victim of a kidnapping. On the other hand, it could've just been random violence."

"Either way, I want to know," she said. She had stopped crying now, and her mouth was set in a firm, straight line.

"We *all* want to know, honey," Karen Drummond said.

She nodded, closed her eyes, and leaned her head back on the couch.

I glanced out of the sunporch windows, through the curtains. A dark blue sedan turned the corner down the street.

"Hey, Dad." Nicole's voice rang out from the kitchen. "I think we've got something."

"That's great, honey," I shouted back. "Jake, could you come out here, please, on the double? Ladies, if you'll just stand up and move slowly out of sight to the back of the house. Cassidy and Karen, it'd be best if you two and Nicky went upstairs."

Marcia straightened up in her chair. "What's happening, Frank?"

"I think we're about to get company," I said.

16

The two detectives took their time getting out of their car and coming up the walk. Ferrier was looking over the front of the house. Upwood carried a little notebook. I should have known they might be looking for me again. I'd made sure I hadn't been followed earlier, especially when I picked up Karen Drummond from the Omni, but out of habit I'd carelessly parked my truck behind Marcia's car in the driveway (Jake had hidden his Jeep in the garage). All the two cops had to do was look.

They rang the doorbell. Marcia went to answer it. Toronto and I had quickly split a cold beer from the fridge into two glasses and raided the game drawer to spread a few chips around the table and deal two hands of stud poker.

"Look who's here," Marcia said as she ushered the two detectives into the kitchen.

"Hey, guys. Long time no see, I said. "Awfully late for a social call, isn't it?"

Toronto discarded only one card and picked up a new one. Going for the straight or the flush?

"We were in the neighborhood," Ferrier said. "Saw your truck." He watched for a moment, while I picked up a four and a jack to go with my two sevens and a queen. "Didn't know you had an out-of-town guest. How you doing, Jake?"

"Stupendous." Toronto nodded in his general direction. He was wearing his pale brown gas station attendant shirt with the sleeves cut off. The name patch on the shirt said CARL. Out of the corner of my eye, I caught Carol Upwood ogling his biceps.

"Really has been a long time since I seen you last. Was over that business in Leonardston, wasn't it? You were playing cards then, too, if I recall. You and I lost a game of hearts."

"Good memory."

"You and that Commonwealth's Attorney over there still an item? What was her name again?"

"She and I are still friends," Toronto said. With him, no one was an item.

"In town on business?"

The question might've been loaded, but Toronto didn't miss a beat. "Nope." He pitched a couple of white chips from his pile into the center of the table. "Social."

"Some hunting, maybe."

"Maybe."

"You bring that bird of yours?"

Toronto shook his head. Smiling, he said, "Nahhh. Frank here needs a little remedial help with his redtail."

It wasn't true, of course, but I nodded.

"Still haven't got you to take me out hunting with your bird, Frank," Ferrier said. "We need to do that."

"We do," I said. I threw three chips on the table to raise Toronto.

"I see you've moved on a bit yourself," Toronto said, appraising Carol with a wink.

"Yup. They've got me tutoring brilliant young detectives for the locals now."

Carol actually blushed.

The two detectives watched Toronto see my bet and raise me three. Considering that neither one of us had any idea how much we were playing for, it seemed like a bold move.

"Well, I know you didn't just stop by to watch us play poker and drink beer, Bill," I said.

"No, sir. As a matter of fact, we didn't. I got the envelope you dropped off for me earlier."

I nodded. "Makes for interesting reading, doesn't it?"

"Most definitely. Where'd you get the articles and the picture?"

"That's the real interesting thing. The articles came courtesy of the missing Cartwright Drummond."

"S'that a fact?"

"The picture took some professional private detection."

"I'll bet. I sure as heck hope you aren't tampering with any evidence."

"Moi?"

He said nothing, took a long, cold look around the rest of the kitchen. "We also had a few more questions for Cartwright Drummond's mother and wondered if maybe you might've bumped into her this evening."

"The doctor?" I did my best to feign ignorance. "I thought she was still talking to you guys."

"We stopped by her hotel to see her, but she's not in her room."

I shrugged.

He eyed Marcia, who'd been hanging in the doorway listening. "How 'bout you, Ms. D'Angelo? You know who Dr. Drummond is?"

Marcia nodded.

"Haven't seen her today, have you?"

"Sorry, Detective. I can't help you."

"Ummm." He watched Toronto raise me another two and call.

"All right, folks, sorry for barging in on you so late." He turned toward the door. "Good evening, Jake, Ms. D'Angelo. Frank, you think we might have a word with you outside?"

I took a sip of beer. "Absolutely." I winked at Toronto. "But I'm taking my cards with me."

I followed the two detectives back outside and down the walk to their car. Upwood leaned against the bumper. Ferrier had produced a toothpick from somewhere and rolled it between his lips. Steam came from all our mouths. I wished I'd slipped on a jacket.

"Frank, listen," he said, taking the toothpick out. "I don't need to know everything you're doing, but I sure as shootin' expect to be kept informed, especially if you get anything solid or something important develops."

"I'm afraid I'm just trolling the periphery on this one, Bill."

"Yeah? You seem to be laying things out pretty nicely for someone who's just trolling."

"Maybe a bit too nicely?" Carol added. She looked at Ferrier and nodded. Suspicion, thy name is woman.

"Anything new on the girl? Ransom note? Calls?" I asked.

They shook their heads.

"The clock's ticking."

"Tell me about it," Ferrier said. "Here's the thing. My hunch is there's gonna be all sorts of shit hitting the fan around here pretty soon over this. You get my drift?"

"Uh-huh."

"You'd best remember how to duck."

"Thanks for the heads-up."

"Oh, and one more thing."

"What's that?"

"Since when you think you going to beat a man's straight with only a pair?"

17

Again it was a night of little sleep. I got up early the next morning, this time to take a jog. The day was shaping up to be picture-perfect for spring: bright blue sky, the air already warmer than the night before. Nuthatches, Carolina wrens, and even a few bluebirds sang along my route down Rugby Avenue onto Rugby Road. Out of curiosity, I decided to detour down through University Corner, behind the old medical school, through the parking lots and over Jefferson Park Avenue to the parking garage across from the primary-care building where I'd discovered Cartwright Drummond's rental car.

I was stunned to see a small crowd gathered on the sidewalk. Behind them, in a row along the curb, were two large satellite trucks and three or four television vans. Apparently, this spot had become media central for the unfolding drama and mystery of the disappearance of Cartwright Drummond. Three officers manned a barricade, keeping the curious away from the trucks. Across Lee Street a TV crew was busy setting up for an interview. The reporter, a dark-haired twenty-something male wearing a trench coat and tie, looked more like a made-up Humphrey Bogart than any of the real detectives downtown. I couldn't help musing about the image people would see on their screens— early-morning steam from the "brave" announcer's breath, the stark gray image of the concrete garage. What a fractional depiction of reality it would be. I slipped past the crowd and kept jogging. The last thing I needed was some orange-faced reporter shoving a microphone into my face.

"Hey, Pavlicek."

I winced and turned to see none other than Jed Haynes, standing to my right with his hands in the pockets of a university warm-up jacket. He must have been in the crowd of bystanders and broken away when he saw me. I waited while he came abreast of me.

"It's all over the grounds. Everyone's been talking about it since the other night."

"Entertainment for the masses," I said.

"Is she dead?"

I took a long look at him before I answered. His cheeks were ruddy and narrow, his hair pleasantly disheveled. Anger still smoldered in his eyes, but it seemed to be more under control now.

"What would make you say that?" I said.

He shrugged and pointed to the second story of the garage. "I saw a lot of cops and a van that was marked 'Forensics' up there the night they found her car."

"You get around, don't you?"

He shrugged.

I said nothing.

"Well? What do you think? She dead?"

"Like I told you before, I'm not a cop, Jed. I'm out of it. Better talk to the police. I know they'll want to be talking to *you*."

"They already have. And I'm supposed to be going back down to talk to somebody else this morning."

I glanced around. Bet somebody's keeping an eye on you, too, I thought. But I saw no one.

"They won't tell me anything," he complained. "They just keep asking more questions."

"Maybe it'll make you more humble," I said.

"But did they find her body?"

I ignored his question, turned, and broke into a jog again, crossing the street to make sure I put as much distance as possible as soon as possible between myself and the big trucks. Thanks to the likes of Willard Abercrombie, Cassidy Drummond's fear was fully realized: the investigation had gone media.

Nothing would be sacred now; nothing would be free from potential exposure. Not even the minutest details of a young girl's life. Hey, I make my living asking questions too, but even I stop at bra sizes.

Speculation is cheap. Whatever happened, on the slim chance that Cartwright Drummond might still be alive, time was running out.

An hour later, showered, shaved, and halfway presentable, I appeared on Marcia's doorstep once again. I was there to collect Nicole, who'd spent the night at Marcia's behest to keep Cassidy company. The plan called for Toronto to follow Nicole and me over to my office in his battered Jeep, then we would go over the computer files they'd uncovered the night before. Nicole had no classes today, so I'd told her she could come help out if she wanted. There was no plan to leave Cassidy and her mom or Marcia without protection, though. Toronto, foreseeing the need to relieve himself of full-time security duty, had, the day before, made what he called "an arrangement."

The arrangement answered the door.

He was at least six-eight and more than three hundred pounds, most of it muscle. His head was bigger than my midsection. His jaw appeared capable of crushing small aluminum cans.

Toronto stood smiling right behind him. He was decked out in black combat boots, green coveralls, and a Virginia Tech baseball cap that in some parts of C-ville might have invited a fistfight, although I doubted anyone would dare challenge Toronto.

"Frank, I'd like you to meet Mr. Earl. Mr. Earl, this is the fella I was telling you about. My old partner, Frank Pavlicek. Best damned PI around."

Mr. Earl grinned and took my hand in his giant paw. He shook it like it was a rag doll. I felt fortunate to get it back.

"Mr. Earl is Samoan. You might remember him. He spent a couple of seasons at right guard for the Philadelphia Eagles a few years back."

I didn't remember but figured the safe thing to do was nod. "Right. Sure."

Mr. Earl nodded back. We all nodded. Toronto ushered me into the kitchen while Mr. Earl went about checking the window casings.

"This guy for real?" I said when we were out of the big man's hearing.

"Saw him kill a pimp in New York last year with his bare hands. Dude had been whoring out strung-out teens, one of whom happened to be his sister's baby girl."

"Okay . . . I guess. He armed?"

He nodded. "Beretta and a shotgun. Don't worry. I've worked with Mr. Earl a lot. He owes me a big favor."

"What's his first name?"

"Don't ask him," he said.

"Roger that."

At my office a half hour later, a letter had arrived along with the usual assortment of bills and junk mail. Addressed to me personally, presorted standard, the stationery bore a shiny gold foil edge and the almost garish image of an equally golden eagle. The communiqué was a bold request, as he put it, from none other than Congressman Tor Drummond himself, an opportunity to donate a certain amount of money to his campaign war chest and thereby be designated an honorary member of what he called his Eagle Council. He was even planning a little get-together for this group of the local faithful—an outdoor speech and pep rally two days hence at the amphitheater on the east end of the city's downtown mall.

The amount of money wasn't that large—eagles must have lost some of their lofty status in the present climate. That I had somehow made it onto the congressman's mailing list was a bit ironic, given that the congressman and I had not parted on the best of terms. Also surprising, given my political leanings, which could best be described as apolitical.

I selected a Krispy Kreme from the dozen we'd stopped to pick up along the way and took a bite.

"You guys need a woman around this office more often to help keep you straight," Nicole said, wadding up a stray napkin Toronto had left on the table and tossing it into the trash. "You know how much cholesterol there is in this junk you're eating?"

"We don't want to know, do we, Jake?"

"Un-huh," he grunted.

"How'd you and Cassidy get along?" I asked her.

"Awesome, considering she's going through a lot right now."

"That's good. I'm afraid what's not good is the fact

the cops don't seem to have much new information and no one's found her sister's body yet. If there's any chance that Cartwright's still alive, the longer it takes to find her, the worse the chance's that she will be when we do."

Toronto finished off his third doughnut, plugged in Cartwright Drummond's laptop, and booted it up. "Okay," he said. "We're going to have some solid info here for you in a few minutes. I was also thinking, Frank, long as I'm gonna be here, you need any help with Armistead while you're on this case? I might as well make myself useful."

"I'd say you're pretty useful already, but thanks very much."

"Armistead's been a little testy lately . . . don't you think?" Nicole said. "You think she knows you're getting ready to release her?"

I shrugged.

"Could be," Toronto said. "The more I work with hawks, the more I wonder just how much they know."

"Dad," Nicole said, "if you and the police think something bad's happened to Cartwright Drummond, we need to make sure we document and bag any evidence."

"Bag any evidence?" Toronto cocked a brow and looked at her with teasing admiration.

"Girl wants to be an investigator," I said.

He shook his head. "You know, Frank, passion's wasted on the young, isn't it?"

She punched him playfully in the shoulder. "It is *not*," she said.

"In youth we learn," I said, trying to remember the von Ebner–Eschenbach line. "In age we understand."

They both ignored me and set to work with the computer. I flipped open the file Nicole had prepared

for me, to which I'd added the newly acquired copy
of the photo of Tor Drummond standing with George
and Norma Paitley. The folder was in chronological
order, as well organized, I thought, as any I'd ever
received as background when I worked as a cop. Nicole had printed most of it from the Internet: photos
and news clippings, a handful of op-eds, even a couple
of spin pieces from Torrin Drummond's Web site regarding his current bid for reelection. A five-year-old
article from a national business magazine profiled
Drummond's business interests, which ran from publish-
ing to biotechnology, transportation to forest redevelop-
ment. Drummond's sex scandal figured prominently, of
course, with several tabloid exposés and a number of
essays. Opinions ranged from apologetic disappoint-
ment to incredulous disdain.

"Okay, you ready, Frank? Here's what we've got,"
Toronto said a few minutes later, rubbing his hands
together.

They'd shown me some snatches of sentences the
night before, mostly gibberish, nothing too useful.

"We broke the password and got into her current
E-mail pretty easily. Nothing too spectacular there.
Reconstructing her deleted files, we hit pay dirt,
though."

"You can do that?" I asked.

"Sure," Nicky said. "People think when they delete
something it's automatically erased from their hard
drive, but that's not true. It's only moved to a different
sector, waiting to be overwritten by another file. Until
that happens, you can still recover it."

"We found two recent E-mails that looked interesting, both from the same address," Toronto went on.
He turned the laptop screen so I could read it.

> *Picture me, a secret amphibian,*
> *Sprung from kingdom chain,*
> *Species yet unfound.*
> *Fashioned whole,*
> *Heir to code,*
> *Conscience,*
> *Reason,*
> *Blur too*
> *fast for sound.*
>
> —*SA*

"Looks like a poem," I said. "Free verse—not much in the way of iambic pentameter. 'A secret amphibian.' Strange."

"Sounds like it could be your swimmer," Toronto said.

"Maybe."

"But here, check out the second E-mail. It's a little more straightforward. Came from the same address."

meet me. twelve-thirty a.m. i've got big news.

"That's it?" I said.

"That's it."

"When did she receive these E-mails?"

"Both around the same time," he said. "Two days ago."

"The night she disappeared."

"She must've read them, because they'd both been opened," Nicole said.

"Somebody read them, at least," Toronto said.

"Can they be traced?" I asked.

"You bet." Toronto rubbed his hands together again. "That's where things really begin to get interesting. You wanna tell him, Nicky?"

My daughter picked up some more pages just coming off the printer. They'd obviously pulled them from some server somewhere. "The mailbox they came from belongs to a foundation in Richmond. It's called Second Millennium. The foundation's purpose is to help support disadvantaged kids from the inner city. It apparently doles out grants and scholarships to private schools, even pays parents or guardians for some kids' living expenses," she said. "And guess what?"

"What?"

"We found out who's behind the foundation—Congressman Torrin Drummond."

"But that doesn't make any sense. Why would he have sent his own daughter E-mails like this from some foundation address?"

"I don't think our man sent them," Toronto said. "Best I can tell, he's not involved in the day-to-day operation of the foundation. He doesn't use that E-mail box. There's a woman in Richmond who does, though. We just got the data on her. Works full-time as a nurse." He picked up another sheet of paper. "The foundation's only address is a post office box, so my bet is she runs the thing part-time from her house or something."

"What's her name?"

"Name's Roberta Joseph." He handed me the paper. Listed were complete addresses, both home and work, and phone numbers.

"You guys make this too easy for me," I said.

"You think this woman's involved, Dad?" Nicole said.

"I don't know. Seems like a stretch to me. Tell you what, Jake. Keep your cell phone handy. I may need your backup and we may need to move in a hurry. Let me know if we hear anything else from the police.

Nicky, I'd like you to make copies of all this stuff and drop it by Ferrier's office. Don't talk to anybody. Just put it in an envelope and leave it for him. Great job. And thanks."

"Where are *you* headed?"

"Richmond. To do a little surveillance on this Joseph woman and to track down a certain gossip reporter who used to work for Tor Drummond," I said.

18

Ninety minutes later, I found Roberta Joseph's home address on the west end of Richmond. It turned out she lived in an apartment complex only a mile or so from the interstate. The brick-and-frame units were nicely set back from the road in a neighborhood of single-family dwellings. Brick walkways, the same color and texture as the bottom half of the buildings themselves, connected the various apartment units. Her building was the farthest in back and looked out on some woods and the corner of a small reservoir.

I parked where I could see her door and waited. A wreath of fresh-cut flowers hung from the door of unit 214. No sign of any activity. The morning newspaper was still rolled into its receptacle.

I made sure my .357 was tucked away beneath my jacket, climbed out of the truck, and went and knocked on the neighbors' doors. Two were at home: a middle-aged guy with a beer belly rubbing sleep from his eyes and a steely-eyed seventy-something retiree watering the flowers on her front stoop. I explained who I was, but simply told them I was searching for a teenage runaway. I asked if they'd seen any suspicious activity or any strangers around the building in the last forty-eight hours, being careful not to mention any specific apartment numbers. Both shook their heads. They each took my card and promised to call me if they did.

I went back to the truck and watched and waited some more. About ten minutes later the door to apartment 214 opened and an attractive woman, about my age, with short blond hair stepped out to get the newspaper. She yawned and stretched for a moment, as she scanned the front page. Everything about her looked petite, even her feet and hands. She wore running pants and an unbuttoned man's shirt over a white tee. Didn't look like much of a kidnapper to me. She turned and went back inside.

I thought about it, climbed out of the truck, and rang her bell.

"Just a minute!" a woman's voice called from inside.

A few seconds later she opened the door.

"May I help you?"

"Mrs. Joseph?" I asked.

"Yes, I am."

I gave her my card. "If you can spare a few moments, I'd like to ask you a few questions."

She read the card, then searched my face a little doubtfully. "What's this about?"

"Just routine, I hope. I was trying to get some information on Second Millennium. I understand you're involved with the foundation?"

"Yes, of course. Has one of our kids gotten in trouble or something?"

I hedged a bit. "Possibly. May I come in?"

She looked at me cautiously for another moment. "Do you have any other type of identification?"

I produced my private investigator's registration complete with DMV mug shot. She examined it thoroughly before handing it back.

"All right," she said. She stepped aside to open the door. "Just give me another minute. I need to go upstairs and finish helping my daughter get ready for work. We both leave for the hospital in a little while."

Daughter? Could it be a ruse? Did she have Cartwright Drummond bound and gagged upstairs and was she planning to come back down with shotgun blazing? I searched her eyes for any duplicity. "Of course," I said.

She led me into a living room, white walls and a cathedral ceiling. "Sit down, please. I'll only be a short while. My daughter has some . . . special needs." She ascended an open stairwell to the second floor and disappeared down what appeared to be a hallway.

Special needs. I wasn't quite sure what to make of that, but I'd find out momentarily, I supposed. I sat down in a black rocking chair next to a contemporary sofa.

The room was fragrant with the smell of cleanser and quite bright. Two skylights let in sun overhead, which shone on several framed black-and-white photographs. They were mostly landscapes, but a few were of people. Since they were neither framed posters nor signed, I assumed Roberta Joseph was the photographer. A couple of the images showed a girl about my own daughter's age, quite different from her mother, if this was Roberta's daughter. The girl's hair was dark. She had a wide nose and pretty dark eyes. Her features made her appear Eastern European, and large blotches were visible on her skin. Something about her looked vaguely familiar, but I wasn't sure why.

Roberta Joseph reappeared at the top of the stairs. She wore clogs now, but they didn't seem to interfere with her coming down the steps.

"I'm sorry," she said. She sat down on the edge of the sofa. "Now. What can I do to help you?"

"You said your daughter has special needs?"

"Yes. She's autistic, partially disabled, and mildly retarded. At least that's what all her testing shows. She rarely speaks."

"And you said she works with you?"

"We both work at the hospital, yes. I'm a critical care nurse and Averil works in the cafeteria."

"I see. Is this your daughter in the photos?"

"Yes."

"You took the photos?"

"Uh-huh."

"She has quite an expression, which the photographer seems to have captured perfectly."

"Thank you," she said, maybe surprised by the compliment. "You said you wanted to know something about Second Millennium?"

"Yes. Do you work for the foundation?"

"Yes, I do. I run most of it, actually. We're not that large."

"And its purpose is?"

"We donate money to needy families for their children, mostly here in our community, and in a couple of other areas across Virginia."

"How do you find out about these children?"

"Direct referrals. As I said, we're quite small. We're not a government agency. We've built up a small network of doctors and nurses in the area, and we also are sent names by some of the local churches. In fact, it's why I work as a nurse."

"Who provides your funding?"

"Our donors prefer to remain anonymous," she said.

She'd obviously been asked the question before. I

wondered how Toronto had made the connection to Drummond. Bank records? Maybe I didn't want to know. "Can you tell me where the foundation's office is?"

She shrugged. "That's no secret. It's here. I've turned a third bedroom into a small home office. We like to keep costs down so that the funds we have mostly go to benefit the children."

"Do you use the Internet?"

"Sure."

"Send much E-mail?"

"Some. Look, Mr. Pavlicek, I really would like to know what this is all about."

"I'm trying to track down the source of some suspicious E-mail messages," I told her.

"Messages? What kind of messages?"

"They've surfaced in an investigation involving a missing person," I said. "They appear to have originated from your foundation's E-mail account."

"What?"

"Who has access to your E-mail, besides you, Ms. Joseph?"

"Well, no one. Unless you count Averil, my daughter. She does send E-mails from time to time. Usually with my help. She has some friends she likes to correspond with. But I can't imagine why or how she would be sending the kind of messages you seem to be talking about."

I glanced at the newspaper she had set on the coffee table. On the front page was a story about Cartwright Drummond's disappearance.

"Are you sure these E-mails are coming from my account?"

I wasn't sure of anything. But Toronto knew what he was doing. "They appear to be."

"I'm sorry," she said, "but I don't know anything about them."

She didn't seem threatened by my questions. She seemed to be telling the truth. If Roberta Joseph truly knew nothing about the E-mails sent to Cartwright Drummond, and her daughter was as she described, it was improbable the messages had emanated from this home. Maybe whoever had sent them had hacked into her account and used the box as a conduit to funnel their rantings to Cartwright. Which meant we'd have a much harder time tracking the person down. But that still didn't explain Second Millennium's connection to Congressman Drummond.

"You mind if I take a look at your office?"

"Of course not."

She led me from the living room around a corner, down a back hallway to what the building's architect had obviously meant to be a spare bedroom or small family room. The room was dim. She switched on an overhead light.

Lavish plants hung from the ceiling and ferns grew on the windowsill. A nondescript desk and chair, a large filing cabinet, a cork bulletin board with a map, and a personal computer. Otherwise, the office looked unremarkable.

"Any of your clients ever visit here?"

"The kids? No."

If I'd still been a cop, I would've directed her not to touch a thing and gotten a team in to look for fingerprints. Maybe I could still get Ferrier to have that done. "Okay. Thanks very much," I said.

She switched off the light. I followed her back toward the living room. There was a thud on the stairs as we rounded a corner by the front hall, and I looked up to see an overweight young woman, with the same pretty hair and eyes I had seen in the photos on the wall, coming slowly down the steps. Her gait was slightly irregular, as if one leg were shorter than the other.

"Averil, I'd like you to meet our guest," Roberta Joseph said.

The woman descending the stairs smiled through large white teeth and stared at me without saying a word. She reached the bottom of the steps and made her way to stand in front of us. Her skin didn't look as bad as in some of the pictures, but it was obviously abnormal.

"Pleased to meet you, Averil," I said.

The girl said nothing. She just kept right on staring at me with that fixed smile.

"Averil loves meeting new people—don't you, honey?" Roberta Joseph said, taking her daughter's hand. "She understands a lot more than she's able to communicate verbally. We get along fine most of the time. She does excellent work at the hospital. She likes music and photography, even books."

"Books?" I said.

Her mother nodded.

Averil's gaze never left me. What connections, I wondered, were being made in her mind? What was she seeing in my face, in my expression, that could cause her so much interest? But then I remembered why I was here.

"Well, thank you, Ms. Joseph. I'm sorry to have taken up so much of your time. It seems a computer hacker is using your screen name to send the E-mails. You might want to change your password."

"Yes, absolutely. Will you be able to find this person?"

"Not easily, I'm afraid."

Averil, her smile disappearing, was suddenly pointing to something on my jacket. For a second, I thought she'd noticed my gun, but then I followed her gaze to a spare pair of leather jesses I had tied in one of the loops on the front.

Averil kept pointing.

"My daughter seems fascinated with something on your clothing," Roberta said.

"These . . ." I held them up for Averil to see. "These are called jesses, Averil."

The young woman nodded slightly.

"I use them when I go hunting."

Without inhibition she stepped forward and ran her fingers over the leather. Then she smiled.

"I apologize, Mr. Pavlicek. Averil's a little forward sometimes."

"That's okay," I said.

The girl stepped back.

"I'm sorry we couldn't be of more help to you," Roberta said.

"I appreciate your time. Just one more question. It may have nothing to do with anything . . ."

"Of course."

"Does the term 'Secret Amphibian' mean anything to you?"

" 'Secret Amphibian'? No. Why?"

"It was contained in one of the E-mails."

Roberta Joseph shook her head and shrugged.

Averil rocked on her heels. "C-c-cake," the girl said. Her smile had disappeared as she mouthed the words. Her voice was flat.

I looked to Roberta.

"Averil! You spoke. Good for you."

"C-c-cake," the girl repeated.

"Cake?" I said.

"I'm sure she's talking about the cake they baked yesterday at the cafeteria. Isn't that what you were doing when I came in to get you to come home last night, Averil? You were helping the assistant chef with a cake."

The girl gave no indication that she understood her mother's question. She seemed to have forgotten I was there as well. She stared straight ahead, as if she were looking across some vast distance.

"Well," I said, "thank you both again for your time."

"It was our pleasure." Roberta Joseph showed me to the door.

Averil stayed where she was, swaying slowly back and forth to some silent beat, her eyes suddenly closed.

19

Diane Lemminger worked at a cable TV news affiliate in Richmond, where she had managed to parlay the infamy from her affair with Congressman Drummond into a career as an on-air host. A development not without irony or precedent. The show, appropriately enough, was about politics and scandal and was called *Government Offense.*

When I told the receptionist in the lobby what I wanted, she eyed me with disdain. Apparently, private investigators were pretty far down the social ladder from television personalities in her book. She closed the glass window to her partition and got on the horn to announce my presence to whatever powers there were. I took a seat on a shapely leather couch with a nice view of a fountain and a court-yard garden.

After a couple of phone calls, the receptionist slid her window open again.

"Someone will be with you shortly." She smiled, then turned back to her obviously more important work. The partition slid closed with a dull *clump,* and I wondered vaguely if the glass was bulletproof.

I took in the plush surroundings. The cell phone in my pocket burst to life. I pulled it out, immediately recognizing the Caller ID number on the display screen.

"Hi, Bill."

"Pavlicek, what in hell are you giving me now? We got a girl in a world of trouble, probably dead. We're trying to find her, or what's left of her, as soon as possible, not to mention the media all over our backs, and we've got you hiding her mother and her sister somewhere and sending me poetry."

I looked around the lobby. The receptionist wore transcription earphones while she typed, but I lowered my voice anyway. "Pulled those E-mails off of Cartwright Drummond's laptop," I said.

"You what?" He seemed to be fumbling with the phone for a couple of seconds. "You know, if Abercrombie finds out about this—"

"I think it's a dead end, for now at least. Looks like someone may have hacked in and used the E-mail account, but I've got an address and a room you guys need to dust for prints."

"I want that laptop. *Now.* You hear me?"

Boy, did I hear him. Those digital cell phones get great reception. I had to pull the handpiece away from my ear to keep from suffering ear damage from the string of profanity zinging across the line. "You through?" I said when he finally stopped.

"No. But *you* may be."

"I'll have Jake bring you the computer," I said and pushed the button on the phone to break the connection. It immediately rang again, but I shut it off.

The receptionist hadn't looked up from her typing. I contemplated the fountain again, and the courtyard, and the fine Oriental carpet on the floor of the lobby. Maybe I should consider a change in career, I thought, set myself up as some sort of media expert like one of those ex-detectives plying the late-night talk shows. Maybe I needed a vacation.

Fifteen minutes later, a tall, good-looking young black man who said he was a production assistant ushered me past a couple of vacant sets, down a hall, and into Diane Lemminger's office, a softly lit rectangle, furnished à la Madonna—minus the bed, of course. A display on one wall showed several photos of Lemminger with various notable politicians she'd interviewed, including a certain curly-lipped former President of the United States.

"Diane's still in the studio," the assistant said, "but she'll be through in just a minute."

"Thank you."

He bade me sit down in a canvas director's chair next to a chaise filled with oversized pillows and closed the door behind him as he left. Less than five seconds later, the same door opened and in stepped a tall, slender woman with brown hair swept back over her shoulders. Makeup caked her cheeks. She wore a red sweater top, a dark skirt, stockings, and pumps to go with her projected self-importance.

I'd never watched her news show, but she was easy to recognize from the photos on the wall. Not to mention that for a while there, her photo had been plastered all over every TV screen and supermarket tabloid in America. Her azure eyes assessed me with a look of mischief. Her pretty mouth dimpled to one side in a wry smile.

I stood up as she said, "You must be Mr. Pavlicek."

Her slender fingers were moist.

"Sorry about the perspiration," she said, wiping her hands with a tissue. "Always happens when I'm under the lights." Her accent was smoothly Southern, not that different from Marcia's but with a deeper tone and an unmistakable hint of sultry. I caught an updraft of her perfume.

"So," she said. She draped herself across the chaise. "You don't mind if I lie down, do you? I'm whupped. Please, sit."

Sit, boy. Yes, ma'am.

I took my chair again as she eased onto her side with her head on one of the pillows, slipped off her shoes, and curled her legs under her in a feline motion. "You told the receptionist you're digging into Tor Drummond's background. Who are you working for, McCartney's campaign?" McCartney was Drummond's opponent in the upcoming election.

"No. I'm not working for any candidate."

"Oh?" Her smile disappeared. "Who do you represent, then?"

"Others."

She went right for the jugular. "These *others* must be really interested in Drummond for you to drive all the way down here from Charlottesville. Does this have anything to do with Cartwright Drummond's disappearance? It was our lead news item again last night."

"That depends," I said.

"Depends?"

"I understand you know Cartwright and Cassidy Drummond."

"Of course. I used to see the two of them all the time."

"Have you had any contact with Cartwright Drummond since your breakup with the congressman?"

"Yes. Cartwright contacted me last month, in fact. Would you believe it? She called me all the way from Japan."

"What about?"

She surveyed me for several seconds without speaking. "I'm working on a story," she said. "Have you heard of my show?"

I shook my head. "Sorry, don't get a chance to do much TV."

"Ummm . . . too bad for you. Anyway, this story involves Tor Drummond. We've been doing a series of exposés on Virginia politicians regarding their ties to big business or special-interest groups, whatever. I've been saving Drummond for last."

I'll bet you have, I thought. She seemed about ready to lick her chops. Part of the reason her affair with Drummond had come to light, according to the newspapers, had been their very heated breakup. Ms. Lemminger, apparently, had made quite a bit of noise. Looking at her now, I could believe it.

"And Cartwright wanted to talk with you about your story?"

"Yes. That's what she said."

"How did she know about the piece?"

"Oh, that's easy. I sent out a letter several months ago to several of Drummond's supporters and confidants, offering to let any of them tell their side of the story."

"Did any others take you up on it?" I asked.

She smiled again. "A few."

"If you don't mind my saying so, Ms. Lemminger, some might accuse you of having a certain bias when it comes to Tor Drummond."

"Absolutely. That's why people watch, isn't it? I think I have a good idea what people want." Her eyes searched mine. She shifted slightly on the couch, revealing a little more leg. "Sometimes I have an especially good idea what people want."

"Uh-huh. Who else responded to your letter?"

She decided to examine her nails. "I'm sorry. My sources must remain confidential."

"But not Cartwright Drummond."

"Well, the poor thing's in trouble, isn't she? She might even be dead."

"That she might."

"I don't think her troubles have anything to do with our conversation, if that's what you're implying," she said. "The information we discussed was strictly background."

"Background. What kind of background?"

She waved her hand at me as if to dismiss the gravity, if there were any, of the information. "I suppose if you want to learn that you'll just have to watch my show. We'll be taping in a couple of days. It'll air this weekend." She uncoiled from her chaise, stood, and came around to the back of my chair.

"If Cartwright Drummond is still alive, she may not have until this weekend," I said.

She leaned over so that she was almost speaking into my ear. "All right," she said softly. "I'll give you a tidbit. Ever hear of a foundation called Second Millennium?"

I decided I better play dumb. "No. What's that?"

"It's just one of three or four foundations supported by Tor Drummond's money. The Drummond family has always been very philanthropic."

"So?"

"I'm sorry," she said, her voice lilting upward. "Can't tell you anymore."

"Listen. You don't understand. This might be very important." For a moment, I thought about telling her about the E-mails, but decided I'd better keep it to myself.

"I understand your concern. But I assure you, if I had anything I thought could help find Cartwright Drummond, I'd take it to the authorities."

"Even if it meant losing your story?"

She said nothing. She stepped around in front of me, placed her hand on the arm of my chair, and bent down to look into my eyes. "Frank, you know, I'd really like to help you, but . . ." Her fingers began to gently massage my wrist. The Chanel Number 5 went from trace to thick cloud.

I picked up her hand and put it back on the arm of the chair. "Maybe I should ask the cops to pay you a visit, then."

"Oh, pooh. I told you, I don't think I can be of any help to them."

"What about the rest of the Drummond family? They're under enough duress as it is. Running with some new scandal on the congressman now will only add to it."

"I'm very sorry about that. I really am. But if I don't air these little tidbits, trust me, someone else will."

"You seem to think television is more important than reality."

"Reality?" She suddenly grunted in disgust, let go of the chair, and stood. "Let me tell you something about reality. About a young woman who works for a man she believes in, a man who represents all of her ideals about service, and justice, and doing what's right." Her face grew red. "How she makes the stupid mistake of thinking she's in love with this man, but he uses her, and when she needs him the most, he turns his back on her and walks away. *That's* reality for you."

"I see." I rose from my seat, walked to the door,

and pulled it open. "Thanks for your time, Ms. Lemminger and for the information."

"You're entirely welcome. Anytime."

"Maybe you'll finally get the story you're after, then."

"Maybe you'll be part of it, Frank," she said.

20

I drove back out toward Richmond's West End. I thought about everything I'd learned so far, about what Diane Lemminger had said, and decided I wasn't about to leave Richmond until I tried to find out more about Second Millennium. The E-mails and the TV reporter's upcoming exposé had to have some link to Cartwright Drummond's disappearance.

Roberta and Averil Joseph worked at Physicians' Specialty Hospital. In the afternoon sun, the facility seemed to glow with the power and authority of modern medicine, all contained in a futuristic brick-and-glass structure that had once been an architect's dream. I parked in the visitors lot and entered the lobby.

Since it was the peak of visiting hours, the elderly volunteer behind the reception desk was occupied with at least three different groups of people who'd come to see their relatives or friends. I swept by this entourage without even looking at the desk. I didn't know exactly where I was going, but it wasn't hard to give the impression that I did.

Around a corner, a set of double doors brought me into a long hallway. About halfway down this corridor was a sign that read CAFETERIA, with an arrow pointing to the right down another hall.

Should I start with Averil? I didn't want to be seen

as unscrupulous, attempting to talk to her without her mother present, so my head voted for finding her mom. But I hadn't eaten anything since the doughnuts that morning, and my stomach voted in favor of the cafeteria. The stomach won. At least I could always claim a legitimate reason for my visit. You know, gourmet Pavlicek, driving five miles out of his way just for a taste of hospital food.

After one wrong turn I managed to locate the cafeteria, a spacious affair with salmon-colored walls and tall windows facing the parking lot. A few dozen customers were eating dinner: families with children, a man and a woman in tailored business suits, an elderly couple who seemed to be stooping in prayer over their meal. The food was served assembly-line style, as you might expect. I found a tray, picked up a salad and a drink, and began to work my way down the line in search of an entrée, only to come face-to-face with Averil Joseph.

She was helping to serve pork chops, mashed potatoes, steamed broccoli, and some sort of rice and bean casserole. Another worker stood next to her, a fifty-something woman with gray hair and a flat face. She and Averil seemed to be operating in tandem.

Averil showed no sign of recognition as I slid my tray in front of her and asked for the pork chops. She dutifully took the plate I handed her and scooped a couple of pieces of meat neatly onto the side, then handed it to her coworker. Averil wore an oversized green apron and a thin paper cap with elastic around the edges. I picked up the plate with the rest of my food from the other woman and moved on down the line, keeping a close watch on Averil out of the corner of my eye.

She seemed to try not to be too obvious about it,

but by the time I reached the desserts, she had cupped her hand over the side of her companion's head and was whispering something in the older woman's ear. Apparently Averil could communicate, at least in some fashion, when she needed to. Since there was no one behind me in line, the other woman had no food to serve at the moment. She disappeared into the kitchen, leaving Averil standing at her post in the serving line alone.

I paid the cashier, then stepped back along the counter.

"Averil. Remember me?"

The girl stared straight ahead as if she hadn't heard me.

"My name is Pavlicek. I just visited your house this morning. Remember?"

Her face turned to me then, but not in the way you would expect. She didn't look me in the eye, or even acknowledge that I had spoken her name. Instead she stared at my jacket and the jesses still attached there.

I took them off and gave them to her. "Here. Remember these?"

She turned the leather straps over in her hand as if they were a magic amulet.

"Do you send E-mail a lot, Averil?"

She said nothing, but for the briefest moment she smiled.

"Just what do you think you are doing?" Roberta Joseph's voice came from behind me. Her department must have been closer to the cafeteria than I thought.

I turned to see the nurse in hospital scrubs covered by a half-length, multicolored coat, standing next to the gray-haired cafeteria worker. She had her hands on her hips. Her hair was neatly tucked beneath a surgical cap, and her face looked grim.

"I was speaking with your daughter," I said.

"I thought I told you this morning we didn't know anything more about your questions," she said.

"I know, I know. But Averil here seems to have developed a sudden interest in E-mails."

Roberta Joseph's eyes narrowed. Then she turned to the older woman. "Can you excuse us, Lena? Thanks for coming to get me." The woman shot me a look that could've melted lead and disappeared again into the kitchen.

"There's a private dining room over this way," Roberta said. "We can talk there." She turned to her daughter. "Averil, you okay?"

The girl nodded.

Her mother took her by the hand, leading us toward a far corner of the cafeteria. The elderly couple seated in the corner stared, but most of the other diners ignored the three of us.

We came to a closed door on which was a sign that read CONFERENCE ROOM. Most likely it was used by various departments within the hospital for meetings, at lunchtime and otherwise. At this particular moment, however, it stood vacant. We went in, Roberta closed the door behind us, and we all took chairs around a long table.

Averil had begun to grin again.

"Before we go any further, I want to know just exactly who you are working for," her mother said.

"Cassidy Drummond," I said.

She stared at me and said nothing, but she swallowed. Hard.

"Look, I know Drummond's behind your little foundation, all right?"

"How do you know that?"

"I have sources at the bank," I lied. Truth was, I

didn't even remember what bank Second Millennium used, although that information was probably buried somewhere in the reams of background material Toronto and Nicole had printed out.

She must have bought it. Her shoulders slumped, and the fight seemed to drain out of her. "This is not good," she said. "Tor's not going to be happy."

"Why not? Because I've exposed his philanthropy? What's the harm in that?"

She shook her head. "You don't understand. You've opened a real can of worms."

"Okay. Tell me about it."

"I can't. I shouldn't even be sitting here talking to you."

"Look, Ms. Joseph. You know Cartwright Drummond is missing, right?"

"Of course." She pushed a stray wisp of hair off her face.

"I've got copies of two messages sent from your foundation's E-mail address to Cartwright the night she disappeared, one of which looks like an invitation for Cartwright to come meet someone, someone she knew. Did you send those E-mails?"

"No. I did not."

"Do you know who sent them?"

"I do not."

"You said your daughter has access to your account."

"Yes, but that's ridiculous—" Roberta turned to face her daughter, who was seated next to her, and took both of the girl's hands in her own. "Averil," she said, "do you remember someone named Cartwright Drummond?"

The girl stared blankly at a spot across the room.

"Look at me, Averil."

The girl obeyed and focused on her mother.

"Have you ever heard of Cartwright Drummond?"

It took maybe three or four seconds, but eventually Averil gave a slight but distinct nod. She remained expressionless.

"Have you sent mail with the computer to Cartwright Drummond?"

We waited, but Averil gave no indication that she even understood her mother's words.

"Your daughter ever write poetry, Ms. Joseph?" I asked.

"Write poetry? No, not that I know of. She did attend a speech class at her developmental learning center last year. I think they may read poetry to the classes sometimes. In fact, I remember them saying they thought it might help stimulate language development in the students."

"Can you get the address and the name of the teacher for me?"

"I suppose. Maybe this is all just some mistake. If Averil sent some random E-mails, I'm sure she meant no harm."

"If you don't mind my asking, where's Averil's father?"

She folded her hands on the table and stared at me. "He's not in the picture. We never married. I've raised Averil on my own."

Suddenly, quite deliberately, her daughter reached over and placed a hand on top of her mother's. The nurse smiled.

"Averil understands quite a bit, it seems," I said.

"She understands my gestures and my emotions."

"Back to the foundation. Are you sure you're the only person who ever uses that E-mail box?"

"Yes."

"Would you be willing to supply me with the foundation's address list?"

"I can't do that," she said.

"Why not?"

"Because the list contains many of the names of the foundation's beneficiaries, and we like to keep that information confidential. You wouldn't believe how many requests we get in that we have to turn down."

"I'm running out of time here. The police now have the E-mails too. It's just a matter of time before they subpoena all your records. I'm trying to find Cartwright Drummond."

She looked at her watch. "I'm sorry, but I really do have to get back to work." She let go of her daughter's hand, pushed away from the table, and stood and started toward the door. Like a dutiful puppy, Averil followed.

"What if it were *your* daughter who was missing, Ms. Joseph?"

She hesitated for just a moment, then turned to face me. "Please stay away from me and my daughter, Mr. Pavlicek. I hope we won't have to repeat this line of questioning."

"I strive to avoid redundancy," I said.

Roberta Joseph took her daughter by the hand again, spun around, and the two of them were gone.

I called *Ferrier* this time. From my cell phone on the way back to Charlottesville.

"Oh," he said. "Isn't this the private dick who hung up on me earlier today?"

"Sorry about that, Bill. I was, uh, in the middle of an interview."

"I'll bet."

"Listen—those E-mails I sent you? They came from

a foundation in Richmond. I've been looking into it, and you guys need to get some people on this right away. I—"

"Save it, Frank."

"What?"

"I said save it. We're shut down."

"What are you talking about?"

"There are a lot of folks in crisp dark suits walking around our office right now. They're taking over the investigation. They're also convinced this is a kidnapping and they're pretty convinced they know who did it."

"FBI?"

"Uh-huh," he said. "And they're sure looking forward to talking to you."

21

The hospital security video was less than clear. Shadow clouded a big chunk of the screen, because the camera lens was positioned so as to pick out license plate numbers of vehicles entering and exiting. It was difficult to say, for example, who for certain had been driving a particular vehicle, but there was absolutely no doubt that at 1:16 A.M. on the night Cartwright Drummond disappeared, her rented Nissan Maxima with the D.C. plates had entered the hospital parking garage. And right behind her another vehicle had entered, a black Jeep Cherokee, bearing California plates and registered in the name of Jed Haynes.

"I guess if it walks like a duck—" Ferrier shrugged.

The FBI agent in charge of the case went to switch off the tape. I figured she was in her mid-thirties, although she looked older, with a touch of gray in her hair, small wrinkles around the edges of her eyes, no makeup. She also looked like she could bench-press more than a lot of guys I knew. Her name, she said, was Agent Christine Packard.

Outside, the night air was sweetened by the smell of sumac and sassafras. Much warmer than the night before. But here next to Ferrier and Upwood's desk in the detectives' room at Charlottesville police headquarters, we might as well have been inside a concrete bunker on the moon.

"That's not all," Packard said. "We obtained a search warrant to go over Haynes's Jeep, and we've got particles of her blood dried into a plastic door-knob, more on a piece of rubber under the dash. And as you know, Haynes's alibi gets a little fuzzy after one a.m."

"So for some reason Cartwright Drummond drove to the hospital parking garage that night and Haynes followed her in his Jeep," I said.

"That's the way we see it."

It was only a two-minute drive from the house off Fourteenth Street to the parking garage at the medical center, so it sounded plausible.

"But Tor Drummond's other daughter says Cartwright left the house out in Ivy just after midnight. It doesn't take an hour or more to get to Haynes's house from there, especially at that time of night, with hardly any traffic. I'd say twenty minutes tops. What was she doing for almost an hour?" I was thinking about the E-mail message—*meet me. twelve-thirty a.m.*

"Who knows?" She tapped a thick green file folder she was holding on her leg. "Maybe she stopped for gas. Maybe she had a hankering for some Milk Duds or a Slurpee."

"If she did, there would be a receipt, or someone would've seen her."

"We're checking."

The case was far from airtight, but I had to admit it looked bad for Haynes.

"How about inside the girl's car?" I asked. "You have any evidence there that you can tie to the swimmer?"

"Not yet. We figure he cut her in the Jeep, then drove her someplace in the Nissan, which was when she spilled the little bit of blood there."

"You think she's still alive, then?"

"Absent a body, we're still going on that assumption."

"You pick up Haynes yet?"

The agent nodded. "Got him down the hall. We've already questioned him for close to two hours. He's sticking to his story for the time being."

"Look at it this way, Frank," Ferrier said. "You did a good job of bird-dogging the kid for them."

I said nothing.

"That's right," Packard said. "You talked to Haynes before anyone else did, didn't you, Pavlicek?"

"So?" I said.

"Seems kind of odd, don't you think? You're in early on the case, claiming to represent Cartwright Drummond's twin sister. Now, according to Detective Ferrier here, you claim your client doesn't want to be found. Oh, and the mother suddenly seems to be missing too. . . . You make a deal, did you, with this Haynes kid? The two of you split the ransom?"

"What ransom? What are you talking about?"

"C'mon, Frank, let's drop the charade. You're caught."

I looked at Ferrier, who was staring blankly at his hands. "You guys are in fantasyland—you know that?"

She pulled a plastic bag containing a piece of paper from the folder she was holding.

"So this little note you left demanding two million dollars in bearer bonds—that's a fantasy?"

"I don't know what you're talking about. Where did you get that?"

"I suppose you don't remember leaving it on the

desk when you went to try to intimidate Congressman Drummond in his office."

"Whatever it is, I didn't write it."

"I suppose that's why your fingerprints are all over the paper."

Stupid, I thought. Really stupid. I'd lost my temper and Dworkin had aced me.

"Pretty good scheme, though. Take a wealthy public figure like Drummond. His daughters are just back from out of the country. You and Haynes must've been planning this one for a while. And, hey, you've got to admit, Pavlicek, your public service track record hasn't exactly been star caliber. Was it more than just the money? Maybe revenge too?"

Another detective passed through the room, trailed by Haynes's roommates, both of them looking a lot more serious and respectful than the last time I'd seen them. Nobody noticed me. The detective led them down the hall, around a corner and out of sight.

"You talk to any of those jokers yet?" I said.

"We're just about to take their statements," Packard said.

Ferrier stood up. "Look, Agent, I don't know what's going on here, but I've known Frank for a couple of years now, and as far as I'm concerned, he's clean. Looks to me like someone's trying to set him up to take the fall for this."

"Your opinion is duly noted, Detective."

A door slammed around the corner and footsteps approached the big room. Jed Haynes appeared, being led by another agent.

"Potty break," the FBI guy snickered in our direction.

"Hey!" Haynes said, catching sight of me. "Ask this guy. He'll tell you. Pavlicek, you talked to me before these turkeys did and I told you the truth—I didn't do anything to Cartwright. I wouldn't. I—"

"Can it, pal." The agent strong-armed Jed down the hall in the direction of the men's room.

I didn't have anything to lose at this point, so I called after them. "Hey, Haynes, you ever hear of someone—a swimmer, maybe—calling himself the secret amphibian?"

The young man turned with his escort. "The what?" he said.

"The secret amphibian."

"Never heard of him."

"You write poetry, Mr. Haynes?"

"Huh?"

"Poetry—you know, 'admittedly an eloquence so soft,' that sort of thing."

"What do I stinking care about poetry?"

"I didn't think so," I said.

They turned and continued along the hallway.

"What is that?" Agent Packard said. "Some kind of code between the two of you?"

"No, ma'am. Part of *my* investigation."

She snickered.

"What about these E-mails and the newspaper articles and other stuff that Frank has come up with?" Ferrier said.

She dismissed the idea with a wave. "We'll follow up on them. Looks like some kind of a smoke screen, if you ask me."

Ferrier sighed, shaking his head.

Willard Abercrombie just happened to trail by, his eyes flaming, his face capillary-rich with venom.

"You," he said, pointing a finger at my face. "I always knew it." Then he turned and fled.

"Am I under arrest or something?" I said.

Packard glared at me. "Give us the girl, Pavlicek. And tell us where her mother and sister are too. It'll go a heck of a lot easier for you if you do."

"I want an attorney," I said.

22

Armistead rose upwind, her talons extended, and parachuted onto my fist. I fed her the morsel for which she'd come. Her amber eyes were fixed on a point on the hillside above where Nicole and Toronto were attempting to flush a squirrel we'd sighted almost half an hour earlier as it scrambled to blend in among the bark and branches. After stalking the quarry from various treetop vantage points for several minutes, Armistead seemed to be trying to tell me it was time to move on in search of easier game.

I'd spent more than three hours the night before under detention at the Charlottesville Police Department. An hour for my lawyer to get there, and another two being cross-examined by Agent Packard and a couple of tall characters who looked like they were fresh out of the academy. Once, when I told them about the paper trick Dworkin had pulled on me, I thought I saw a seed of doubt enter Packard's eyes, but it passed. I refused to divulge the whereabouts of Karen and Cassidy Drummond. The lawyer did a good job of blustering on about civil rights. In the end, they had to let me go, if only because they had no other physical evidence to link me to Cartwright Drummond beyond the fake ransom note. I'm sure they also figured that if they kept me under surveillance I'd eventually lead them to Cartwright, her mom, and her sister. When it came to Cartwright, at least, whether she were dead or alive, I was hoping to oblige them.

The day was a carbon copy of the one before—bright blue sky with little wind. Toronto and I had been up since dawn trying to piece together the information we had on Second Millennium. We needed to clear our minds, so we decided to take Armistead out to a patch of woods I knew near Lake Albemarle to hunt squirrels. Nicole showed up as we were about to leave and she wanted to tag along.

There had been a silver Ford Taurus, two men inside, parked just around the corner from my apartment since I'd gotten home last night. Toronto said he caught sight of them again, a couple of hundred yards behind us, as we drove past Foxfields, out Barracks Road toward the lake.

Toronto and Nicole came crashing through the thickets down the hill.

"I'll bet she'd've had him by now," Toronto said, "if it weren't for the three of us stumbling around down here."

Maybe, but maybe not. Normally, there was a natural selection aspect to any hawk's hunting. Birds of prey, like all wild hunters, are opportunistic. The young or the old, the weak or the diseased, often become their targets, which, in the balance of things, tends to strengthen particular species populations overall. But this bushytail was obviously at the height of his evasive prowess. A team of dogs might have been more successful in flushing the intended quarry from his den, but they might've had difficulty with such a survivor.

Secretly, I even felt relieved. Hunting fox squirrels wasn't even legal here in Albemarle County, the only exception being if the hawk happened to stalk one while after gray squirrels, as was the case now. Fox squirrels, much larger and stronger than the grays, represented the outside limits of the hawk's abilities. Armistead had taken one other fox during our time together, and it had been a fierce battle to the death.

Still, if the redtail could down this kind of prey, she could easily handle almost any other potential game when I returned her to the wild in what we hoped would become her future habitat. A mature, healthy female, Armistead was ready to find a wild mate and begin sitting her own nest.

From the spot where we stood we could see across to the lake, where a few early-season anglers were casting their lines.

"Why don't we head on down through that pasture up ahead? Looks like prime rabbit ground to me." I cast off the redtail. She flew on ahead to perch on the speckled limb of a dead oak that had been stripped of almost all its bark. Nicole jogged along to stay close to Armistead while Toronto and I hung back along the side of a well-worn trail.

A man emerged from the woods along the trail, carrying a fishing pole.

"Well, well," he said. "Fancy meeting you way out here, Pavlicek."

His name was Beauford Sloan and he could've been a stunt double for Wilford Brimley, so close was the resemblance.

"How you doing, Beauford?"

"Fair to middlin'."

"Jake," I said, "this is Beauford Sloan. He's a retired cop from Charlottesville and also a private investigator."

Toronto nodded.

"Jake's my old homicide partner. Lives over in Leonardston now. Helps me out from time to time."

"You don't say," Beauford said. The two men shook hands. "You fellas out here hunting?"

I pointed downwind to the distant tree where Armistead perched. "Got the hawk up after squirrels."

He nodded. "Word's all around town that you've got yourself in some kind of brouhaha over this Drummond thing everybody's talking about."

"That would be correct," I said.

"Well," he chuckled, "you know how it goes. Keep casting 'em, partner." He nodded at the two of us and disappeared on down the trail.

Toronto and I headed off after Armistead and Nicole.

"One thing's been bothering me," I said after Beauford was gone.

"What's that?"

"The blood on that rental car, especially the fingerprints. Wouldn't you have thought the kidnapper or killer would've thought to wipe those away? They were in plain view, as clear as day."

He shrugged. "Perp might've been in a panic. Had to leave in a hurry."

"Maybe. But the doors were all locked."

"You're thinking the scene was staged?"

"I don't know. It's a possibility."

"Something I don't get," Toronto said. "If the feds think you and Haynes look good as kidnappers, why don't you just let them know where Cassidy Drummond and her mom are and get yourself off the hook?"

"Because Drummond's trying to hide something, and now he's trying to frame me. He must be getting pretty desperate. By keeping him from knowing where the rest of his family is, I can keep him off-balance and there's a better chance he'll make a mistake."

"What about Haynes? You said the video and the physical evidence were pretty incriminating."

"I know. The fibbies are obsessed with what they think is a slam-dunk case. But a lot of the pieces just don't fit."

"Where are you going now with this E-mail thing?"

"I'm not sure. It really does look like whoever sent those messages knows what happened to Cartwright Drummond and is probably responsible. And then there's the poem."

I had taken the paper out and looked at the words again before falling into bed the night before. *The Secret Amphibian*. Was Averil Joseph, autistic and seemingly retarded, capable of writing those words? If so, what did she mean? Even if she did turn out to be the writer, so what? Cartwright Drummond may have been as mystified as anyone by her strange message.

"Hey, guys!" Nicole was almost a hundred yards ahead of us by now, following Armistead as she stooped low over the edge of the pasture. "Are we hunting here or what?"

We jogged to catch up. The sun had risen above the trees, and the chilled air was warming. By the time we got to Nicole, Armistead had already taken her rabbit.

"You guys missed it," she said.

I let the hawk feed for a bit, then called her off the rabbit using a lure. This might be one of the last times I ever do that with you, girl, I thought, and here I am, too preoccupied with a case.

The idea of letting my first bird go was bittersweet. I didn't have to, of course. I could keep this redtail and hunt with her for many more seasons. But Armistead, like most raptors flown by falconers, lived more on the edge of being wild. I'd decided the biggest thrill in the experience was to train her and see her prepare for the day when she would fly free and alone in her environment—I hoped for many years to come. A part of me also harbored the hope that she would remember me after she'd gone.

"All right, girl." After feeding Armistead another piece of her kill, I slipped her hood over her head and pulled the braces snug using my teeth. Jake bagged the prey and we began the walk out with Armistead riding on my fist.

"You two were talking more about the Drummond case, weren't you?" Nicole said.

"Girl must have bionic hearing," Toronto said.

"How come those guys were following us in their car?"

"That's a long story, honey. We're playing hardball now," I said. I scanned the woods and the nearby hills, wondering from where they might be watching.

"I hate it when you do that, Dad. I'm not a child. I deserve to know what's happening."

I said nothing.

We walked in silence for a couple of minutes. A few cottony clouds had appeared, but overall the sky remained an electric blue. We crossed from the warmth of the sunlit pasture into a forest of box elder, witch hazel, and black gum. Up ahead you could see the forest clearing, and beyond that a highway, and down the shoulder a ways, my truck. No sign of the G-men or their car.

"They said on the news this morning they had questioned a couple of suspects in the disappearance," Nicole ventured as we broke out of the trees.

"Let's just drop it, Nicky," I said.

"Arggghh!"

Her frustration was loud enough for every federal agent, not to mention angler and otherwise, within a mile or so to hear.

23

I spent the rest of the day on the phone in my office, trying to run down any lead I could think of regarding George and Norma Paitley and Second Millennium. Nicole had two classes and a lab. Toronto passed the time at the workbench in my office cruising on-line with his own laptop. Then he sat typing some code into the computer for a while. He also set up shop on the couch and finished fashioning a new set of anklets I'd begun making for my next bird.

We ate a late lunch from a vending machine off the lobby. "Things going to be okay over at your place?" I asked him as we chewed our prefab chicken sandwiches. "It's a long time to be away."

"Got it covered," was all he said.

Later, the guys in the Taurus parked across Water Street must have been getting bored. Around four o'clock they were replaced by a fresh crew: a guy and a gal in a minivan. Attempting to blend in.

Around six-thirty I finished making my calls and looked at Toronto.

"Nothing," I said. "I talked to three different people with D.C. Metro, fifteen current and former neighbors of the Paitleys, a human resources manager with George Paitley's old employer. No one seems to want to speculate whether or not the couple might've been the victim of worse than a hit-and-run. 'Tragic' seemed to be the most common adjective. One guy said they still haven't even changed the lane markings where it happened after all this time—says the intersection is a death trap."

"What about the woman from South America the Paitleys' son talked about?"

"Nada."

"Too bad," Toronto said.

"You want to hear how I got nowhere on Second Millennium, too?"

"Not if you got nowhere."

"Right," I said. "Well, it'll be dark in a little while. About time to lose these newbies across the street, don't you think?"

"I was beginning to think you'd never ask."

"I thought we'd head over to Marcia's first and pick up your Jeep."

"Good deal. I've got an extra set of plates I keep in the back. They won't be able to trace those to me."

"Wonderful."

"You got something in mind for the folks in the van? 'Cause if not, I could always just go down there and shoot them for you."

"I don't think that'll be necessary," I said.

There is an old coal tunnel that runs from the basement of the warehouse where my office co-op is. It's dark and dingy, and at night, it's frequently home to squatting wildlife. Not many people know about it. The entrance is covered with a big sheet of wallboard, but if you know where to remove a few screws, you can slide the board and make an opening big enough to squeeze through.

The tunnel runs under the railroad tracks behind the building and connects to another old warehouse on the other side. The second warehouse is used by the city to store mowing equipment and trucks that are rarely used. Even better, there's a bus stop on the opposite corner, shielded from the view of anyone watching my building. There's another stop off Grady Avenue just half a block down from Marcia's house.

I stepped into the hall. The building had emptied out for the day. No one ever went to the basement anyway, except the janitor, and he finished making his rounds and went home promptly at six. We left all the lights on and the computer screen burning brightly in my office. I'd already gotten everything I needed from my truck in the parking lot. Toronto had a small suitcase loaded with an assortment of flashlights, tools for breaking into things, and a couple of weapons.

For once, the plan went like clockwork. We made our escape, caught the bus, and were being let into the back door at Marcia's place by a nodding Mr. Earl about half an hour later.

"Everything all right here?" I asked.

Nod.

Mr. Earl and Toronto clasped hands.

"Frank!" Marcia called out. She hurried into the kitchen from the living room. The sunporch was off limits now, and all the drapes were drawn in the rest of the house. "We were beginning to get worried."

I kissed her lightly on the lips. She was wearing a plush terry bathrobe and slippers.

Karen Drummond came thumping down the back stairs, followed by her daughter.

"What's happening?"

Toronto headed out to the garage with Mr. Earl to check on the Jeep. Marcia and the rest of us stood around the kitchen island. I gave them a capsule summary of my interviews with the Josephs and Diane Lemminger and the developments with the FBI.

"We've been trying to cling to hope about Cartwright," Karen Drummond said.

"I understand."

"It's worse than knowing for certain that she's dead. It's like living inside a tornado—a tornado that never stops."

Marcia put her arm around her friend's shoulder.

"No one knows where we are still, right?"

"Let's hope not."

"Frank, maybe we should just go to the FBI," Marcia said. "If they think you're involved—"

"I've thought this through," I said. "The congressman's definitely trying to hide something. He knows we're on his trail if he and his people are plugged in to the investigation, which I'm sure they are. By now, they've seen the articles about the Paitleys and the copy of the photo. I'm sure they know I've been asking a lot of questions about Second Millennium too. Whatever he's trying to cover up, it's something big enough to take a wild stab at framing me for Cartwright's disappearance."

"Big enough to kill for?" Karen Drummond said. Her face was set like stone.

"Possibly."

"You think that's what Diane Lemminger's exposé is going to be about?" Marcia said.

"Yes. Either that or something related."

"You think Tor knows about the upcoming show?"

"Maybe. Maybe not. Diane said she had talked to Cartwright, but we don't know how much Cartwright may have told the congressman."

"If Tor Drummond wanted to stop a reporter from airing something, especially Diane Lemminger, you'd think he'd figure out how to go after her, not his own daughter."

"What can you tell us about Second Millennium?" I asked Karen Drummond.

"Nothing really," she said. "I've seen the name before, of course. It's been around a long time. Tor's family has always supported numerous charitable causes. Millennium wasn't one of the bigger charities. They help children, but I think they like to keep a low profile."

"Ever wondered why?"

"No, come to think of it, I haven't. I guess I always just assumed it was because of the nature of the families and the situations they became involved with. A lot of broken families. Children with only one parent, or no parents."

"Children with only one parent, like Roberta Joseph," I said.

"What do you mean?"

"Just thinking out loud."

It was quiet for a moment.

"All right," I said, "I'm still operating under the assumption that Cartwright is alive and we need to find her as soon as possible. Anything solid we find, we'll pass on to the FBI, but we aren't going to wait for them. Your husband's been in Congress a long time. He may have friends there, strings he can pull. While he's trying to cover up something else, he may be hampering the investigation."

Toronto and Mr. Earl came back in from the garage.

"Everything ready with the Jeep?" I said.

"Ready and waiting," Toronto said.

"Karen, do you know anything about your ex-husband's schedule this week?"

"A little."

"Now that all this has happened and his trip is off,

do you think he will be up in Washington, or staying at the house out in Ivy?"

"I don't know. He only rented the Ivy house after he moved out of our home in Richmond. He's back and forth between Charlottesville and Washington all the time, I think, and he's always stayed in an apartment up in D.C. when the House is in session. But with Cartwright missing and all, I would have no idea where he'd be right now."

"All right." I stretched, stifling a yawn. "We'll just have to take our chances, then."

"What are you going to do?" Marcia asked.

"Jake and I are going to do a little late-night hunting," I said.

24

The moon hung full in the sky as Toronto and I made our way on Barracks Road out of the city and into Ivy horse country. We passed miles of white board fencing, gates, and side roads, backed by fields and outbuildings and substantial houses, all of which appeared to glow with an almost unearthly pallor. The ghostly hulks of the Blue Ridge, visible off and on at various twists and turns of the road, loomed like sleeping guardians.

"I don't like going in without a layout," Toronto said.

"Me either. This is kind of a spur-of-the-moment thing."

"You said there's security?"

"There was, last time I was there. Although I'm not sure they'll be so beefed up when neither the congressman nor any of his family is at home. I'm hoping for just a caretaker or something."

"Long as he's not a caretaker with a shotgun."

We turned onto a long dirt road that followed the banks of the rock-strewn Mechums River in a wide arc back toward the way we had come. It was not the way I had approached the Drummond house before. Soon the dirt turned to pavement again, and we rolled along in the darkness, our headlights blazing a path. When I noticed a familiar landmark up ahead, the

distant hillside from which Nicole and I had observed
the house, I cut the lights and pulled the truck off
onto a grassy shoulder.

"How far?" Toronto asked.

"I'd say about half a mile, across this field. It looks
like there are woods on the other side. We'll have to
get through there, then, if I remember correctly, work
our way across another field to approach the house."

"Great . . . just great." He was slipping out of his
sneakers into black combat boots that rode high up
on the legs of his fatigues. "That way they can get a
clear shot at us."

"All the money I'm paying you and you're still
being a pessimist?"

"Right, baby. Go ahead and subtract some from my
outrageously humongous bill." He shot me a funny
look.

"Now what?" I said.

"Didn't you ever bust in anywhere when you was
a kid?"

"I must've been away at a cub scout convention
that week."

"Uh-huh. Well, in my neighborhood, *we were* the
cub scouts."

I didn't have an answer for that, so I said nothing.
I made sure my .357 was loaded and slid it into the
shoulder holster under my coat. Toronto wore his .44
on his waist and also carried a little sawed-off number
that looked like a cross between an Uzi and a Gat-
ling gun.

"What's the current mandatory sentence for armed
robbery in Virginia?"

"I don't know," I said. "Guess I'll have to study up
on that."

"How about an alarm system? Did you see one when you were in there before?"

I nodded. "But it didn't look too complicated. Probably a walk in the park for you."

"We'll see." He slipped on a pair of black gloves with cut-out fingers.

Toronto had told me stories of when he was young, running with what we now would call a gang, knocking over houses in Yorktown Heights just for kicks. Sometimes they would lift a television or a stereo; sometimes nothing at all. Of course, all this was before a stint as an Army Ranger rehabilitated the young man's ways. I doubt Yorktown Heights was a part of his history that made it into his application to join the police academy.

"Let's go," I said.

We walked through the trees nearest the truck and squeezed through a rusty barbed-wire fence. Before us lay the newly plowed field. The darkened soil, with the turning, still emitted a faint acidic breath of loam. We made our way awkwardly across the furrows, Toronto dragging a bushy branch behind us to erase our tracks.

On the far side we entered woods again. Here the trees were smaller, mostly pitch pine in rocky soil, but the bed of needles cushioned our step. After five minutes of descending a gradual slope, I caught my first glimpse of the brown grass of the field and the driveway and the house rising above. The main gate to the compound, which had been wide open a couple of days before, was closed and chain-locked, which, along with the relatively rural location, must've discouraged enough to keep them away. There were no lights on that we could see, inside the house or any of the outbuildings either, but bright floods lit a good deal of the property. We came to the edge of the woods.

"What do you think?" Toronto whispered.

"I think we need to get closer," I whispered back.

Our best approach appeared to be back up along the slope to our left, where a triangular section of pines jutted into the field and came within fifty yards or so of the back of the house. Five minutes later we reached that point in the woods and lay on our stomachs side by side beneath a thicket. Toronto produced a small pair of binoculars from somewhere, and we took turns sweeping the entire property for any signs of life. There were none. A few early-spring crickets had begun to chirp near the pond, but otherwise the place might as well have been locked up for the season. No cars in the driveway—we would check the garage before making our entrance, though. No dogs or cats or animals of any kind. No outdoor implements or other tools left standing.

Toronto looked at me and I nodded.

He produced a small handgun from somewhere else that was actually a pellet pistol with a customized silencer. There was a short *zip* like the sound of air releasing from a tire, followed quickly by the sound of glass and bulb breaking, and then another. The back of the house and the field we needed to cross went dark except for the moon.

We waited some more. No sound came from the buildings. No movement, no other lights being turned on in alarm. I looked at Toronto and shrugged. He lifted his eyebrows in a bemused expression.

We both turned and stared at the house a little longer. Still nothing.

Without looking, I tapped him on the shoulder,

crawled from beneath the bushes, and entered the field. I focused solely on the house, but I could hear Toronto's breathing beside and just behind me. The approach from this side of the main structure was relatively unencumbered by shrubs or ornamental plantings. We had to negotiate a drainage ditch and a low, easily hurdled stone wall, but that was it.

We made a quick sweep of the driveway to check for vehicles. The garage doors were solid, but there was a large window on one side of the building. A quick beam from one of our flashlights revealed the same Chevy Suburban I'd seen Drummond's security goons driving, but whether that meant the two were still camped out on the property or had merely left the vehicle there was impossible to tell. Since they'd locked it up inside and it was clearly a working car and not a family one, I held out hope for the latter.

We moved across the patio to the French doors leading into the kitchen. The floodlights aimed toward the far side of the house bathed the patio in a faint reflective glow. We both switched to latex rubber gloves, and I stood lookout while Toronto checked out the security system. Then he pulled a jackknife and some other type of tool out of a pocket. He ran something along the edge of the door and leaned on the lock. There was a soft pop. He motioned me over and within five seconds we were in.

Silence. The kitchen was still as a tomb. From what I could tell, when my eyes adjusted to the near darkness, it was also spotless. Probably the result of a cleaning service. Toronto found the control panel for the security system next to the door. I moved over to the coffeemaker and used my penlight to check out the contents. It too was spotless—and empty. Jake swept his little beam across the stove, even looked into the garbage. We looked at one another and nodded. Nobody home.

I motioned for Jake to follow me toward the front of the house. Cassidy Drummond had indicated that her father's office was connected to a landing on the main staircase. We passed down a hall floored with inlaid bricks and cedar crossbeams, turned left and made our way across a sunken family room, up a couple of steps to a foyer next to the front door, and there found the stairs, an open flight of treads minus risers with a handrail and banisters to one side. The landing stood only a few steps above the main floor, and the double doors to Drummond's office were held shut by a simple tubular lock that took Toronto all of three or four seconds to open.

Congressman Drummond's home office was nowhere near as large as his office in town or probably, for that matter, the one in Washington, either. Still, the room was elegantly appointed, with built-in bookshelves coated in black lacquer, thick carpet, heavy drapes, an oversized computer monitor, laid out with keyboard on a workstation custom-built into a corner of the room facing one of the windows. We shut the door behind us, pulled the drapes closed, and flipped on our beams.

"Okay," I said in a low voice, "I'll take the room while you go through the computer."

"Ever-ready E-file snooper at your service." Toronto smiled, made a show of flexing his shoulders and cracking his knuckles, sat down, and brought the big screen to life.

I started with the congressman's desk. It too was locked, but without even looking away from his screen Toronto produced for me a little tool that looked like a cross between a corkscrew and tweezers. After a minute or so of poking, twisting, prying, and prodding, I managed to open the desk.

"Tsk, tsk . . ." Toronto scolded, typing on the keyboard and clicking the mouse, his eyes never leaving the computer. "You scratched the wood."

I went through all the drawers. Drummond seemed to be obsessively tidy: paper, pens, other paraphernalia were all neatly organized. There were a few travel brochures touting luxury hotels on St. Croix—maybe the congressman was planning another trip—but all else seemed to be mundane stuff. The deepest desk drawer contained a metal frame from which hung several boldly labeled file folders. There was one for bills, one for insurance and investments. Drummond had recently spent more than ten thousand dollars for a painting and some vintage bottles of wine at a celebrity charity auction. His credit card bills showed several restaurant charges and purchases from catalog retailers. He also seemed to fuel his vehicles, or have them fueled, at one of the same stations I frequented. His bond and mutual fund portfolio was impressive, if only because the current total of the accounts listed stood at more than three million dollars. The last file in the drawer was marked CORRESPONDENCE—PERSONAL FILES.

"Find anything?" I asked.

"Nope. Dude doesn't seem to use his computer much. Doesn't even use word processing."

"Probably old school, not like us progressives."

He grunted.

"How about his personal E-mail? Can you get online and check his screen name?"

"Not without time. Got a new program that'll maybe sniff out the password, but with this clunker of

a CPU, it might take four, five hours. I can write down
the E-mail addresses he uses, and maybe Nicky and I
can hack into them back at your office. What're you
holding there?"

I had pulled the last file from the desk drawer. It
was pretty thick.

"Apparently Drummond likes to handwrite his personal letters. How about you take one stack and I'll
take another?"

I sat in Drummond's desk chair while Toronto
spread his pile out on the floor. I read through two
letters Drummond had received from his daughters
while they were in Japan. The letters contained little
news, were almost cryptic in fact. Either they commu-
nicated with their father only out of obligation or they
gave the details of their lives overseas by E-mail or
phone calls. The main excuse for even sending the
letters at all appeared to be photos the girls had taken
of some sites in Tokyo.

"Gotcha," Toronto suddenly said.

I looked up from reading. "You have something?"

"Maybe. Didn't you say the woman who ran that
foundation was named Roberta Joseph?"

"Yes."

"Got a note here from her to Drummond, along
with copies of some checks. The note and the dates
on the checks are from last year."

"Let's see them."

He brought them over and we spread them out on
the desk.

The note was hard to decipher.

> *Dear Tor,*
>   *Did you make an error on these checks?*
> *Shouldn't those for* A *and* P *be less than the*

*checks for the general fund? I assume you may
have been in a hurry and just transposed the numbers. Unless you're changing the arrangement. I'm
holding on to them until I hear. Just let me know
what you want to do. I can deposit them in the accounts, if you want, transfer the money, and we
can make the adjustments next month.*

Roberta

There were photocopies of seven different checks
on two pages, four on one, three on the other. All
were in Drummond's handwriting and from his personal account, all made out to Second Millennium
Foundation. On five of the checks, the words GENERAL
FUND appeared on the notation line. The other two
had letters handwritten on the same line, a different
one for each check: *A* and *P*. Most interesting of all,
however, in the top corner of one of the sheets, the
one with the three checks, including those bearing the
letters, Drummond, or someone else, had printed a
word in dark pencil on the copy: PAITLEY.

"What do you make of it?" Toronto said.

"Looks like our Ms. Joseph's managing several different accounts. And one or more of them have something to do with some dead people."

He lined up the copies. "You think we should
take them?"

"We'd be contaminating potential evidence."

"Right, like we haven't already done that."

I pointed toward the corner where Toronto had
been working. "There's a fax machine over there.
Looks like it's turned on. Let's see if it has a copy
function."

We had just finished copying the last of the checks

when Toronto cocked his head. "Hold on a minute. Listen . . ."

I heard nothing.

"Did you hear that?"

"No, I—" But now the sound became much more distinct—the low murmur of an engine and the sound of tires on stone. A car was coming up the driveway.

We scrambled to put the letters back into the file the way we had found them. Should I take the letter I'd just been reading? I skimmed the rest of it to look for any other bombshells, but there didn't appear to be any. I stuffed it back into the file along with the rest of the correspondence.

Toronto had already shut down the computer and was busy restoring everything else in the office to the way it was when we arrived. I finished returning all the files, then closed and locked the desk. We clicked off our lights and went to the window. I drew the drape aside and looked out.

Unfortunately, the view from the office window failed to show me the approach to the front of the house. I could see out to the woods, the moon and stars overhead, and on the mowed field grass the bright swath of brilliance, now unmoving, from a pair of headlights. A vehicle was definitely there, but it appeared to have stopped only partway up the drive.

Toronto edged around my shoulder to have a look. "What do you think, mate?"

"Whoever this is belongs here. They came right in through the main gate."

"What are they waiting for?"

"Maybe they picked up on the fact that the lights were out in back."

He furrowed his brow. "We need to get out," he said. "Now."

No argument from me. "How about the side of the house closest to the trees? It's still dark there. The headlight beams don't reach up that far."

Toronto nodded. We pulled open the drapes and made our way out of the office, locking the door behind us again. We descended the stairs but didn't head back toward the kitchen. Instead, we crossed a dining room and entered another short hallway that led down a short flight of steps into a recreation room with a wet bar, pool table, big-screen television. Through a door on the far side was an exercise room with a weight machine, exercise bike, and treadmill. There were also two large windows facing the woods.

You could still see the glow from the unmoving headlights further out on the grass. There were sensors on the windows, but Toronto took out a pair of clippers and a little magnet and quickly dispatched them. One thing we hadn't taken into account, though. The house was built into the hillside, split into multiple levels. The drop from these particular windows looked to be at least fifteen feet.

But it was too late to worry about that. Just as we raised the window on the cold night air, the moan of a garage door rising, followed by the ignition of the Suburban's engine, came from the far side of the house. The security boys had been home all along.

Toronto went first. He swung his legs out the window and hung from the sill for an instant before dropping with a grunt to the ground. I was right behind him. I thought I'd timed my drop well enough to minimize the height as much as possible, but my foot must have caught the edge of a rock when I hit the ground. A jolt of pain shot through my leg. I didn't think the ankle was broken, but I'd sprained it badly enough. Toronto grabbed my arm and began running for the woods with me hobbling along, partially supported by his bulk, as best I could.

"Remind me to get you to the gym more often, buck," he whispered. "You gotta learn to let those knees flex a little more when you land."

I wanted to tell him I knew that already; I thought I'd been doing just that. But there were bigger concerns at the moment. I tried to stay low with him as we entered the safety of the woods and began making our way uphill through the trees.

A few yards in, I pulled him to a halt. "Hold on just a minute," I said. "I'd like to get a look at whoever is in that car."

"What are you, nuts? If those guys in the 'Burban know what they're doing, they'll be out here sweeping this hillside with their high beams in a couple of minutes."

"It'll only take a second. Where are the binoculars?"

He shook his head, but plucked out the glasses and handed them over.

From our new vantage point almost the full length of the driveway was visible. A dark Corvette, its headlights still blazing, idled about three-quarters of the way down the incline. The team in the Suburban had driven out to meet it in the same way they'd driven out to meet me, but there seemed to be a much more extended conversation occurring, as if the participants knew one another. Mr. Turnip was standing in front of the bigger vehicle pointing at the house, while his partner leaned on the fender right behind him. I switched my focus to the driver of the Corvette, a woman in a leopard-skin jacket with a shapely profile, standing with her arms crossed in front of her.

It was none other than my good friend Diane Lemminger.

25

"Call for you, Señor Pavlicek," Juanita Estavez said early the next morning. "Line one."

It was a standing joke between us—Juanita didn't answer phones. She was, however, the therapeutic receptionist, listening ear, and all-around organizational spark that kept me and the other semimarginal businesses in the office co-op from sinking into anarchy.

"Somebody famous?" I asked.

She smiled, showing bright teeth. "No, but you have important visitors. From the FBI. I think they're searching your office."

"Great. I've got a business to run, we're still towing the two turkeys in the minivan around with us, and now this."

"Looks like the feds got us surrounded." Toronto, who was standing next to me, smiled. He'd made sure to remove his laptop and any traces of his presence before we left the office the night before. Returning from Ivy, we'd trailed Diane Lemminger to the Holiday Inn out by the interstate on Fifth Street. Fortunately, the guy working the front desk was a friend of mine, a very dark-skinned paraplegic named Bebo Walter. I'd first met Bebo when I happened to catch one of his wheelchair basketball games over at the old MAACA gym on Park Street; since then, he'd become a good source for me. I gave him twenty bucks and he promised to let me know as soon as he detected any sign that Lemminger was about to check out or leave the hotel.

Afterward, Toronto and I had driven across town and hidden the Jeep in Marcia's garage again, then walked a few blocks to catch a bus to take us back downtown. A little after midnight, we snuck up on the minivan parked across the street from my office and rapped on the window with a box of Krispy Kremes for the two agents. Almost as good as Eddie Murphy in *Beverly Hills Cop*.

"They show you a warrant?" I asked.

"Sí, Señor. I wouldn't have let them in otherwise. . . . Oh, and someone else—he drop this off for you," Juanita said. She reached in her drawer and pulled out a pale blue envelope. No return address. Inside was a crude drawing of an eagle, or maybe a hawk, and two words in capital letters: FLIGHT CANCELED.

I know a handful of antifalconry, supposedly animal-rights types in town.

"What is it?" Toronto asked.

"Someone with a sick sense of humor."

"Thanks, Juanita." I limped around her desk and tossed the envelope and its contents into the wastebasket behind her.

"What happened to you?" Juanita said.

I grimaced. "Stepped on a garden rake."

"A garden rake?" She looked skeptical.

"Gardening," Toronto said.

The two of us walked up the stairs out of earshot. "How you wanna handle this?" he said.

I shrugged. "Not like my office hasn't been searched before."

"I only need to send a fax and spend a few hours

on-line and I'll be able to tell you anything you want to know about those Second Millennium accounts."

"You know I've been thinking about that. Why don't you let me talk to Bill Ferrier, get him to do it for us this time? That way, it'll be nice and legal if it comes down to pinning something on Tor Drummond."

"Be still my hacking heart. All right, if you say so, boss." He glanced up the stairs. "We've still got a problem though. What about the Gestapo upstairs?"

"I'm thinking divide and conquer."

"Yeah?"

I checked my watch. "Ferrier's usually having coffee about this time at a place across the mall. I might just pay him a visit. Meanwhile, you could go on up to my office and—without interfering or being in any way threatening, of course—do your best to intimidate the living bejeezus out of whoever's there."

"Bejeezus," he said. "I can do."

"How's it feel to be on the sidelines?" I did my best to smile brightly for so early in the morning.

Bill Ferrier glared at me from behind his cup of coffee.

"Sit down," he said.

The morning crowd at Chaps was light. My favorite hangout on the mall, Chaps offered coffee and dough-nuts, but specialized in multiple flavors of homemade ice cream, shakes, and malts, not to mention the fifties memorabilia plastered everywhere in pleasant disorga-nization, cool metal-and-vinyl booths, even an authen-tic Rockola Princess jukebox.

"As you can see outside, I don't travel alone any-more." The guy and the gal from the minivan had

changed shifts again with the original crew. I guessed
one or both of them would be somewhere in sight.

He checked over my shoulder. "Tall guy leaning
against the storefront and reading the paper at ten
o'clock."

"Sounds like one of them."

"What do you expect? You're fuckin' with the feds
and a congressman here, Frank. Why don't you just
let it go? If Karen Drummond can put you in the
clear, why not let the feds worry about her and her
daughter?"

"Maybe later," I said.

He shook his head. "Mother and daughter must
really be worried someone's after them or something
to want to hang around with you," he said.

"Maybe they just needed a break from being the
nightly feature at six, ten, and eleven."

"Uh-huh. What, you their press secretary now,
too?"

I said nothing.

"What happened to your leg?" he asked. Guess I
hadn't done a good enough job of disguising the limp.

"Garden rake," I said, trying to sound a little more
convincing than I had with Juanita. "Stepped on it at
first light when I was going out in the backyard to
check on Armistead."

"Right. I heard there was a break-in at Tor Drummond's estate in Ivy last night."

"Really? Hate it when stuff like that happens.
Bumps up the crime rate."

"Someone slipped in and out right under all his security—a real professional job."

"Must've made someone look bad. Hear any more
about Haynes?" I knew Bill wouldn't let go of an

investigation like this entirely without keeping tabs on it.

He shrugged.

"Bet he's not confessing, is he?"

"Nope. They had to let him go. No body, no other evidence, for now, and the video's inconclusive—can't prove he was driving the Jeep. I suppose they're hoping one of the two of you leads them to the girl."

"They still seem pretty convinced that this is a kidnapping."

His eyes searched the restaurant to make sure no one else was listening. "That's because there's been another note," he said flatly.

I stared at him, trying to absorb what he'd said. "Not from Tor Drummond's office again, I hope."

He shook his head. "They're keeping this under wraps, but it showed up at police headquarters. Came in the regular mail, Charlottesville postmark."

"What did it say?"

He lowered his voice. *"I have Cartwright Drummond. She is alive and I will keep her until it is time."*

"Until it is time. Time for what?"

"Nobody knows."

"Sounds like it might be a hoax."

"Maybe, except that inside the envelope was a Polaroid of someone bound and gagged. Not a very good picture, but looks like it could be her."

"She's still here in the area, then."

"Quite possibly."

"So why are they still dogging Toronto and me?"

His voice remained calm. "Could've been you sent the picture, Frank."

"Right," I said. "Either that or the tooth fairy."

He looked down at the table. "I know. I know."

"What about Haynes?"

"Still the prime suspect."

"You've got to admit, the evidence so far doesn't look good for the kid."

"I hope you don't plan to try to dog him yourself."

"Who, me? Why do that when I've got the feds? Don't pay my federal taxes for nothing."

"What's going on, Frank?"

"I told you. I think Drummond's dirty and there's a connection."

"Okay," he said. "Just for the sake of argument, let's say you're right and maybe this case is more complicated than what it first appears. Absent a dead body or any other physical evidence, we still gotta go with the facts we've got in front of us."

"I've always been a believer in facts."

"C'mon, Frank. When are you going to tell me what you're working?"

Two families noisily entered the ice cream parlor looking for doughnuts: a father and mother and another mother alone with six or seven children in tow. We were seated in the back booth nearest the bathrooms, and I faced away from the group and the door, but I still kept my voice down.

"Drummond's dirty," I said. "He may or may not be good for his daughter's sudden invisibility, but the guy's hiding something. Might even be seeing it on TV soon."

"Well, hallelujah, hoorah. Next time I really want to know something I'll just park my butt over at the local station and sic one of their people on the case. Man, oh, man, by the time they get through with you and me this go-round, you'll be serving five to seven up in Orange County and I'll be camped in a stilt house, crewing on a sportfisherman out of Oregon

Inlet to supplement my pension. Who's the brilliant TV type?"

"Diane Lemminger."

"Lemminger? Isn't she the one who . . . ?"

"One and the same."

He thought about that. "She's got some cable show out of Richmond now, don't she?"

"It's called *Government Offense*."

"You know what she's got on Drummond?"

"I don't know for sure, but it has something to do with that foundation where those E-mails came from. You know if the FBI's looking into that?"

He shook his head. "Don't know. They weren't too thrilled when they heard you'd pulled it off the hard drive. If somebody wanted to, they could think you all did some tampering. Could try to make a case for obstruction."

"Obstruction of what, if they aren't looking into it?"

"Guess it all depends on a person's perspective."

"Cartwright Drummond was suspicious of her father."

"We know that."

"Yeah, but she might've been onto something."

"I'm listening."

"I think it might be the same something Diane Lemminger's so charged up about, something to do with Second Millennium." I took three pieces of paper from my pocket, copies of the checks and the note from Drummond's file, and slid them across the table so he could read them.

He looked them over. "Where'd you get these?"

"You don't want to know."

He shrugged. "Doesn't look like all that much to me."

"People don't usually keep separate bank accounts without a reason," I said.

"Maybe," he said. "But it could also be an innocent reason."

"Maybe."

"I'm not liking the sound of any of this." Ferrier's voice was now barely above a whisper. His coffee was long gone.

"Me either, believe me."

"What if this has nothing to do with Cartwright Drummond's disappearance? What if we're looking at two separate problems?" he said.

"Somehow I don't think so. I think Drummond's made a public career for himself out of smoke and mirrors."

"What's so new about that?"

"It's new if people died for it."

We stared at one another for a long moment.

"I'll see what I can do," he said.

26

I was crossing Water Street in front of my office, beginning to get in a rhythm with my limp, when Tor Drummond's yellow Hummer rumbled to life from the curb. His security men, who'd been talking to the remaining FBI agent by the silver Taurus, jumped back into their dark Suburban. This was obviously no campaign stop. There wasn't a microphone or a reporter in sight.

Drummond turned on his flashers and pulled to a halt right in front of me. He opened the hatchlike door and stepped out.

"Hey, Pavlicek!" His cowboy boots and jeans were jet black. He wore a white turtleneck sweater and a camel-colored cashmere sport jacket.

"Hey, yourself."

The boys riding shotgun in the second vehicle pulled up behind the Hummer and also turned on their flashers. Turnip and his friend, the same two I'd met before. They sat behind the glass, expressionless.

"Been waiting for you. I'd like to ask your advice about something, if you can spare a couple of minutes," the congressman said.

I peered up and down the sidewalk. "I look like Lucy to you? Sorry, the advice booth's closed right now. Besides, I don't really have a couple of minutes to spare. Unless you're here to tell me where your missing daughter is."

"Aw, c'mon, now, don't be like that. We may still be able to help each other."

"Why? So you can try to set up me up for Cartwright's disappearance again? No, thank you."

"I'm really sorry about that. Mel gets a little carried away sometimes. He's only trying to protect me."

"Yeah. From whom?"

He held out his hands. "Just a couple of minutes. That's all I ask."

"If you've got something to say that might help find your daughter, you're better off telling the FBI. And you can try siccing them on someone besides me while you're at it."

"I'm here because I want to talk to you, Pavlicek. No one else. Don't you understand?"

I looked up to see a sharp-shinned hawk, smaller and quicker than a redtail, swoop from a tree around the corner of the library after a wren. It was rare to see sharpshins in the city, rare to see one at all unless you knew what to look for. Drummond saw me briefly staring and followed my line of vision. He might've seen the birds too.

"All right," I said. I cocked my head in the direction of his goons in the trailer vehicle. "Lose the safety patrol and you can take me for a spin around the block."

He crossed his arms and looked at me. Then he snickered and gestured toward his bodyguards. They neither questioned his intentions nor his actions. Immediately, the Suburban backed up and pulled around us, roaring off down the street. They turned right onto Second Street and disappeared.

"Okay, then?" he said.

I went around to the passenger side, found the handle, and pulled open the hatchlike door. I'd never ridden in a Hummer before. It felt like crawling into a cross between an M1 Abrams and something out of *Star Trek*. Tan-and-blue leather interior, giant silver gearshift, dials and controls. Computer monitor in the center of the dashboard to show us exactly where on the planet our little blip was located, using the global positioning system.

Drummond saw me staring. He patted the steering wheel. "Never ridden in one of these babies before? Here, let me show you how this works." He pushed a button and tweaked some dials to pull up a street map of C-ville on the screen. Impressive.

"Personally, I prefer the Joe method."

"Joe method?"

"Yeah. He's the guy at the gas station, knows where everything is, but no one ever stops to ask him directions."

He turned the flashers off with a smirk, shifted into gear, and we moved away from the curb. I felt like one of the title characters in *Kelly's Heroes* expeditioning in my own tank down Water Street. I checked the side mirror just to make sure the FBI folks in the Taurus were following us—didn't think the congressman would try anything foolish with them around. They were. I also leaned into the seat and felt the comforting butt of the .357 beneath my jacket, just in case.

We reached the intersection of Ridge and Main, by the Lewis and Clark statue. He turned right down the hill. At the bottom we turned onto Preston Avenue.

"I saw you limping," he said. "What'd you do, hurt yourself?"

"Seems pretty obvious, doesn't it?"

"What happened?"

"I'm in a risky profession."

He grunted. "Saw that bird you were looking at, too. One of the detectives—Ferrier, was it?—told me you keep one like it yourself."

"Not exactly. Different species."

"A man of nature. You know my record on the environment is one of the strongest parts of my . . ." He stopped himself in midsentence. "Never mind. I suppose whatever I say must sound like platitudes to a man like you."

He had that right.

"So," he said, "I understand you're keeping Karen and Cassidy's whereabouts a secret."

"Who says I even know where they are?"

He smiled. "I thought you were hired by Cassidy."

I said nothing.

"You think this evidence they've got against Jed Haynes is conclusive enough? I told you before what I thought of the young man."

"I think it's more likely someone's trying to make everyone think Haynes has either killed your daughter or is keeping her somewhere."

He twisted his lips into an odd shape. "Interesting theory. I hope you don't think I'd have anything to do with something like that."

"Your chief of staff's trying to frame *me,* isn't he?"

"Ummm. Guess you've got a point there," he said.

I shook my head and leaned back onto the leather headrest. The Hummer kept moving toward Barracks Road. "Doesn't it bother you, Drummond, that your own daughter and your ex-wife don't trust you?"

His turn to say nothing. But he seemed to grip the wheel a little tighter.

"Look," he said after a few moments, "you seem to be the kind of man I can do business with."

"Oh, yeah? What kind of man is that?"

"Independent. Tough and smart. I've employed a number of private investigators over the years, but most were disappointing."

"Disappointing how?"

"They weren't willing to take risks."

"You trying to hire me, Congressman?"

"Maybe. After all, I'm just as interested in finding out what's happened to Cartwright as Karen or Cassidy is."

"Maybe even more interested."

"What do you mean by that?"

"What's Cartwright got on you that's got you so worked up?"

He shrugged. "I don't know what you're talking about."

"I'm talking about Second Millennium. I'm talking about George and Norma Paitley."

"Oh, yes, I've heard you've been down bothering Roberta Joseph and her daughter."

"You told me you'd never heard of the Paitleys."

"That's right."

"Really? How come I turned a photo of you standing arm and arm with them over to the cops then?"

There was a slight, barely detectable hesitation to his answer. "Good God, man. You know how many people I've had my picture taken with over the past fifteen years?"

"I've also had a chat with Diane Lemminger."

His face lost a little color when I said that. He stared, expressionless, through the windshield.

"You're the one who sent me to her, told me Cartwright had been talking to her, remember? She said she's working on a story about you."

"Good God, my friend, I hope you don't believe anything she's got to say these days. No one takes that show seriously. Like I told you before, she's gone and become a harlot to the highest bidder with a camera."

"Some might say the same about politicians."

He shook his head. "I suppose it serves me right. I mean, for what I—for what Diane and I—did together. She'll probably take whatever she thinks she's got to the tabloids before she's through."

Drummond had learned to affect true humility and honesty so well, talking with him was like getting lost in a house of mirrors.

"Funny, because she's here right now in Charlottesville."

"Here? What for?"

"I don't know. I was hoping you might be able to tell me."

"I haven't a clue. Probably trying to dig up more dirt on me."

"Maybe just visiting old friends," I suggested.

"You really think I may have had my own daughter kidnapped or killed, don't you?" he said.

"You sure act like it."

"Is that what Cassidy thinks too?"

"When she decides to talk to you again, you'll have to ask her."

He nodded. The sky was beginning to clear overhead as we waited in a line of cars headed down the hill toward the light at the big intersection with Emmet Street. The trees were infused with a shadow of spring green where the budding tips of new leaves grew fatter every day.

"You spent much time around hospitals, Pavlicek?" he asked.

"Some."

"You know I trained as a physician, don't you?"

"Are you saying doctors aren't capable of murder?"

"Not at all. I'm only trying to get you to appreciate that there is often a finer line between life and death than most of the general public realize or want to even think about. Doctors must think about and deal with that line almost every day."

"How do you deal with it up in Washington?"

He didn't answer. Which was about the most honest thing I'd heard him say.

We were looping around onto the 250 Bypass, heading back in the general direction from which we'd come. We drove in silence at the posted speed limit toward my office. Almost every driver we passed turned and gave the Hummer a look. Drummond appeared oblivious. I checked the side mirror for our FBI tail again. Still there.

"Someone broke into my house out in Ivy last night. Have you heard about it?" he said.

I shrugged. "Too bad. Anything taken?"

"Nothing that I could see. Whoever it was broke into my desk, though, and went through my papers."

"Guess you'd better shore up your security out there," I said.

"Exactly what I'm thinking. Which is why I thought I might offer you and your friend I've heard about— what's his name?"

"Toronto."

"Toronto, then—a chance to work for me regarding this whole affair. I can certainly pay you a lot more than you're probably getting now."

"Not interested," I said.

"You sure? You might want to think about it."

"I've thought about it. Not interested."

He looked perplexed, disappointed. We climbed the hill to Lewis and Clark again and took the left onto Water. Eased back downhill toward the big parking garage where the Suburban sat idling at the curb.

"Looks like your shock troops are ever vigilant," I said.

"That they are. The price of freedom—isn't that what we say?"

"The price of freedom."

He pulled to a stop in front of my building. I unbuckled, opened the door, and climbed out.

"I guess I was wrong about you," he said.

"Yeah?"

"I'll have to add stupid to the list of qualities."

"Yes, but I'm as loyal as your first puppy," I said and closed the door.

27

Back in the office, the searchers had vacated the premises. Everything looked neat and tidy. Toronto sat at my workbench, staring into his laptop.

"How did it go?" I asked.

He shrugged. "Dudes didn't seem to find what they were hoping for. And then, for some reason, they decided it was time to leave."

"Can't imagine why."

"You think it's my deodorant?" he said.

"Bugs, cameras?"

"Already swept for them."

I picked up the phone. "Think they've tapped this line?"

"That'd be my guess."

I put the phone back in its cradle.

"Here," he said, handing me one of the many cell phones he always seemed to have at his disposal. "Certified secure."

I wanted to find out exactly when Diane Lemminger's exposé on Drummond was supposed to air, so I called the studio in Richmond and was surprised when they connected me with a man who said he was her agent.

"She's not here," he said, between bites of some kind of food he was eating. "They've stopped taping, anyway. I guess you musta heard the news."

"News?"

"Yeah-h-h . . . it sucks. Didn't you hear? Her show's been canned. You believe it? I'm telling you, there ain't no justice. Seemed like her numbers were on the rise too. Now I'm over here making sure we at least get paid what we're due."

"Who canceled the show?"

"Who do ya think? Some honcho from New York supposedly calls last night out of the blue. I don't know, man. Shit happens."

"Diane know about this?"

"Sure she does. Told her myself. Good thing too. She was hanging around my place last night, and she might not've taken it so well over the phone—you know what I mean? I tried to console her, but, hey, what can I say? Little sweetie wasn't in the mood. She took off like a bat out of hell."

"Thanks for the info," I said.

"Hey, wait a minute. What'd you say your name was again?"

"Pavlicek."

"Right, Pavlicek. Hey, listen. You see Diane, you tell her from me this shit about her show being axed ain't got nothing to do with talent. Tell her to call me. A face and tits like hers're gonna end up on somebody else's screen in a heartbeat. I can practically guarantee it. This game's full of nothin' but whores."

After I hung up, Toronto and I compared notes. I decided I'd better pay a visit to Diane Lemminger, then shoot down to Richmond again with the copies of the checks we'd taken from Drummond's office to see if I could learn more.

"Oh, almost forgot," Toronto said. "Nicky called."

"Good. I was wondering what had become of her. What's she up to?"

"I don't know, but I'd see if I could get her back over here if I was you."

"What do you mean?"

"She wanted to know if I could use my sources to find out more information on Jed Haynes. You know, stuff that isn't public."

"Great. As if I don't have enough troubles," I said.

I dialed Nicole's dorm room and left an angry message on her machine.

"What are you gonna do?" Toronto said. "I guess she figures she's just trying to help."

"If she calls or comes by, you tell her I said to stay away from Jed Haynes. The FBI's all over that kid. Who knows what he's up to? Might even be dangerous. And if they catch her working a case without a private investigator's registration, it'll be a long time before she'll do any official investigating in this state."

I left the office and headed out Fifth Street toward the interstate. Big clouds played hide-and-seek with the sun today. The air smelled of impending rain. The silver Taurus stayed back a discreet distance a few cars behind me.

Diane Lemminger's Corvette was still in the parking lot at the Holiday Inn. I edged into a space close to the front and strode in through the entrance. The lobby was quiet. Bebo Walter sat looking at a computer screen behind the desk.

"How about them Hoos?" I said. Bebo and I were both big fans of the university sports teams.

He looked up. "Hey, Pavlicek. How ya doin'?" He reached across the specially built low counter to shake hands.

"Man, don't you get any time off? Your boss must be a slave driver or something."

"Yeah," he chuckled. "Maybe I oughta put in for more overtime."

The fact that Bebo managed the place didn't exactly bode well for such a proposition.

"Can't find good help. It's the stinking economy. Unemployment's too low around here."

"Could be worse," I said. "Could be no business."

"I suppose. Your little pigeon is still in the coop, far as I know."

"Good to hear. Anything else interesting?"

He glanced around, lowering his voice. "Yeah. This fella came and stood outside the front door about a half hour ago. He dials his cell phone and the switchboard lights up. I pick it up, and he asks to be put through to your lady with the Corvette's room. I put him through, he stands there talking for a minute, and then he comes inside and heads upstairs."

I thought about it. "What did he look like?"

"Squat, muscle-bound guy."

"Blow-dry hairdo?"

"Yeah, that's him. You know who he is?"

"Unfortunately. Anybody else show up?"

"Nope. Just the usual. Checkouts, that sort of thing."

"Blow-Dry still upstairs?"

"Nope. Left about five minutes ago. You just missed him."

"Thanks very much, Bebo."

"You got it," he said. "Anytime."

The night before, he'd written Diane Lemminger's room number for me on one of those little yellow sticky notes. I took the elevator up to her floor. The room was about halfway down the corridor on the right.

"Who is it?" she called when I knocked.

I heard her shuffling around inside, obviously checking me out through the peephole.

She opened the door. "Well, well, well. I must've won some kind of popularity contest this morning."

She was drunk, or at least she appeared to be. Her long hair draped haphazardly over the shoulders of her blouse. The skirt she wore looked as though she'd slept in it. The liner around her eyes was bright but a little jagged, as if it had been just recently applied with an unsteady hand. I smelled no booze, but she was certainly on something.

"Well, don't just stand there," she said. "Come on in."

The sheets on the king-sized bed were in disarray. An expensive suitcase lay open on the floor with clothes and other articles strewn about. Around the corner in the bathroom I could see a sunken whirlpool bath with the taps open and steam rising from the tub.

"You feeling okay?" I asked.

"Marvelous," she said. "Just marvelous. So what? You want to ask me s'more questions?"

"Maybe you'd better sit down first."

"Okay," she said. "Okay." She sat down on the edge of the bed.

"I heard what happened to your show."

"Ya did, huh? Isn't that just dandy?"

"I'm sorry."

"Yeah. " Her eyes grew listless. "Me too." Then they brightened. "So whatcha want to ask me, big Mr. Private Investigator? Go ahead. Ask away."

"What were you doing out at Tor Drummond's place late last night?"

"Tor? Oh, yeah. Tor's lackey was just here. What a dick he is."

"You were out at Tor's house, in Ivy, last night."

"Right, right. I wanted to tell him . . . I wanted to tell him to go fuck himself." She giggled.

"What about the exposé you were planning to do about him?"

"What about it?"

"You said it had something to do with the Second Millennium Foundation."

"Sure. Second Millennium . . . Tor Drummond's nursery . . . He's a great man, you know. Donates a lot of money to all sorts of causes. Takes care of all those unfortunate kids . . . Second Millennnemm. . . ." Her voice trailed off in a slur.

"What about Second Millennium? What were you planning to talk about in your story?"

She lay back on the bed and closed her eyes. Then she rolled onto her side, folding her legs up in a fetal position. "I don't know. I don't . . . I'm really not . . . feeling so good . . ."

"Maybe you need to see a doctor." I moved beside her.

"I don't know. I—" She began to tremble.

"Miss Lemminger?"

She didn't answer.

"Miss Lemminger?"

Her breath was slow and labored. I felt her forehead. Ice cold.

I picked up the phone on the bedside table and dialed 911.

28

"Did you know she was a diabetic?"

Carol Upwood and I leaned against the fender of her white Mustang parked in front of the hotel. After calling for help, I'd dialed the front desk and told Bebo to expect an ambulance and to direct the paramedics up to Lemminger's room. Then I'd tried Bill Ferrier, but Carol had answered his phone instead, saying Bill had told her he was headed up to D.C.— which I hoped meant he might be working something behind the scenes for me. Two paramedics and a pair of firemen had come and gone, checking vitals, hooking Diane Lemminger up to an IV, and whisking her away. The hood of Carol's Mustang was still warm.

"Nope. I found the insulin with her name on it in the bathroom. They'll probably want to check and make sure it's okay," I said.

"You think she just screwed up her dose or what?"

"I don't know, but I've got some concerns."

I told her about Dworkin's visit.

"You sure it was Drummond's chief of staff?" she said.

"I'd put money on it, and I'm not a betting man."

"All right," she said. "I'm going to want to talk to the guy inside to verify the description. I'm sure you've also got some speculation as to motive."

I couldn't tell her about my observation of Diane

Lemminger out at Drummond's place the night before, of course, but I described my most recent conversation with the congressman and dropped hints about the TV exposé on which she had been working.

Carol heaved a sigh. "I know what Ferrier would say if he was here: 'We'd all better walk pretty careful on this one, pal.'"

She glanced over at the silver Taurus. The agents inside had stirred a little at the sight of me exiting the hotel with the paramedics and Lemminger on the stretcher. One punched a number and spoke rapidly on a cell phone.

"You guys may've been bounced off the Cartwright Drummond case, but this is still your jurisdiction. I'm talking about attempted murder here."

"I understand." She shook her head. "Can't wait to see what happens when Abercrombie hears about this. What am I going to tell him?"

"You'll think of something."

"I'm still not clear how you managed to tail Lemminger here to the hotel."

"Trust me. You don't want to know, Carol. The important thing is, she might be dead now if I hadn't," I said.

She grunted in disgust. "The last guy who asked me to trust him turned out to be a child molester."

"What can I say? You've never been married, have you?" I knew she'd had an on-again off-again boyfriend for a few years.

"Nope. Not sure I'll ever want to be, either."

"Just wondering. You ever think about what it'd be like to have a child?"

A breeze stirred the decorative landscaping at the base of the building and blew a lock of hair across her eyes. She brushed it back, and a smile appeared on her lips. Maybe it was a sad smile. "Of course," she said.

"Seems to me kids usually trust their parents."

"That's true."

"But when that trust is broken . . . I don't know."

"What's that got to do with Diane Lemminger?"

I shrugged. "Maybe nothing."

"You're up to something, Pavlicek. I can smell it. You'd better be careful it doesn't come back to bite you."

I gave her my best innocent stare.

She flexed her arms against the car. "Lemminger's a pretty well-known person. Once she hits the ER at the hospital and they realize who she is, this'll be all over the news."

"Hopefully they'll keep us out of it," I said.

"Hopefully." She snickered and looked at her watch. "You know, if you'd let Bill and me in on some of your secrets, maybe we could help."

"Thanks for the thought, Carol."

"Bill told me about the little chat you and he had earlier," she said.

"You think that's why he's gone to D.C.?"

"He wouldn't say."

"Hey," I said, "thank you. You didn't have to come."

"Thanks yourself. Remember what I said about Abercrombie."

She hopped in the Mustang and the engine roared to life. I stepped away as she nodded at me and zoomed out of the lot.

Plans change.

The guys in the Taurus turned out to be not as easy to ditch as their backups. This time I chose the rural approach, a short patch of abandoned logging road that runs along the back side of Carter's Mountain not too far from Jefferson's Monticello. I shifted the Ford into four-wheel low and hit the dirt with some speed. Even with our ground clearance, the run was treacherous at forty miles per hour.

"You know," Toronto said, after one particularly big jolt that ricocheted his head off the ceiling, "I'm kind of fond of my teeth in their present location." You had to give the FBI agents credit—they hung in there for half a mile or so. It might have been a blown tire, a stump, or a broken axle that grounded them. I didn't stick around to call AAA.

A steady drizzle began as we drove out 250 toward Ivy. Fog descended and all but obliterated the pastures and trees and homes we passed. Despite the pea soup, about half a mile from Tor Drummond's place, I clicked the headlights to high beam and left them there.

The gate was closed and locked, as it had been the night before. But now, instead of sneaking in the back, we drove right up to the stone pillars. Toronto jumped out with an oversized pair of bolt cutters, quickly snapped the chain, pulled the wrought-iron gate open, and hopped back in the cab.

"That oughta get somebody's attention," he said.

He was right. I had just punched the stick shift into second gear when the incandescent beams of the Suburban, coupled with amber fogs, shot into our eyes, headed down the driveway from above to block our path.

"I hate guys who hide behind big bumpers," Toronto said.

"Not me with the Ford, I hope."

"Nah. You're on the cusp. I give you a pass."

The larger vehicle rushed down at us. For a second, I thought a game of chicken might be appropriate, but then I thought better of it and let us coast uphill until we stopped. The Suburban suddenly braked too.

An even more blinding beam from a spotlight sticking out of the Suburban's passenger window broke across Toronto's face. He didn't flinch.

"Please step out of the vehicle!"

The voice spoke through a bullhorn.

Toronto shrugged. I shrugged. We opened our respective doors and stepped out into the rain.

I slipped on my coffee-colored outback hat, which, next to my long yellow slicker, might have made me look like the Marlboro Man, if my jaw had been more square. Jake had donned only a Virginia Tech windbreaker over his sweatshirt and jeans for the occasion. His .45 in its shoulder holster was hard to miss.

Turnip and Robot climbed down out of the Suburban onto the crushed stone too. They both wore olive trench coats, no headgear. The Robot balanced a pump-action shotgun in his hands, pointed at the ground, as if it were a baton. It wasn't quite the shootout at the OK Corral, but the four of us did meet face-to-face in the blinding light somewhere between the bumpers. Drizzle, made visible in the brightness, swirled all around us like cold dust.

"Forcible entry," Turnip said. "That's a mistake."

Toronto shrugged. I shrugged.

"The congressman's not at home."

"Really? Well, I guess you two fine fellows will have to do, then," I said.

"That a fact? Who's your buddy?"

"His name's Jake Toronto. Don't worry. He's not quite as mean as he looks." I tried to say this with a smile.

Turnip wasn't buying. His staring companion stifled a twitch.

I didn't look at Toronto, but I could almost imagine his mouth twisting into a sardonic half-grin.

"Had a chat with a woman a little earlier today named Diane Lemminger. You two know who she is, don't you?"

Both tried the blank-stare routine. Turnip's companion had a hard time pulling it off, however. He rolled his tongue around inside his mouth as if he was about to bite it off, and it made his cheek bulge.

I went on. "I understand she talked with you two gentlemen as well, just last night, which surprised me, knowing how loyal you are to your boss and all."

"She tell you that?" Turnip asked.

"Maybe not in so many words."

"Maybe you two was the ones broke in out here last night."

I smiled. "Or we could just be good at following people."

He folded his arms across his chest and glared down at us. The incline of the driveway put the two security guards about half a foot above Toronto and me.

"Say we did talk with Lemminger," he said. "So what?"

"She's run into a problem. She was taken to the hospital in a diabetic coma."

The guards stood impassively in the rain. The rain had started to trickle in streams down their faces.

"We don't know nothing about no diabetic coma."

"No? Then what was Mel Dworkin doing visiting her room just before she came down with the blackout routine?"

They didn't answer.

"Oh, and the cops might be interested in what you

three were talking about last night, right here, at about this same spot, in between your headlights and hers."

Robot started backing away toward their truck.

"Hey, where you going?" his companion said.

The bigger man suddenly looked scared. "I didn't sign on for this kind of crap," he said under his breath.

Clearly, Turnip faced a situation. His wingman was deserting him, right in the face of the enemy.

"You boys hold on for just a second," he said. Then he turned and caught up with his partner. They kept their backs to us and their voices low, but Turnip gestured violently with his hands and words hissed out like a pent-up release of steam.

"We're wasting our time," Toronto said softly without looking at me.

After a minute or so of talking, they finally got around to ambling back in our direction. Robot lost the shotgun, throwing it into the backseat of the Suburban. Their faces were so wet by now that they almost looked like a pair of mangy pups. Not that we must've looked much better.

"Lemminger wanted us to go on TV, okay?" Turnip said.

"She tell you her show had been canceled?"

"Yeah, but I knew her from back when she worked for the congressman. She said if she got some taped interviews, she'd have a better chance at pitching it to one of the networks. We told her we'd have to think about it."

"What did she want you to talk about?" I said.

"What d'ya think, pea brain?" He jerked his thumb toward the main house, which was dark inside, as it had been the night before. "About all of Drummond's extracurricular activities."

"Such as?"

"She wanted us to start with the high-priced whores. Said something about needing more eyewitness accounts."

I nodded. Everybody's breath had turned to steam. "How long you been working for Drummond?"

"Seventeen years. Jimmy here just started this year."

"Did Lemminger give you any idea what else her story was about?"

He shook his head. "Not really. Isn't that enough?"

"How much money she offer you?"

"Ten grand apiece."

Robot, who'd now proved to the world he could talk, said, "I'm glad we didn't take it."

"Shut up, Jimmy," his superior said.

"You been working for this guy seventeen years. You must've seen a lot of things," I said.

Turnip stared at me like I'd just walked in from some other dimension. "I've seen a lot of things."

"The congressman's daughter, the one who's missing. He got you guys mixed up in it?"

He shook his head. "We've got nothing to do with that."

"Oh. Well, I guess I'll just take your word for it, then."

We stared at one another.

"What about Drummond himself? He doesn't need you guys to pull off something like that."

"I don't think so," he said.

"Why not?"

"Because he was pretty pissed when he found out we didn't follow her when she left here that night."

"Could've been an act."

He shrugged.

"Why was the congressman having you follow his daughters?"

"I just do what I'm told, pal. I've never been paid to ask a lot of questions, like you are."

"Really? I guess I'll take that as a compliment."

A look passed through his eyes then. It was a look of cold steel hatred. But there was also another dimension to it—call it professional assessment. As his eyes cut back and forth between me and Toronto, they seemed to accept the reality that the odds of him surviving a violent encounter were not good at the moment.

"You say someone's trying to put the brakes on Lemminger?" Robot said. "Drummond's still a doctor, ain't he? He might've done something like that."

I sensed Robot's term of employment might soon be coming to an end.

"Tell me more about this break-in you had out here," I said. Figured I'd play along with my earlier story for consistency.

Turnip crossed his arms. One pro to another. "Last night someone went in through the kitchen. Disabled the alarm and everything. Nice piece of work, actually. Cops said so too. Wouldn't mind catching the guy who did it just to have a beer with him." A sickly smile crept across his face as he stared at Toronto.

"You check with the congressman to see if anything was missing?"

"Yup. Nothing, he says. Looks like whoever did it was just snooping around."

I shrugged. "Maybe it was kids or something."

He chewed on his lip. "Sure, that could've been it. Kids who'd taken a crash course in disabling twenty-thousand-dollar alarms."

The rain came down harder. The drizzle was turning to wind-driven droplets, an accumulation of which dripped steadily from the brim of my hat.

"So what we appear to have had here, gentlemen, is a professional exchange of information. Would you be in agreement with that?"

"I suppose."

"Got anything more, Jake?"

Toronto said nothing. I guessed his eyes had never left Turnip, even when Robot had toted the shotgun.

"I suppose that's about all we had to talk to you fellas about, then, for the moment. You might want to let the congressman know we dropped by."

"Oh, I'll be sure to pass on your regards."

"Sorry about your gate," I said.

"Me too," Turnip said.

"Occupational hazard."

"We all got to have an occupation," he said.

29

Ash-colored clouds clung to the Blue Ridge like ghostly tumors. Rain pelted the windshield as Toronto and I made our way back into the city. It was going on three days since Cartwright Drummond's disappearance. If she were being held by someone in the Charlottesville area, as the postmark on the envelope containing the note and photo seemed to indicate, she could be somewhere within only a couple of miles' radius of our current location. A bulletin on the radio told about the FBI taking over the case and said agents had been searching some dorm rooms at the university. They must have traced the delivery of the envelope and narrowed down the possibilities.

I picked up Toronto's cell phone and punched in the number for Nicole's room again. She answered on the second ring.

"Dad," she said, "I've been trying to get ahold of you. I left a message over two hours ago on your office machine."

"Don't use that line anymore, Nicky."

"Why not?"

"Because it's probably tapped."

"Oh."

I gave her the new cell phone number.

"You're not going to believe who I've been talking to."

"Nicky—"

"I have a friend who has another friend who's on the swim team with Jed Haynes."

"Nicky, we've got a problem."

"What's that?"

"I need you to back off on this, honey. I really appreciate your help so far, but the FBI is all over the place, and there may even have been an attempted murder. More people could get hurt."

"But, Dad—"

"No buts. You're not a registered private investigator. You're smart as a whip, but you don't have the proper training. The FBI catches you talking to Jed Haynes or anybody else about this, you'll be in hot water, to say the least. Not to mention that you're not trained in self-defense or firearms or . . ."

The lecture was falling on silence, so I shut up.

"Are you through?" she asked softly.

"For the moment."

"I know someone, the FBI or whatever, has been watching Jed Haynes. We saw them. They were posing as students, but you could tell they really weren't. They were just hanging around as if they had no place to go or nothing to do.

"Cassidy was right. Haynes is a jerk, but he has something to give you and he says he wants only you to have it."

"Nicky—"

"I've got it all arranged," she said. "The FBI, no one's going to be able to track him or see that we're talking to him. We're supposed to meet him in an hour."

"Nicky, this is not—"

"Please, Dad. I promise I won't talk to anybody else after this."

I glanced across at Toronto, who was shaking his head and shrugging. "Kids," he said.

"Where?" I asked.

"Scott Stadium." The largest venue in the area, the football stadium seated more than 60,000 fans on a game day.

"When?"

"As soon as it gets dark," she said.

Dion and the Belmonts were doing "The Wanderer" on the truck radio as my headlights shone off the rain-soaked pavement of Alderman Road. Very few people, students or otherwise, were on the streets. The stadium loomed like an ancient acropolis in the darkness.

"The kid better have something important to get us all out here like this," I said.

"I think he does, Dad."

We'd picked Nicole up outside Alderman Library. Before that, I'd dropped Toronto off a few blocks from my duplex and he'd walked in, without being detected by whoever might be keeping tabs on the place, to tend to Armistead. I keep pieces of fresh quail in a separate freezer, used only for that purpose, in my storage room. I picked him up a half hour later at a spot over on Rose Hill Drive.

"Kid better know what he's doing, too, as far as losing the people who are tailing him."

"He said he's sure he can lose them," Nicole said. "And if anybody's trying to watch us, we'll be able to see them."

"I'll make sure of that," Toronto said.

"I'm still not too keen on you being here, Nicky," I said. "Jake and I could've done this by ourselves."

"I told you. He said he wants to talk to you, but he's not sure he trusts you and he does trust me."

"So what's the source of this sudden trust in you?"

"I listened to him, Dad. I didn't beat him over the head by machine-gunning him with a bunch of questions. Like I said, he may be a jerk, but I think he's basically harmless."

"We'll see about that."

We drove across to Stadium Road and pulled into the construction entrance. Renovation was still going on on a portion of the upper deck, and several large trucks and a crane were parked against a tall wall of plywood and wire. I cut the lights and backed the pickup between a Dumpster and a panel truck, hoping it wouldn't be noticed by any university policeman who might happen to wander by.

I pulled on my slicker, still wet from standing in Tor Drummond's driveway talking to the turnip. Nicole had on a red raincoat with dark hiking boots.

"You guys ready?"

They both nodded. We stepped out into the rain.

It was cooler now and the air was filled with the rich smell of loam and stagnant water and gasoline. I carried both my sidearm and a flashlight on my belt, but I didn't want to use the light unless it became absolutely necessary. Lights from the street coupled with a few bright security lights farther up the parking lot cast a dim glow over the area, and once our eyes adjusted to the semidarkness, we could navigate with caution.

Just as Cassidy said Jed had told her, there was a narrow break in the construction fence about seventy yards south of the entrance, wide enough to slip through. We stepped inside and about twenty yards later came to a six-foot chain-link fence—easy enough to scale. I turned as I did and looked behind me at the dim outlines of sloppy footprints we had left in the mud, hoping the rain would continue long enough to obscure them or wash them away.

We found the closest entrance and began to walk up the gradual incline of switchback ramps on the exterior walls that led to the top of the stadium. We were under cover now and watched through the glow of the streetlights far below as the rain came down harder. At the top, the wind swirled mist along the girders. The university grounds were nothing but a haze of lights, shrouded in fog and rain.

We crossed another wide ramp to the nearest portal, which brought us out into the rain again, only inside the stadium now, to the railing of the aisle at the bottom of the upper deck. The wind subsided for a few moments. Instantly, Toronto crouched low and positioned himself against the inside rail so that he became virtually invisible. Nicole and I turned to the right, as she said Jed' had told her to do.

Barely enough light filtered into the stadium to make out the seats and section numbers. Two sections over, however, it was possible to distinguish a lone figure seated about halfway up.

"Guess that's our man," I said.

I scanned the other rows of seats as far as it was possible to see around the stadium. No sign of FBI or anyone else. I pulled Nicole behind me and we approached with caution.

When we got within thirty feet or so, I could tell it was Haynes. He looked like a car bomb survivor. His hair and clothes were soaking wet, dirty and disheveled. Across the center of his forehead ran a big smudge of grease. We came to within about ten feet of him, I held out my hand, and we stopped.

"Funny place to meet," I said.

"Tell me about it. I been friggin' freezing up here waiting for you guys." He blew on his hands.

"How'd you lose your FBI people?"

He shrugged. "I know the grounds. They don't. Simple as that."

Maybe it was just me, but this Jed seemed like a much more contrite individual than the one I'd first encountered. Of course, being detained and questioned for hours and having your every move shadowed by the feds does tend to have that kind of effect on a person, not to mention being soaked to the bone.

I waited. Jed looked at his fingernails. "I don't care what anybody tells you. I didn't kidnap Cartwright," he said.

"That seems to be a popular line these days. Her father's saying pretty much the same thing."

"I don't care what he says—I didn't do it."

"If you say so."

"Hey, Nicky, you said your old man would believe me if I just told the truth."

"That's right," she said.

He shivered and rubbed his arms and legs. "I'm sick and tired of this crap, of these guys following me around and everything."

"Sometimes part of the object of surveillance is to let the suspect know he's being observed. It increases the pressure. Causes him to make a mistake," I said.

"Yeah, well, I ain't about to make any mistakes. You can tell those assholes that."

"I'll be sure to pass on your compliments next time I see them."

He tugged at his ear, which sported a small gold ring at the moment, and ran his fingers through his wet hair. "You want to know something? I really thought when they brought me in and stuff, that it was like some kind of joke or something."

"I guess they grilled you over the car."

"Geez . . . you don't even know, man. One dude, I thought he was going to send me to death row or something. Wouldn't even let me go to the bathroom or nothing. I thought I was going to piss in my pants."

"I guess these last few days have kind of put a crimp in your plans."

He snickered.

"How's the swim season going for you?" I said.

"It was going great till all this happened. Now Coach says I won't be allowed to swim with the team till it gets cleared up."

"Too bad."

"You think Wright's okay?" he asked.

"I don't know. She might not even be alive anymore."

He stared blankly into the wind and rain.

"You all right, Jed?"

"Yeah. Jesus." He shook his head as if to clear it.

"What have you got for us?"

He looked at Nicole.

"It'll be okay," she said.

He focused on me again. "There's something I want to ask you," he said. "I hear you used to be a homicide detective."

"That's right. A long time ago."

"How do you know when someone's losing it? I mean, you know, about to go off the deep end and do something crazy?"

"What do you mean?"

"I don't know . . . like what kinds of things do they do and stuff?"

"There's no easy answer to that, Jed. Some people

are better at masking their emotions than others.
Some are sociopaths who seem capable of totally shut-
ting off any feeling. Why? You think you know someone like that?"

"I don't know, man. I don't know."

"Does this someone have anything to do with
Wright's disappearance?"

"Maybe. Listen, one thing I didn't tell you before . . .
Wright, she can get a little crazy sometimes. You
know, she comes up with all sorts of wild ideas."

"What are you talking about, Jed?"

"I've got something to give you."

He wiped his hand on his pants and fished in the
pocket of his jeans. He pulled out a small object and
rolled it in his fingers, examining it. Then he held it
out to me. "Here," he said.

I stepped up to him and took it from his hand. It
was a round post earring, looked like white gold or
silver, with a distinctive blue dot, maybe turquoise, in
the center.

"Where'd this come from?" I asked.

"I think . . . I think it might be Wright's," he said.

"Do you know if she was wearing it the night she
disappeared?"

"I don't know, man. I told you, I never saw her."

But I knew at least three people who would know
the answer to that question. And maybe the cops
could ID it from the Polaroid. "Where did you get
the earring?"

"On top of the clock radio in my room. This morning. But it wasn't there when I went to bed, I swear."

"Have the police or the FBI gone over your room?"

"Yeah, man. Twice."

I thought about it.

"Have you gotten your car back, Jed?"

"No way." He shook his head. "Bastards said they had to run more tests or something."

"Normally who else but you has access to your car?"

He shrugged. "A few buddies. I let people borrow it. The guys at the house."

"You said you didn't know Cartwright was coming to see you the night she disappeared."

"That's right."

"The next morning your car was right where you had left it the night before?"

"Yes."

"No sign of a break-in?"

"No."

"You notice anything different about the vehicle— mirrors changed, gum wrappers on the seat—that sort of thing?"

"I don't know. I didn't even pay attention. That's what I told those guys from the FBI, too. The next time I drove it was on my way to class and practice that afternoon when you came to talk with me, and I was in a hurry. Besides, even if I had noticed something I wouldn't have thought anything about it. Like I said, I let lots of different people drive my car."

"Wouldn't they have had to get the keys from you, though?"

"No, not necessarily. I been through this with everybody already—all of us have to keep an extra set of keys hanging on a rack in the kitchen at the house. Parking is like hell around there. Sometimes we gotta switch the cars all around, or back somebody else's out of the way. It just doesn't make any sense, that blood or whatever they said they found in the Cherokee."

"And it only costs fifty cents to make a copy of a key."

The wind gusted and swirled, blowing heavier sheets of rain against the top of the stadium.

"Why are you giving this to *me,* Jed?"

He looked at Nicole, then back at me. "Because she said I could trust you." He rubbed his nose. "And because you stood up to me. Not many people do that."

"Your parents know you're in trouble?"

"Yeah, right," he snickered. His eyes picked out a spot among the rows of seats. "My old man's a computer company executive. Sometimes I almost forget what the guy looks like. He goes overseas a lot."

"You're from California, right?"

"San Francisco."

"Your mother work, too?"

"Mom's an accountant—she's great when she's around, which is more than Dad, but not all that much."

"They going to come out here?"

"I told them not to."

"Well, they must be proud of you—your swimming awards and all."

"They're proud. Mom used to come see me swim quite a bit, but not since I came to school out here. Dad, he checks in on an occasional big award ceremony or something. I don't think he's been to a meet since I was a sophomore in high school."

"I'm sorry."

He said nothing.

"Who do *you* think put the earring on your clock radio?"

He seemed to be on the verge of saying something, but he stopped. He stood up, rubbing his arms. "I

really don't know. Look, man, I'm freezing to death."
His feet stuttered down the concrete steps past us. "I
gotta go."

I pointed at his back to signal Toronto. Haynes
dropped into the nearest portal, and was gone.

30

Marcia D'Angelo's kitchen was quiet, save for the hum of the dishwasher. Mr. Earl and I stood in the faint glow of a dimmed row of track lights overhead. Nicole had been safely deposited back at her dorm. Marcia and Karen and Cassidy had apparently gone to bed.

"Maybe your boy is just trying to snooker us with the earring," Toronto said into my ear, which was pressed into the cell phone. He'd called to say he was camped out just down the street from Haynes's house, off Fourteenth Street. He was watching the FBI watch the place. The feds in the commandeered apartment across the street had apparently perked up considerably at their subject's sudden reappearance.

"Guess it wouldn't do much good to check this thing for fingerprints," I said.

"Nope. If anybody's partial, besides yours and Haynes's, is on the thing, best you'd get would be a smudged mess."

I grunted my agreement. "All right. Well, let me know if anything important happens."

I crept up the stairs to Marcia's bedroom and knocked, half hoping to find her under the covers in a state of partial undress—a wicked thought under the circumstances, I knew.

"Yes?" Her voice sounded small and indistinct.

"It's me. Frank."

"Come in," she said.

I opened the door and entered her room. The light was on in the corner and a fully clothed Marcia, a peaceful smile on her face, sat in her rocking chair, clutching a worn Bible, the kind that might have been acquired in some long-ago confirmation class—white leather cover with gold trim on its pages. Cassidy Drummond, in jeans and one of Marcia's old sweatshirts, was sitting cross-legged on the floor in front of her. Both women's eyes were red with tears. I felt like the bad wheel on a lopsided tricycle.

"We've just been having a little discussion," Marcia said.

"Don't mean to interrupt, but I've got something important."

"Of course." Even in her plush bathrobe and slippers, Marcia radiated a sense of calm. She smiled at me tenderly.

"You two all right? I mean, everything okay around here?"

"Doing better," Marcia said.

Cassidy nodded. The younger woman looked at me searchingly for a moment, then back at the floor.

"How are *you* doing?" Marcia said.

"Tired and wet, but making progress."

"How much longer do you think this can go on?"

"I wish I knew." I went over, leaned down, and kissed her softly on the forehead.

She squeezed my hand.

I turned to Cassidy. "You think you're up for a few more questions?"

She nodded, brushing a tear from her cheek.

I squatted down to her level, pulled the earring from my pocket, and held it out for her. She stared at it for a moment, then took it from my outstretched fingers.

"You recognize it?" I asked.

Her lips began to tremble. "Yes," she said. She put her hand to her mouth and her eyes brimmed with more tears. "It's Wright's." Her voice was barely above a whisper.

Marcia rose from her chair, bent down on one knee, and put her arm around Cassidy's shoulder.

"Was she wearing it the night she disappeared?"

Cassidy nodded. She broke down. Marcia wrapped her arms around the young woman and she sobbed into her shoulder.

"What's going on here?" We all looked up to see Karen Drummond standing in the doorway. "I heard a noise."

"Frank's found something," Marcia said.

Dr. Drummond stepped into the room and knelt down next to her daughter as well. "What is it?"

No one said anything. Cassidy tried to force back another sob.

I pointed to the earring she was holding in her fingers. "I needed to get a positive identification on the jewelry," I said.

Karen Drummond stared at it as if it were a mysterious object from another universe. "Oh, my gosh," she said.

"Your daughter was wearing this earring the night she was abducted?" I said.

"Yes, I'm pretty sure she was."

But then, instead of grief, her expression changed to one of anger. "Haven't you people put us through enough already? What's happening? Why is this taking so long? Why can't you find the monster who took my daughter?"

"I'm working on it, ma'am. So is the FBI."

"We've done everything you've asked. We've been camped out here in secret for more than three days now. And nothing. Now you come in with this."

"I know."

Cassidy pulled away from Marcia's shoulder. "It's okay, Mom." She took her mother's hand in her own. "I know it'll be okay."

She and her mother embraced.

After a few moments Karen Drummond turned to me. "I'm sorry," she said. "I'm exhausted and I can't sleep and this just never seems to end."

"Sure," I said.

"Find her, Frank. Please. I don't care who has her, whether it's Tor or this boyfriend or whatever. I don't care if we have to go to the FBI," she said. "Find her soon."

Back in the truck, parked in an empty slot among hundreds of other vehicles in a university parking lot, I looked out upon a streetlight and a steady drizzle. I picked up the cell phone and dialed Ferrier's number at home.

"You are becoming one unpopular person downtown, my friend," he said after I identified myself.

"Yeah, but I think we're getting close." I explained about the meeting with Jed Haynes and the earring and the fact that both the FBI and Toronto were keeping an eye on the kid.

"This thing's giving me heartburn," he said.

"Carol talk with you about Diane Lemminger?"

"Right. Now we have an attempted murder investigation on our hands. Abercrombie's about to shoot into orbit."

"Any luck with what we talked about earlier?"

"Yeah. I ran down the info on those accounts from the checks you showed me and on this foundation, Second Millennium. The foundation was formed back in 1984. The accounts have all been opened since the foundation started, the first in '84, the others at later dates. All the accounts, by the way, are controlled by Tor Drummond."

"Hang on a second." I suddenly remembered something Diane Lemminger had said in her delirium about Second Millennium—"Tor Drummond's nursery." "Can you give me the exact dates the foundation filed for incorporation and when the first account was opened?"

"Yeah, sure." He fumbled with some papers for a moment. Then he read the dates off.

"Bill, I need you to meet me down in Richmond."

"When? Tonight?"

"Yes, as soon as you can get there. I'm driving down there myself now."

"Where?"

I gave him the address and directions to Roberta Joseph's apartment.

"What's going on, Frank? You know I can't—"

"Second Millennium was formed and the first account opened less than two weeks after George and Norma Paitley's accident. I think I know the story Diane Lemminger was working on," I said.

31

Only one light appeared to be on inside the Josephs'
apartment. Through the closed blinds, I could make
out its dim illumination coming from the area of the
kitchen. No one had responded when I'd rung the bell
the first time. I tried it again.

Still no answer.

It was almost eleven o'clock at night. No sign of
Ferrier yet. Were the Josephs still at work? Maybe
they were asleep already, but somehow I didn't think
so. The other units all seemed quiet. A heat pump
whirred away outside one, in unison with the distant
swish of traffic. The rain had ended, and a clearing
breeze followed. The air smelled of forsythia, the brick
sidewalk was still slick, and water dripped from an
overhang and from shrubs and small trees.

I stepped off the stoop and made my way around
back. Beyond the corner of the building, it was much
darker. The light hadn't been from the kitchen after
all, but the hallway. There was a deck and a sliding
glass door with vertical blinds.

What to do, go in or wait it out? Two B&E's in one
week—kind of pushing the envelope here, partner, I
thought. But if I waited until Bill got here, we'd have
to go obtain a warrant. I looked around at the neighbors. All quiet. *Find her soon.*

The sliding door was locked, but there was no bar

across the flashing. I pulled out my pocket tool, flipped open a blade, and went to work on the mechanism. After a minute or so, I managed to engage the lever and turn it to open the lock. I pulled on the handle and slid the door open a few inches, pausing again to listen before entering. So far, so good.

Inside, silence. A dim glow from the light down the hall. Cardboard boxes were strewn about the floor, some old jars and dented pans, no kitchen table or chairs. Pictures had been taken from the walls. It looked like someone either already had or was in the process of vacating the apartment. I slid the door shut behind me.

The phone was still in place on the kitchen wall, however. I went over and picked up the receiver. Still a dial tone. Curious.

I took out my penlight and stepped past the kitchen counter. The beam swept over open cupboards and drawers, all empty. The dishwasher was open, but there were two drinking glasses and a food-encrusted cereal bowl left on the racks.

I moved down the hall under the light to the living room with the cathedral ceiling. Empty, discolored carpeting. All the photographs of Averil and all the furniture were gone. Reversing course, I headed back down the hall toward what had been Roberta Joseph's office, at the end of the corridor. The door stood slightly ajar. I withdrew my gun.

I took a couple of steps forward until I could see into the room, then pushed on the door. It swung about halfway open and then came to rest against something—another box, it appeared. Another step, cautious. I pointed the gun and scanned the room with my light. Nothing. The pictures and plants and all personal effects were missing. Nothing behind the door. But the computer was still set up on the desk and the office chair remained. Even more curious.

I sat down in the chair and looked for the switch to turn on the computer. Behind the unit, a power strip lay on the desk along the wall. As I reached around to flip the switch, my hand brushed up against something hard that had obviously fallen behind the monitor among the tangled cords. It felt like a small book. I pulled it out.

A photo album. Roberta Joseph, in her haste to leave, must've dropped it. I opened it and began flipping through the pages. Each one contained a black-and-white photo. Several were of Averil, others of people I didn't recognize; a few were cityscapes or images of a beach.

One of the last pictures caught my eye. I stared at it, trying to make sense of what I saw. It was similar to some of the others, a candid of two people, taken in this very room, in fact. In the picture Averil sat smiling at the keyboard. But there was another person seated next to her—they seemed to be posing for the camera as if they were shaking hands. My eyes took in the face of Penn Hersch before I realized the significance of what I was seeing. The same dimpled cheeks and gel-slicked hair. Penn Hersch, who was Jed Haynes's roommate.The resemblance between Hersch and Averal Joseph was also hard to miss.

I thought I heard a thump out by the stairs. I slipped the photo out of its album sleeve, stood up, and tucked it into the back pocket of my pants, and raised my gun. Of even more concern, however, I suddenly heard voices down the hall, someone fumbling with keys to open the front door.

I sprinted down the hall and managed to duck around the corner into the kitchen just as the front door swung open.

"I told you it was the other key," the louder of the two voices said.

"Yeah, well, the boss said it was the other one." I recognized the first voice as the turnip's. The other was his partner in shadowy security.

My only problem: the sliding glass door was about ten feet across the room and a large open area connected the space in between with the dining area, which opened directly to the area around the front door. I was trapped.

But I had a loaded .357 in one hand. What the heck.

I stepped around the corner again into the light, in full view of my new company.

"Welcome to the party," I said, with the gun trained directly at them.

Their eyes went wide with fright and surprise. "Holy shit," the turnip said under his breath. "Just what we need." He raised his hands in the air and his robotic sidekick did the same.

"You want to tell me what you two gentleman are doing here?" I said.

He shook his head. "Man, you don't know what you're getting yourself into, big fella."

His partner's gaze slipped for just an instant to a spot behind me. As I think of it now, I must have turned a little and taken a step back into the shadow of the kitchen. Too late, I saw an arm flashing at me from the concealment of the doorway I had failed to notice on the opposite wall. Too late, I realized the hand held a syringe like a dagger, felt the pinch of pain in my neck where it entered.

I managed to stop its advance, at least temporarily,

by gripping the strong fingers with my free hand, swinging the barrel of my gun wildly at the assailant with the other. But I felt the arm release and seem to disappear, and my whole body went numb. My head began to swirl in semidarkness. Then three pairs of hands were upon me, and I was sinking down, farther and farther into a deeper darkness on the floor. The hands grabbed me by the jacket and pulled at me violently. They seemed to be in a great hurry. I felt myself sliding, bumped my head against something hard, and the next thing I knew I was alone outside somewhere on a rain-soaked lawn.

I heard what sounded like a shout. Unable to move, unable to speak, I stared as if through a mist at fast-moving clouds against a black canopy sprinkled with stars, my own killing sky. Very soon even the stars disappeared, and I was falling into total darkness, heartbeat and shallow breathing, and suddenly I remembered something the Secret Amphibian had written about a light too fast for sound.

32

Voices again. Marcia D'Angelo's merged without meaning into Bill Ferrier's and Nicole's and someone else's. A dream? They didn't seem to know I could hear them. My head throbbed with a pulsing rhythm. My ears ached and my mouth and lips felt like they were on fire.

"Hey, he's waking up," Nicole said.

I opened my eyes to the speckled white ceiling of a hospital room. A male doctor in a long white coat stood at the foot of my bed. Next to him, in sport coat and tie, Ferrier grinned, shaking his head. Marcia, with Nicole standing behind her, sat in a chair beside the bed. She picked up my hand and held it. I realized there were two tubes sticking out of my arm.

"How are you feeling?" the doctor asked.

"Like someone took a crowbar to my skull." I managed to form the words, but my voice came out as a croak.

"That'll wear off soon. You'll be feeling better in a few hours. The drug's being purged from your system. Lucky for you, your friend came along and found you. And also lucky for you, whoever did this to you didn't get quite enough Veronol into your bloodstream to finish the job. It's a powerful enough barbiturate to have either killed you or left you in a permanent coma."

I nodded, absorbing the news.

"Where am I?"

"You're at MCV Hospital, in a room reserved for VIP patients." He glanced at Ferrier. No doubt the detective had pulled some strings. "My name is Dr. Grinell. I'm a toxicologist and the medical director of the poison control center."

"How long have I been here?"

"Since last night." The filtered sunlight streaming through the smoky glass seemed to indicate it was early afternoon.

"Can I get some water or something?"

"Of course."

We went through a little rigmarole of Marcia pouring me a cup of water and the doctor helping me to adjust the bed so I was sitting a little more upright.

"Okay to talk with him alone now, Doc?" Ferrier said.

"I don't see why not." The physician looked at me. "You're in pretty good physical condition for your age, Mr. Pavlicek. That's been of great benefit to you in this instance. Whatever you're doing, keep it up. Just don't go around getting stabbed with any more needles."

I nodded. The doctor left the room, closing the door behind him.

"Well," Ferrier said, "here we all are."

"And glad of it," Marcia said, still holding my hand.

"What do you think he meant by 'for my age'?" I asked.

She shook her head and rolled her eyes.

Ferrier cleared his throat. "Uh, you wanna explain to me, Frank, how come I found you almost dead on the lawn outside that apartment?"

"Did you get them?" I asked.

"Get who?"

"The guys who gave me the shot and dragged me out there."

"No. I saw two characters run away when I shouted from the parking lot, but after I took one look at you I figured I better call the ambulance and stick around until it got there."

"You made the right decision," Marcia said.

Ferrier crossed his arms. "Who were the two men?"

I looked over my shoulder, realizing I was wearing nothing but a hospital gown. "Where are my clothes?" I said.

"I think they're in the closet," he said.

"Can you get them for me?"

He stared at me for a moment.

"I'll get them," Nicole said. She opened the closet door and began gathering up my jacket and shirt.

"Just the pants," I said.

"Just the pants," Ferrier said.

"Right."

He sighed.

Nicole handed them over.

"Thank you," I said. I searched along the seam until I found the back pockets. The photo was still in the left one. I nodded. "Good."

"You gonna answer my question?" Ferrier said.

"Yeah. Your people got that apartment sealed?"

"We do now."

"I've got a hunch you may find some interesting information on that computer, maybe even some fingerprints." I caught Marcia's eye. "Everything okay up at your house?" I asked.

It might've seemed like an odd question under the circumstances, but she got my drift. She nodded.

I turned back to Ferrier. "Anybody know where Toronto is?"

Nicole said, "I think he's, um, still doing what you asked him to do."

"Okay."

"Are we going somewhere with all these random thoughts?" Ferrier snorted.

"Yes," I said. "First off, I think I know who has Cartwright Drummond, or at least who may be with her."

"Really? Who might that be?"

I pulled out the photo and showed it to him.

"I don't recognize the girl, but the guy . . ."

"Is Penn Hersch," I said.

"Hersch. Isn't he one of Haynes's roommates or something?"

"That's right."

"Where'd you get the picture and who's the girl?"

"Okay," I said. "Here's the deal. I'm pretty certain the Second Millennium Foundation has another purpose besides helping out kids in need."

"Such as?"

"Such as specialized money laundering."

He looked perplexed. "What kind of money laundering?"

"Those letters on those two checks?"

"Yeah, what about them?"

"I think they represent two different people. Each with a special relationship to Tor Drummond."

"What kind of relationship?"

"He's their father."

No one said anything. Marcia was shaking her head in disgust.

Ferrier looked interested. "You're saying Tor

Drummond has been supporting a couple of illegiti-
mate children and using Second Millennium as a front,
mixing up their support with support for a whole lot
of other kids?"

"Exactly. I think that's the story Diane Lemminger
was working on. She come out of the coma yet?"

Ferrier shook his head.

My back hurt. "Can you guys crank this bed up a
little higher?"

Marcia and Nicole jumped up and managed to find
the right button to push to accomplish the task.

"I don't get it," Ferrier said. "This may be tabloid
kind of stuff, but you've been hinting all along that
the congressman might be involved in his daughter's
disappearance or something worse. Then you claim his
man may have tried to off the TV show gal. But why?
Hiding support for a bunch of kids Drummond's sired
out of wedlock may make him a schmuck, but it
doesn't make him a criminal."

"That's where it gets complicated. My guess is Cartwright Drummond knew something about Second Millennium. Diane Lemminger said she talked to her
about it while Cartwright was still in Japan."

"So?"

"I don't know. She might've said something to her
father. And I've got a strong suspicion there may be
more to Second Millennium than just hiding illegiti-
mate children."

"You still haven't told me who this girl in the
photo is."

"Her name's Averil Joseph. Her mother is Roberta
Joseph, the nurse who runs the foundation for Drummond. I think she's the *A* person supported by the
checks."

"So Drummond has the mother of one of his other

kids running the money show. Good way to keep things quiet, I guess," he said.

"Long as the checks keep flowing," I said. "And guess who might be the *P* person?"

He gave a surprised grunt. "Penn Hersch?"

I nodded. "And guess when the 'P' checks started flowing?"

He thought a moment. "They were the first ones, weren't they? Right after the foundation was formed."

"That's right. Which was only two weeks after George and Norma Paitley were killed by a hit-and-run. Which was the newspaper article we found in Cartwright Drummond's suitcase."

"Jesus," he said. "We've gotta find out who killed the Paitleys."

"We've gotta find Penn Hersch," I said.

Ferrier took out his cell phone. "I'm calling the FBI right now. But, Frank, you need to level with me. Do you know who stuck you in the neck with that needle?"

"I've got a pretty good idea, Bill, but—" I shook my head and looked out the window. "Yarak," I said.

"Yarak? Who the hell's that?"

Nicole, who'd sat wide-eyed listening to the discussion, suddenly looked at me knowingly, then bent down and placed her hand on top of Marcia's and mine. She said to Ferrier, "Not who, Detective. What."

Ferrier threw his hands up in a plea for help. "You folks wanna give me some clue what you're talking about here?"

"*Yarak* is a falconry term. It means, the highest state of readiness and hunger, eager to hunt," she said.

33

So that's how it shook out.

What I hadn't told Ferrier was that somewhere in my subconscious darkness of the night before, I'd remembered a little detail of the hand holding the needle that had almost meant my destruction: a missing portion of a ring finger. Mel Dworkin's.

Bright and early the next morning, we were all gathered in a conference room at police headquarters in Charlottesville. Packard and a couple of other FBI agents, Bill Ferrier and Carol Upwood, Toronto and myself. Jed Haynes sat across the table from Upwood and Ferrier. Packard was in command, but since Ferrier was now conducting what amounted to an attempted-murder investigation, Diane Lemminger's as well as my own, she'd agreed to let him open the questioning. There was also the now very much open question of a Paitley murder, so reluctantly, at Bill's request and over Abercrombie's objections, she'd even allowed Toronto and me to sit in. Almost getting killed does wonders for your popularity.

Nicole and Marcia had ridden back to town together, and Nicole was over at Marcia's again to see Cassidy. According to the radio news, Congressman Drummond, his chief aide, and the rest of his entourage were all back in town as well. The congressman himself was scheduled to give a lunchtime speech to his supporters—those special invitations issued to his Eagle Council, one of which I'd received. The outdoor amphitheater, in fact, was just across the way from where we sat. There had been talk of canceling the event, with his daughter still missing and rumors swirling, but apparently Drummond's brain trust had decided to press ahead. The congressman's lawyer had told the media that in addition to his speech, Drummond was planning to hold an impromptu news conference to put out another public plea for help in solving the kidnapping.

Seated at the table, Jed Haynes didn't look nearly as disheveled as the last time I'd seen him. His hair was combed and his face was scrubbed. He tapped his foot nervously on the floor.

Ferrier twirled Cartwright Drummond's silver earring between his fingers. "We think you know where she is, Jed."

Haynes shook his head. "I've told you, man. I don't know. I didn't see her at all that night."

"What about your roommates?"

"What about them?"

"What about Penn Hersch?"

"I don't know. Why don't you ask him?" The cops and the FBI were now watching the roommate, in hopes that he would lead them to the girl.

Ferrier drummed his fingers on the table. "When did you find out Penn was Cartwright Drummond's half brother?"

Haynes's eyes grew large. He looked around at the rest of us. "How did you guys know that?"

"It's going to go real hard for you, Jed, if anything happens to Cartwright."

The young man ran his fingers through his hair. "All right, look. This is all I know. Wright's been pissed at her old man ever since . . . you know, the divorce and everything. After Penn moves in with me, before Wright leaves for Japan, he starts talking about how he knows stuff a lot worse than that about her dad."

"Did he tell her Tor Drummond is his father, too?"

"Yeah."

"The three of you talked about this together?"

"Some. But mostly, Penn and Wright started E-mailing a lot back and forth about it."

"Was that what this Secret Amphibian business was all about?"

He snickered. "Yeah, I guess. Penn started joking how I might be her swimmer, but he was her secret amphibian, and how they were both going to get back at their dad."

"So where's Cartwright?"

"How many times do I have to tell you? I don't know."

"Hell, we've got her bloody fingerprints on her rental car, and traces of her blood in your Jeep. Now you show up with an earring she was wearing the night she disappeared. If you don't know, sure seems to me like someone's trying to make it look like you did it."

"It was supposed to look like that," he said.

Ferrier looked puzzled. "Say again?"

"The whole thing was a setup, wasn't it, Jed?" I said. All eyes turned to me. "Brother and sister wanted to make everybody think she'd been kidnapped. And you were in on it too."

He looked down at the table and nodded.

Ferrier folded his arms across his chest. "What for? What's the point?"

Haynes looked up at him. He shrugged. "They were planning to do something. I don't know, maybe make their father think he was responsible or something, have the whole thing about Penn come out on television, they were saying. But something went wrong."

"What do you mean?"

He shook his head, looked down at the table again, and closed his eyes. "Penn's weirded out or something. He's acting crazy. He won't tell me where Wright is and . . . Jesus Christ . . . he's got a gun." He started crying.

The FBI agents perked up at that information. Packard turned to one of the others. "Call all units," she said. "Tell them the suspect is armed and dangerous, but not to move in. He may try to harm the girl."

The agent she'd spoken to bolted from the room.

Ferrier poured water from a pitcher on the table into a paper cup. He handed it to Jed. Haynes accepted the cup and took a sip. He sat up, wiping the tears from his cheeks with the back of his hand.

"I was pissed at Wright, too, you know. She told me it was over between us. I was just trying to get her to like me again. She's okay, isn't she? She's gotta be okay."

Ferrier held up his hand. "Whoa, boss. Slow down a minute. We've got your buddy covered. He's at the house. You don't think Cartwright's somewhere there, do you?"

"No way. I'd have heard something."

"So who sent the ransom letter and the photo?"

Haynes shrugged. "I don't know anything about any ransom note," he said.

"Looks like your buddy's playing all kinds of games here," Ferrier said.

"We can sort that out later," Packard interrupted. "The important thing right now is to find the girl."

Amen to that.

She looked at Jed. "Mr. Haynes, do you think you'd

be able to place a call and get your friend on the phone with you?"

Haynes nodded. "Yeah. Probably."

She barked an order to the remaining agent. "All right, let's get it set up."

"What are you going to want me to say?" Jed asked.

"It's pretty simple, actually," she said.

Five minutes later, Jed Haynes held the phone in his hand while the rest of us were all wired in, listening through a speakerphone. The agent who'd left the room earlier stood over in the corner with a cell phone to his ear.

"Whenever you're ready, Mr. Haynes," Packard said.

The young man punched in the numbers on the phone. It rang three times. On the fourth ring a voice answered.

"Hello?"

"Penn, it's Jed. That you?"

"Who the fuck you think it is, dickwad? What do you want now?"

"Listen, man. The cops just hauled me in again, raking me over the coals."

"So? You stuck to your story, didn't you? You better have."

"No, listen, man, you gotta understand. They know. I didn't tell them anything, but they know."

"They know what?"

"About you and Wright and all this shit about your father. They even think they know where Wright is."

There was a string of whispered profanities on the other end of the line.

"I just thought I'd better call you," Haynes said.

"Fuck you, man. Don't you get it? Today's the day. Don't you ever come near me or my sister again!"

The line went dead.

Haynes looked at Packard. "Was that okay?" he said.

She held up her hand for quiet, watching the agent with the cell phone, who was listening intently.

Ten or fifteen seconds passed. Then the agent with the phone gave a thumbs-up. "Our boy's on the move," he said.

34

The Ragged Mountain Reservoir sits just off the interstate west of the city, tucked behind a ridgeline at the end of a winding dirt road, beside a summer camp for disadvantaged youth. Only one road provides access in and out of the natural enclave. It is not that long a run back down to Fontaine Avenue leading into the university; the dirt and stone thoroughfare is popular with joggers and athletes in training. At the reservoir itself, a hiking trail encircles the body of water, cutting a groomed path through rocks and fallen trees, and there is a little parking area at the trailhead.

"At least we'll know about the girl," Ferrier said, breathing heavily as we climbed a steep portion of the trail.

"One way or the other," I said.

Several teams of FBI agents, with all their high-tech gear, had already descended on the area, some in vehicles, some on foot, to attempt to create a perimeter. A helicopter, no doubt with the latest in super-magnification surveillance, was a little dot overhead. They'd all tracked Penn Hersch to this location, first in a black Toyota sedan, then on foot along the trail to the opposite side of the reservoir, where he appeared to be approaching an abandoned boathouse. Toronto and Ferrier and I formed a rear guard. A few thin clouds moved across the sky, but the spring sun was otherwise brilliant. It might've been the perfect day for a hike in the woods had it not been for our potentially gruesome mission. Ferrier's radio crackled softly with static and instructions for those in pursuit.

"What's your gut tell you, Frank?" Ferrier said. "This Hersch kid just gone wacko or what?"

My gut and I had not exactly been on speaking terms since I'd encountered that syringe full of barbiturate. "It's whispering that these kids are a lot smarter than we give them credit for," I said.

The trail descended a long projection of forest leading around the northern tip of the reservoir. Ferrier stopped and pointed across the water. Several hundred yards down the far shore, apparently tangled in vines and barely visible through the brush, was the vague outline of what might be the boathouse.

Crack-ck. Crack-ck.

The sound of gunfire suddenly echoed down the shoreline. A figure could be seen running between us and the boathouse. It looked like Hersch. There were shouts on the radio. We drew our guns and began running.

We sped over a log bridge and up and down more steep trail. The bleat of a motorcycle engine burst to life. More shouts over the radio. Above us, the helicopter appeared as if from nowhere.

The sound of the engine again. Higher up the ridge, a bright yellow helmet flashed by for an instant as it whizzed through the trees. Men with weapons drawn, some wearing camouflage, were in pursuit.

We made a beeline for the boathouse. Even up close it seemed to blend into the landscape. You could make out its dirt-encrusted walls and partially collapsed roof. The only approach from the trail, other than chopping through the brush with a machete, was to swing on a vine down a steep embankment to what remained of an older, overgrown path along the water's edge. We made like Tarzan. A pair of agents joined us, a man and a woman, followed by two EMTs doing a balancing act with their equipment and a stretcher.

The building was still as death as we approached. A tattered door hung from its frame, but someone had propped a large piece of siding over the opening. Ferrier held up his hand. He motioned for Toronto and me and the two agents to take up positions, in the little space available, on his left and right flanks. He stepped to the opening, pausing twice to listen. When he reached the door, he grabbed the piece of siding and threw it with a crash to the side.

"Police!"

For a moment he stood with his gun pointed, staring into the darkness of the boathouse. Since he hadn't fired, I assumed that meant no more hostiles. We converged on either side of him.

"Need for medical personnel," he said.

The EMTs rushed ahead of me with their gear. As they passed him in the doorway, Ferrier jerked his head in my direction, beckoning me forward.

Inside the tiny building, next to a burned-out space heater and three almost empty plastic gallon containers of water, Cartwright Drummond lay on her side with her face in the mud. She was gagged. Her hands were bound, her eyes closed, clothing torn, arms and legs badly bruised, and one of her cheeks was caked with a mixture of dried blood and dirt, but there was no doubt who she was. She could have been her sister lying there.

"We've got vitals," an EMT said, ripping open a package of plastic tubing. "But she's in bad shape.

She needs fluids. We're starting her on a drip. Then let's get her out of here."

The other EMT was already on the radio, talking with someone in the university hospital ER.

"What about the chopper?" one of the FBI people suggested.

Ferrier shook his head. "Nowhere for it to land."

The EMTs lifted the patient onto the stretcher. They gathered their gear, the FBI agents hoisted either end of the gurney, and we began the trek out.

I reached for my cell phone and dialed Marcia's.

She answered on the second ring.

"Marsh, it's me. Everything all right over there?"

"Yes."

"We've got Cartwright."

"Oh . . . oh, my gosh. Is she . . . ?"

"She's alive."

"Oh, thank God."

"But she's unconscious, not in very good shape. We're headed to the ER at the university. Pack the Drummonds and Nicole in your car and meet us there."

"Yes, of course."

"Can you put Mr. Earl on the phone?"

She was out of breath now, apparently running up a flight of stairs. "All right."

I handed the cell to Toronto, who explained the drill to his substitute bodyguard, then signed off.

We were all sweating and breathing heavily now. The rush of adrenaline had temporarily overcome the lingering effects of the drug still in my system, but now I felt weak and light-headed. We had to chop our way out, so it was slow going. I tried to assist Toronto, and the two FBI agents who were helping the EMTs bear the stretcher over the steepest and roughest parts of the trail, but I wasn't sure how much good I was doing.

We finally reached the vehicles, where the ambulance driver already had the engine idling. The agents loaded Cartwright in back, the two EMTs jumped in, closing the doors behind them, and the ambulance went screaming off down the dirt road in a spray of rocks and dust.

Ferrier thanked the two agents, who nodded and went running off to join their companions. The chopper was far away now, somewhere out over the interstate. Ferrier put his radio up close to his ear and listened. He pulled it away and turned the sound up for Toronto and me to hear.

It didn't sound good.

"Kid took a couple of shots at the feds, but it sounds like they may have lost him," Ferrier said. "They've got the dirt bike he ditched over near the bypass, but no Hersch."

35

We could hear the cheering and the applause from outside. Ferrier and Upwood leaned against the fender of his midnight-black Mercedes parked in the garage beneath police headquarters. Toronto and I propped ourselves against a neighboring cruiser. The Mercedes was the product of the seizure of a major local drug dealer's estate, one of the few perks in an otherwise thankless job. Ferrier would drive the car for a few months, then move on to another vehicle. In the amphitheater just down the mall, Tor Drummond was beginning his speech to a few hundred of his most loyal supporters.

The roar of the crowd continued, the congressman having announced that his daughter had been found and that he'd just come from the emergency room where she was still unconscious but apparently out of danger. I found out later, of course, that he'd swept in with his entourage and a cameraman in tow and refused to speak with his ex-wife or Cassidy.

"You know we can't do business that way, Frank," Ferrier said.

"I'm not asking you to. All you guys have to do is roll tape when I give you the signal."

"This vigilante crap's already almost got you killed. Now you wanna go back for more?"

I nodded.

The applause gradually died down as Drummond began to deliver his prepared remarks.

"Okay. Let's say I agree to wire you two turkeys. Who're we gonna be listening to? The congressman?"

I shook my head and smiled.

"C'mon," he said. "You want the wires or not?"

"I tell you and you may never make your case. This person isn't going to spill to you, Bill."

"Oh, no? And why's that?"

"Because"—Jake scratched his chin—"he's absolutely certain you won't kill him."

Their eyes locked.

Ferrier pursed his lips. "Shit," he said under his breath.

No one said anything for a few seconds.

"You know," Ferrier said, "if Abercrombie hears about this my ass is grass."

I held out my hands and shrugged.

He turned around and leaned forward and put his hands on the hood of the Mercedes. He stared down into the gleaming finish. "All right," he said. "Carol, let's get 'em both wired."

Minutes later, outside in the brilliant noon, Drummond's voice seemed inspired. Cameras and microphones and media people were present in abundance. The crowd numbered several hundred, a heterogeneous assortment of Virginians, young and old, male and female, black and white, families with children, students, and professionals. Many held signs trumpeting the cause of the man they wanted to send back to Washington to represent all their hopes and dreams, as if one person ever could. Their man was passionate about policies and programs that they desperately wished could provide some palliation for the troubles in their lives. He was flawed but unbowed. Not unlike themselves.

Security was light. Toronto and I, with Bill Ferrier as escort, moved easily around to the back of the stage. Mel Dworkin stood there, among a few other staff and local dignitaries, including the mayor and members of the city council.

I leaned into Ferrier's ear to make myself heard over a new round of applause. "Okay, Bill, thanks. We'll take it from here."

He nodded, looking none too happy about the situation, then turned and made a beeline toward a dark blue police van with its flashers running, the top half of which was visible over on Water Street.

About thirty feet to our right, next to one of the speakers, I spotted my target. The robot stood looking out at the crowd with his arms crossed. I noticed the turnip, too, on the opposite side of the stage, pulling similar duty. I nudged Toronto, and he and I casually strolled over to the robot. As I came up beside him, he saw me out of the corner of his eye. I smiled and gave him a wink. He looked like he was seeing a ghost.

I pulled a folded-up piece of paper from my pocket and held it out for him. "Howdy, friend," I said. "Would you mind taking this note to Mr. Dworkin? It's important he sees it."

He stared at it like he might a can of raw sewage. "Right now?" he said.

I nodded. "Please."

The crowd laughed at something Drummond said and applauded. The robot took the piece of paper from my hand. He walked over to where Dworkin was standing, whispered something in the chief of staff's ear, and handed him the note.

Dworkin unfolded the paper and looked at it. On one side I'd written two words: *Paitley* and *Murder*. He peered back over his shoulder, and the robot pointed toward Toronto and me. I nodded. Toronto stared at him through dark glasses. Dworkin said something to the robot, who moved off down the stage a ways. Then he said something to the person standing next to him and turned and came over to us.

"What the hell's this all about?" he said. His expression betrayed nothing, not even the fact that just a day or so before he'd attempted to punch my own ticket to the boneyard.

"We need to have a talk, Mel."

"Yeah? Well, as you can see, I'm kind of tied up at the moment."

"I can see that. The thing is"—I flexed my shoulders—"my neck's still a little sore, and I was wondering how you happened to titrate the dose."

He glared at me. "I haven't the faintest idea what you're talking about, pal."

"Uh-huh."

In the background, Drummond's voice grew soft, then louder as he stressed a particular point.

Dworkin was to my left. I put my arm around his shoulder and pulled him in close between myself and Toronto. "Well, I've got a proposal I think you might be interested in," I said into his ear. On the other side of him, Toronto, with his hands in the pockets of his parka, managed to twist the barrel of a legally registered snub-nosed .38 from beneath his coat into Dworkin's ribs. Anybody watching would've thought he was merely standing listening to the speech.

Dworkin gave a little start. "Is that so?" he said between clenched teeth.

"It is. And if you want to live, you'll come nicely."

I lifted a decidedly unregistered Saturday night special from my own pocket, cupping it in my palm, and then grabbed Dworkin's fingers as if we were shaking hands. I put the gun squarely into his palm.

"What are you doing?" he said, reflexively grasping the weapon.

"Don't worry," I said. "It's not loaded. Jake's got the bullets in his pocket." I pulled the little gun back and slipped it into my pocket again.

Dworkin seemed to examine his options. He looked over in the direction of the turnip, and at the nearest uniformed officer, a city patrolman standing about fifty feet away. Neither was looking in our direction.

"You guys'll never get away with this," Dworkin said.

"Get away with what? Why don't you go ahead and call one of those cops over? We can explain the whole situation to him. Or even better, go ahead and run. We can blow a two-inch hole in your heart. After all, it's only self-defense."

His eyes grew large. "You want to make some kind of deal, huh?" Dworkin said.

"Trust me. It's a win-win."

"You don't seem to be giving me much of an option."

I smiled and tightened my grasp on his shoulder. "You know there are always options, Mel."

Drummond droned on.

Dworkin thought about it some more. "Okay," he said.

"Not here," I said. "Let's go."

We turned as a unit. I let go of his shoulder, and Toronto pulled his gun back, but only a couple of inches or so. We walked together down the sidewalk over the rise at the side of the amphitheater.

My pickup was there, also with its flashers going, parked right behind the police van. Toronto opened the passenger side and nudged Dworkin in ahead of him. I went around and jumped in behind the wheel.

We didn't have far to go. The old city warehouse across from my office was only a couple of hundred yards down Water Street, on the other side of the railroad tracks.

"Where the hell you taking me?" Dworkin asked.

"You'll see," I said.

We turned left and took the tunnel under the tracks. My cell phone rang and I answered it.

"Frank, it's Marcia."

"Hey."

"It looks as though Cartwright might be okay."

"So I hear. That's great news."

"She's got a lot of bad bruises, though, and maybe a broken wrist. They've got her sedated, and they don't expect her to be conscious for a while. Karen wants to stay with her, but Cassidy insists on going over to see her father at the amphitheater. We're almost there now, in fact. She wants to talk to him."

"I'll bet she does. Is Mr. Earl with you? There's still a crazed kid on the loose, you know."

"Yes, he's right here. Where are you? Can you meet us over there?" she said.

"I'm kind of tied up at the moment, but I'm close by. I'll be there just as soon as I can," I said.

"All right." She hung up.

We pulled into the weed-choked warehouse parking lot. Lucky for us, some city worker had thoughtfully left the door wide open. No one seemed to be around.

We all climbed out.

We went through the open door and meandered between the spreaders and mowers and a rusted-out snowplow toward the back of the building, down some short steps to the plywood opening. Toronto yanked on the wood. I flipped on the bright beam from the four-cell I'd taken from the truck. We shoved Dworkin ahead of us into the opening. He stumbled forward and scraped against a wall.

"Christ!" he said. "What is this place?"

"Old coal tunnel," I said.

"Lovely," he said. "All right. What do you guys want?"

"I want to know why you had George and Norma Paitley murdered."

He folded his arms across his chest. "You guys are nuts, man. I had nothing to do with that."

"Oh, no? The game's over, Mel. We know and the cops know what Diane Lemminger's story was supposed to be about. Your boss has used Second Millennium Foundation as a cover for years to funnel money to children he's fathered illegitimately."

Dworkin drew in a quick breath. Then he shrugged. "So?" he said. "It'll be a big scandal. We've survived big scandals before. Hey, at least the guy's been paying for his mistakes. He's made sure those kids are well taken care of."

"Man's practically a saint," I said. "Where things start to unravel for me, though, is when one of his daughters goes missing and we find this old newspaper article in her bag about the Paitleys' hit-and-run all those years ago. Turns out Cartwright was told her old man's secret by another student, who just so happens to be her half brother."

Dworkin snorted and shook his head.

"So I figure this brother's pretty smart. I figure he was probably raised by foster parents or something, but he wanted to know who his real parents were.

Pretty simple, actually—he followed the money. Found out about the foundation and who was behind it. He even befriended another half sister of his, whose mom had been paid off for years to run the operation. Gave him access to all the records."

Dworkin spat on the tunnel floor. "You're a real ignoramus, Pavlicek—you know that? You can't prove anything. Don't you know me and the congressman had things under control? *We* were getting the real ransom notes. We were ready to pay that kid a hundred and fifty grand to turn over the girl."

"Yeah? Well, I've got a bigger news flash for you. There were no *real* ransom notes. And that's where it really begins to get interesting. For you especially, Mel.

"You see, I figure this brother really wanted to know who his real mom was, too. He got smart. He traced the bank records all the way back and figured out when the checks for his support started. Then he must've started cross-referencing birth records from around the same date. It probably took a while, but he found out who his mother was. Who was she? Somebody who worked for the Paitleys? Maybe one of those indigent people they used to take in. Was that why you had them murdered?"

Dworkin shook his head again. "Man, Pavlicek, you've really flipped, pal."

I looked at Toronto. He'd brought a little canvas bag with him from the truck, and he opened it now. He pulled out a roll of duct tape and a .22 long with a silencer attached.

"What the fuck's all that stuff for?" Dworkin said.

"I'm figuring one in each leg, a couple in the arms," I said to Toronto. "We bind him and gag him. There'll be a fair amount of blood. But there's rats in here. They'll take care of the rest."

"Copperheads, too," Toronto added. "Figure no one'll find him for at least a few days."

"Until the smell gets bad," I said.

"Right." Toronto ripped off a length of tape. Dworkin started shaking. With one hand, Toronto jerked the little twerp off his feet, bent down, and began binding his feet together.

"You fuckin' assholes are insane!" Dworkin screamed. "What do you want? What do you want?"

I bent down to look into his terror-filled eyes. "I'll bet, you and your boss have some pretty good lawyers representing you, don't you, Mel?"

He nodded.

"Probably hard to make any of these accusations stick."

He said nothing.

"You tried to kill me, Mel. I don't take too kindly to that kind of treatment."

"We're just taking care of business," Toronto said.

Dworkin shook his head. "I'll do whatever you guys want. What do you want?"

I coughed loudly and cleared my throat, signaling Ferrier to roll the tape. "All right," I said. "Say the cops'll never be able to put you guys away for any of this. I just need to know, for my own satisfaction, why you had the Paitleys pulverized."

He swallowed hard. He looked at Toronto, who was now working another length of tape around his hands.

"Okay," he said. "Okay. It started out as an accident, I swear. Tor had been banging this girl who lived with the Paitleys. She was from South America or something. No family here, lonely—you know the drill."

I didn't, but I let him continue.

"The girl gets pregnant and doesn't tell anybody until it's too late. So she has the kid. That's when we set up the foundation."

"I'm with you so far. What went wrong?" I said.

"It was an accident, I'm telling you. A couple weeks after this girl has the kid, she shows up one night at Drummond's office with the baby. Says she wants more money. They get into an argument or something—I don't know. She tries to push him, he pushes back. She falls and hits her head. I'm telling you, he didn't mean to kill her."

"What'd you do then?"

He shrugged. "He says take care of it, so I took care of it. I got rid of the body. I phoned the Paitleys and told them we'd paid the girl off and put her on a plane back to South America. Asked them to take the baby boy and have him put up for adoption."

"You mean Penn Hersch."

"Right. That's what his name is now."

"Then what happened?"

"The Paitleys started asking a bunch of questions."

"So?"

"So I phoned some guys I knew, and it was over."

I stared into his eyes. They were colder now. "These guys—that was the garbage truck that killed the Paitleys?"

"I suppose. I never found out until later."

"Your boss know about any of this?"

"He never knew the details. He didn't need to. I was just doin' my job, fellas. I swear."

"Is that right?" I looked at Toronto.

"Sure," Toronto said. "Just doing his job."

"But now Penn Hersch shows up and brings Cartwright Drummond into the equation and everything's hit the fan. That about sum it up?"

"Right," Dworkin snickered. "That about sums it up."

I thought it over out loud. "So Tor Drummond kills Penn Hersch's mother and you have the Paitleys killed. And Penn somehow comes up with that old article—"

"Yeah. The kid's nuts. The congressman even got a bunch of weird notes about the kidnapping. I'll bet now they were from Hersch."

"Wait a minute, you mean he got more than the letter with the photo of Cartwright?"

"Yeah."

"What did you do with them?"

"We gave 'em all to the FBI."

"What do you mean the notes were weird?"

"I don't know. Crazy shit. Drawings of birds and crosses and stuff."

"Birds . . . you mean like eagles?"

"Yeah, I guess so. Kid must've been trying to send some kind of message. Like he was taunting us."

It was quiet in the tunnel for a few seconds. *These kids are a lot smarter than we give them credit for.*

I reached over and grabbed Toronto's arm.

"What?" he said.

"We've got to go."

"What do you mean?" Toronto asked.

"Wait a minute," Dworkin said.

"Jake, we've got to move now. I'll explain on the way."

"What about him?" He pointed down at Dworkin.

"Leave him. We'll tell Ferrier where to come pick him up."

"What the hell are you talking about? You guys can't leave me here in the dark!" Dworkin bellowed.

Toronto was right behind me as I scrambled out of the tunnel with the light.

"Don't leave me here, fellas! Don't leave me. Please!"

Ferrier would have to edit the screams from the tape.

36

You could still hear Tor Drummond's voice echoing down the mall across Water Street as Toronto and I ran through the front door of my office building. Juanita Estavez manned her station behind the receptionist desk. She looked up at us with an expression of concern.

"What's wrong, Señores?"

"Juanita." I slapped the photo of Penn Hersch with Averil Joseph on the desk in front of her. "Do you recognize the young man in this picture?"

She squinted at the picture and began to shake her head. But then she stopped. "Oh, sí. This is the young man who dropped that envelope off for you a couple days ago. I remember because of the way his hair looked."

"You're certain?"

"Uh-huh."

The note that had said, *Flight canceled,* with a drawing of an eagle. Tor Drummond was giving a speech to what he called his Eagie Council.

"Thanks very much, Juanita."

We raced out the door. I punched Ferrier's number on the cell.

"I was right," I said as soon as he answered. "I really think he's going for it, Bill. You better get all hands on deck at the east end of the mall!"

We ran between the buildings and onto the brick pedestrian Main Street. The ankle I'd injured a couple of days before began to throb, and my head spun from the lingering effects of the barbiturate, but I barely noticed. A cop in uniform was standing at the next corner, his radio blaring. I grabbed him and explained quickly, and he ran with us, yelling into his mike.

Half a block away now. Drummond seemed to be winding down his speech. You could see the mass of people clearly applauding, fathers with kids on their shoulders, waving signs.

We reached the edge of the crowd. Behind Drummond and to his left were Marcia and Nicole and Cassidy Drummond, with Mr. Earl still standing guard. Someone had found them all chairs. We ran to the side, where we could get a better view into the bowl.

"If he's here, kid's probably locked and loaded," Toronto said. "He starts shooting, we could have a whole bunch of dead people on our hands."

The spectators roared their approval at something.

"Why don't they pull Drummond off the stage?" I yelled to the cop.

He shrugged and shook his head. He was screaming into his radio. I could see movement near the podium now, a few more cops.

"There!" Toronto said suddenly, pointing at the front corner of the amphitheater to our right. I couldn't see him at first, but then I caught a glimpse of Hersch's face and the back of his head, edging through the mass of clapping and smiling people only a few feet from the stage. He was less than twenty yards from us, but there were dozens of standing bodies packed in between, many straining on tiptoe to get a better view.

"Jake, call Mr. Earl on the cell phone. Tell him to get Drummond off that stage. Now!"

Toronto whipped out his phone and punched a button.

The cop and I dove into the crowd. Someone yelled. Out of the corner of my eye, I saw Mr. Earl rise from the back of the stage, looking at us in surprise, his cell phone pressed to his ear.

We were pushing people away. Suddenly, a siren whooped close by on the street. Everyone else glanced over at the source of the sound, including Tor Drummond, who paused from his closing flourish. Mr. Earl made a lunge toward the podium. But we were all too late.

I remember Penn Hersch, pulling the semiautomatic pistol from beneath his shirt and pointing it at the podium. Screams and shouts. The *pop-pop-pop-pop* as he pulled the trigger. Tor Drummond, recoiling backward from the force of the first bullets striking him in the chest, a look of utter astonishment on his face. The smell of terror. Weapons drawn. Bodies falling, tumbling, scrambling to flee. Others tackling Hersch to the ground.

I groped toward the stage. I remember seeing Marcia and Nicole and Cassidy, along with a group of the congressman's staff in hysterics, racing to bend over Drummond. A doctor, his shirt soaked with blood, futilely attempting to administer CPR. Media photographers still snapping pictures. And high above the teeming, wailing chaos, nothing but a single white balloon, lost by a tearful child, no doubt, sailing upward into an endless blue.

37

No one knows where all the bodies are buried. Maybe none of us really wants to know. If we do, it's only because we want to try to discover what may have been lost, all we might have gained.

Marcia and I stood with Nicole next to Karen, Cassidy, and Cartwright Drummond at the grave in the afternoon sun. The ground seemed to shake as the squad of marines in parade dress thundered off their rifle salute, filling the air with smoke and the smell of gunpowder. We waited while the smoke drifted away. The marine sergeant barked an order, and the flag was removed from the coffin, folded in triangles and presented to Karen Drummond and her daughters. When the last words had been said, the three Drummonds took turns laying roses on the coffin as it was lowered into the ground. The twins wore matching pantsuits, despite the gathering spring heat—Cartwright's visible bruises still had a lot of healing to do. As for the invisible ones, who was to say?

Leaving the ceremony, Marcia, Nicole, and I hooked back up with Toronto, Mr. Earl, Ferrier, and Upwood, who'd been standing back among the throng of mourners. I even noticed Diane Lemminger, wearing dark glasses but obviously feeling somewhat better now, climbing a little shakily into the passenger seat of her Corvette with the aid of a greaseball who had to be her producer.

I wasted the next couple of days in my office, attending to paperwork and returning all the phone calls I'd recently neglected. The inquiries from reporters were relentless, but I finally made a deal with Juanita and had my calls forwarded temporarily to the front desk, where she could intercept them like a tackle in pass protect, stacking messages for me in a neat pile.

Late on the third afternoon, just when I was getting ready to leave for the day, Bill Ferrier darkened my doorstep.

"Hey," I said. "Now that you're halfway famous, maybe you could petition the governor for a few thousand lottery tickets."

He chuckled. "You're the famous one, bud. I'm just a humble public servant." He plopped down on my sofa and set a couple ice-cold bottles of beer on my table, flipping the cap off each with an opener attached to a knife he had taken from his pocket.

I got up and went across to the chair next to him. He handed me a bottle and I sat down.

"I heard Toronto's gone back home," he said.

"Yup. Disappeared back over into his mountains like he usually does. Missed his place and his birds."

He nodded.

"Is Abercrombie still trying to take credit for something?" I asked.

"That's why I had to get out of there." He took a sip from his bottle. "My butt's getting sore from all his attempts to kiss it."

I smiled. "Cost of serving the public, I guess. How

do you think the case against Drummond's chief of staff will go?"

"No idea. The magistrate refused bail. There'll be a hearing tomorrow. It's in the hands of the Commonwealth's Attorney now. But I've got a feeling Mr. Dworkin's going to be spending a long time staring at steel bars."

"And Cartwright Drummond?"

He shrugged. "I understand they're reviewing potential charges. Looks to me like the kid just got carried away. According to her, the hoax was only supposed to last a day or so. She wanted to force her father into a public confession. She didn't know the whole story about the Paitleys or Hersch's real mother until it was too late. That was when Hersch beat her and took her out to the reservoir."

We finished our beers in silence.

Ferrier hoisted himself up from the couch, and when he did, he stood eye to eye with Fauntleroy. He pointed at the stuffed bird. "What kind of owl is that again?"

"European eagle owl," I said. "Largest species on the planet."

"Thing's got the biggest pair of eyes I ever seen."

"For hunting in the dark."

"You ever gone hunting with a bird like that?" he asked.

"An owl? Nope. Not very popular with falconers, unless you like to do most of your hunting at night."

He scratched the shadow of a beard on his face. "You know, when you put it that way, Pavlicek," he said, nodding at Fauntleroy, "that sounds like the perfect kind of partner for you."

*　　　*　　　*

An hour later I climbed to a rocky outcrop up on Buck Mountain with Armistead on my fist and Marcia on my heels. The sun was beginning to drop over the Blue Ridge, a fiery streak of ruby.

"You sure you want me along for this, Frank?"

"Yes," I said.

"What about Nicky?"

"She said she couldn't take it. Just to go do it."

"It'll be dark in a little while."

"I know. And this little lady's hungry. She's going to be one serious hunter."

"Yarak?" she said.

I nodded.

"What if she can't catch anything before the sun sets?"

"Then I'll feed her and take her home and we'll try again tomorrow."

"But if she does catch her own food, you're going to let her go for good?"

"Uh-huh."

"Why now?"

I thought for a few seconds before responding.

"Because it's time," I said. "She's ready. I'm ready for another bird, and it'll soon be the time of year for Armistead to hook up with a mate."

"No sadness at letting her go?"

"There's sadness, yes . . . but I always knew I wouldn't get to keep her forever."

The sky had turned to mauve, and a fat white moon stood just above the eastern horizon. In the shadow of the hills, darkness was rapidly gathering.

I touched Armistead's crown for just a second, a gesture she had only lately been allowing me to do.

"Good-bye, girl."

I let her slip her jesses, for maybe the last time. The

big redtail rose with a mighty beat of her wings to a branch partway up a nearby maple. We had only been kicking through the bush for a couple of minutes when a big brown cottontail jumped out of a nearby thicket and made a dash into the woods.

The stoop was as perfect as I have ever seen. All the mature hawk's hunting skills were on display now. She deftly banked left and right between the trees and, with a wingover at the end, took the prey off a dead run. I hadn't quite wanted it to end this way, such a quick tail chase before success, but what it lacked in duration it made up for in beauty in seeing the creature work at the height of her prowess.

"Wow!" Marcia said. "That was quick."

I made into the hawk over her kill and casually bent down and snipped off her anklets with a pair of scissors.

Normally, I called her off her prize to secure the quarry. But this time I stood back.

"It was time. I told you she was ready."

Marcia squeezed my arm. "What now?"

"We'll back off down the slope and leave her to her dinner."

We began to step cautiously back down the trail.

"Won't she be wondering what happened to you?" Marcia asked.

"Maybe, but not for long."

"Will you ever see her again?"

"It's possible. Redtails are pretty territorial. I picked these woods because I've noticed a wild tiercel out here twice in the past couple of weeks. If they mate, most likely they'll build a nest nearby."

"I'm glad this thing with the Drummonds is over," she said, hooking her arm in mine.

"Me too."

"I almost lost you."

I nodded.

"You think the twins will ever be able to recover from all the trauma?"

"I suppose, in time. They've got a strong mother. And some strong friends."

"I think through all this Cassidy is reaching out for a stronger faith."

"Faith is good," I said.

We'd gotten to the spot where the trail dropped steeply down the hill again. Turning back to look in the gathering shadows, I could barely distinguish the shape of the naturally camouflaged hawk on the forest floor. We watched for a few more seconds. A light breeze stirred the trees around us. Marcia took my hand in hers and we turned to head back down the slope.

"Keee-er, Keee-er—"

I searched out the source of the sound. "It's the male," I said, pointing to the brown form soaring through the dusk overhead. "Mr. Tiercel doesn't sound too happy about our sweetie pie invading his hillside."

"He looks smaller than Armistead," she said.

"He is. Males are about a third smaller than the females. That's why they're called *tiercels,* French for 'one-third.' Fact is, although he's quicker, Armistead can eat this boy's lunch anytime she wants, and there's not a whole lot he can do about it. If he decides to court her, he'll approach her gingerly and bow, maybe even do a little sky dance for her."

"Exactly the way it ought to be," she said.

The hawk above suddenly dropped into a steep descent, then, about halfway through its dive, swirled around into an acrobatic loop-the-loop.

Marcia laughed. "What do you make of that?"

"I do believe our man's changed his tune and decided to show off his stuff for the lady."

"What a way to begin a relationship," she said.

But their dance had only just begun when, as if they'd been figments of our imagination, the two hawks vanished over the ridge.

PENGUIN PUTNAM INC.
Online

Your Internet gateway to a virtual environment with
hundreds of entertaining and enlightening books
from Penguin Putnam Inc.

*While you're there, get the latest buzz on
the best authors and books around—*

Tom Clancy, Patricia Cornwell, W.E.B. Griffin,
Nora Roberts, William Gibson, Robin Cook,
Brian Jacques, Catherine Coulter, Stephen King,
Ken Follett, Terry McMillan, and many more!

**Penguin Putnam Online is located at
http://www.penguinputnam.com**

PENGUIN PUTNAM NEWS

Every month you'll get an inside look at our upcoming books and new features on our site. This is an
ongoing effort to provide you with the most
up-to-date information about
our books and authors.

Subscribe to Penguin Putnam News at
http://www.penguinputnam.com/newsletters